MW00563467

Marilyn Monroe

ON THE COUCH

Inside the mind and life of
Marilyn Monroe

Dr. Alma H. Bond, Ph.D.,

author of the *On the Couch* Series

Although factual information forms the core of *Marilyn Monroe: On the Couch*, this book is a work of fiction, and is not necessarily a complete or historically accurate rendering of Marilyn Monroe's life. The work draws upon some of the published details of Marilyn Monroe's history (*see Bibliography at the end of this book*), as well as speculations about her that have appeared in print. It is also based upon the author's impressions and analysis.

Cover & Interior Design: Tracy Copes; Daft Generation

Published by Bancroft Press
"Books that Enlighten"
800-637-7377
P.O. Box 65360, Baltimore, MD 21209
410-764-1967 (fax)
www.bancroftpress.com

ISBN 978-1-61088-108-1 (cloth)
Bancroft Press / $23.95
Printed in the United States of America

Lovingly dedicated to my daughter,
Dr. Janet Bond Brill, who insisted I write this book.
When I protested that hundreds of books already had been written about Marilyn Monroe,
Janet said simply, "But yours will be different!"

Also dedicated to my wonderful son-in-law,
Sam Brill, for his near-boundless generosity towards me.

PART 1
On the Couch

PREFATORY NOTE

I am Dr. Darcey Dale, a Fifth Avenue psychoanalyst in New York City. I have been in practice for thirty-seven years, and want to tell you about the loveliest, most famous, complicated, and most difficult patient of my long and highly successful career. Treating her is not the work I am most proud of, and I wish I could do it over again and profit from my mistakes. But telling you about it perhaps will give me some insight into the human mind and human emotions, and may help me struggle more successfully on behalf of some other desperate soul.

What I will relate is based on my own summaries of my sessions with her. At the end of each day, I made it a practice, especially with certain patients, to dictate, as best I could recall, the highlights of our appointments together. Sometimes my dictation was lengthy. Sometimes it was brief. It depended on how much time I had that particular day for dictation. In no sense are these summaries everything that my patients and I said during the traditional 50-minute sessions, or what I thought at the time—just what I considered most important.

FEBRUARY 2, 1960

One day in the winter of 1960, my secretary Rivka Ruben informed me that she had put on my appointment calendar an introductory session with a new patient then sitting in my waiting room.

I asked, "What is your impression of the woman, Rivka?"

She thought for a moment and then answered, "I must say, she's not the kind of elegant patient you usually see. Her name is Norma Jeane Mortenson. She's a shy little woman wearing no make-up, with a dowdy babushka over her hair. In fact, 'dowdy' is a good word to describe her."

Fine, I thought. *I'm tired of the glamorous ladies of the Upper East Side whose major concerns are which interior designer they're going to employ for the latest room re-do. This patient may be an interesting change.*

When I walked into the waiting room, I saw immediately what Rivka meant. The little woman sitting there was indeed unimpressive, and I wouldn't have been surprised to discover that she was a woman's maid, or a nanny sent for therapy by an empathic employer.

She was absorbed in a magazine, the cover of which featured the great screen actress and sex symbol, Marilyn Monroe.

I walked over to her and extended my hand. "Good afternoon, Ms. Mortenson. I am glad to meet you."

The woman looked up and, to my shock, a complete transformation came over her. A light seemed to suddenly turn on inside of her, as if she had some radioactive core beneath her skin. Her persona, her body language, her demeanor—indeed, everything about her—changed. She looked and acted like another person, giving off a blazing burst of magnetism and sexuality such as I had never witnessed before. A coat that even the Salvation Army would reject dropped off her shoulders and her babushka was tossed to the floor, revealing sunny blonde curls that resembled white spun gold. She literally glowed.

She leapt up and seized my outstretched hand. "Oh, thank you, Dr. Dale," she said exuberantly. "I've wanted to see you for years, but I was too scared to make an appointment. My good friend Paula Strasberg says you're the one person in the world who can save my life.

"Oh," she added, her cornflower blue eyes sparkling like diamonds, "and please, call me Marilyn."

Her tight, white, knit dress revealed a figure like no one else's in the world. Contrary to my first impression of a woman approaching middle age, she looked younger than what the patient questionnaire revealed—thirty-three years old. At that moment, I realized who she was, and saw first-hand the qualities that enchanted the whole world. When she dropped her disguise, no one alive could have failed to recognize that stunning face and body.

It took me a moment to recover my analytic poise. "Come into my office, Ms. Monroe," I said, "and tell me why you need me to save your life."

I stood at the door of my office and waved her in.

"Oh, no, Doctor," this most celebrated woman said, falling back. "After you."

I have a confession to make. When I was a teenager, I wanted to be a movie star so badly it hurt, and I only gave up the ambition when numerous Broadway auditions gained me not a single callback. I was more dazzled than most at the presence of Marilyn Monroe in my office, and I knew it, which made me cautious. I was as yet undecided whether or not to take her on as a patient, and so I observed her closely as she followed me inside, looked around, and clapped her hands like a gleeful child.

"Oh, how beautiful!" she exclaimed as she bounced around the room, examining every treasure. Usually patients are so self-absorbed they don't even notice their surroundings. But this woman already knew how to get through to me.

"How nice to be in a doctor's office which doesn't look like a morgue!" she continued, gazing with wide eyes at my stained-glass window. I loved my stained glass window, which had been taken, frame and all, from an old country church long vanished. Birds sang eternally on flower-entwined branches that had lit up my office for over twenty years. The deep reds, greens, and blues reminded me of the great stained glass windows of Chartres. I had once been told the glass might have been created by Tiffany, but never had this confirmed, probably because I didn't want to be robbed of the fantasy that I owned a Tiffany.

Other riches surrounded me in my workplace. A Haitian portrait of a weeping woman in deep blues and vital reds hung over the couch. I valued it deeply—it had been given to me by a friend long departed from this earth.

Oriental rugs I personally brought back from China and India provided the same electrifying colors. My couch for patients, the fourth of my analytic career, had recently been reupholstered in a wine and blue Laura Ashley print.

I shook my head. If she had spoken admiringly of my appearance, my articles, my books, or my fame in the analytic community, I could have shrugged it off—all that I was used to hearing. But she had chosen the one thing I couldn't remain aloof from—my "Tiffany"-stained glass. The woman was irresistible.

"Thank you, Marilyn," I said, trying hard to disguise my pleasure. The triumphant look in her huge blue eyes suggested I had not succeeded. "Please sit down and tell me what brings you here today."

Her face fell, and I could see the returning signs of the drab woman I had first met.

"Oh, must I?" she said, with a girlish smile. "I'd much rather look at your lovely possessions and learn how to acquire such objects."

"Maybe another time," I answered.

She ignored my remark and walked around the room, stopping in front of the book shelves. "*Oooh*, all these books! Could I borrow some?"

"They make for difficult reading."

Her face fell again. "I mean, what kind of books are they? I never even graduated from high school, though I've always loved poetry."

I saw that I had hurt her feelings and understood that I would need to be more careful in my choice of words. "We can discuss books another time," I said, gently but with professional firmness. "We have important work to do now. Sit, please."

Marilyn seemed to accept that I would not be distracted. She looked around at the furniture in the room, selected the couch, and sat gingerly down on it.

"In the waiting room," I said, "you said you need me to save your life."

She nodded and was quiet for so long I was afraid she wasn't going to answer verbally. Finally, she began to speak. The words left her mouth so slowly I could barely make them out; they were broken up by an unexpected stutter. "I am often in a—a—d-depression so deep . . . I don't know if I can survive. It feels as if it has always been there and will never go away. The—the—world around me is shrouded in blackness, as if a huge vacuum cleaner has exploded in my face and filled the air with filth. I have no reason to get up in the morning, and if I didn't have to go to the bathroom, I wouldn't leave my bed all day. I often don't. I can't live that way any longer. Can you help me, Doctor? Otherwise, I'll have no choice but to kill myself."

As someone who had absorbed Marilyn's public façade, I was shocked, but as a professional, I responded with instinctive compassion to her desperation.

"I am here to listen to you, Marilyn."

Perhaps I should have said more. But how can one answer such a question? Even my vast experience did not make me all-knowing.

I realized, too, that I had, without noticing, decided to take on her case after all.

She paused again for what seemed like hours. I held my breath. Her mood, however, was quick to change, as I would soon learn. She seemed to brighten all at once and said, "All right. Where should I start?"

"At the beginning," I said.

She repositioned herself on the couch, nodding, and began to talk with relish. She looked positively luminescent, as she often did on the screen, and told me the story of her origins in a frank if somewhat methodical manner.

"I was delivered by Dr. Herman M. Beerman on June 1, 1926, in the charity ward of the Los Angeles General Hospital. I looked him up a few years ago and asked him what the delivery was like. He said, 'Marilyn, I am sorry to have to tell you that you looked like all the other babies I delivered.' I guess that was the last time I was like everybody else."

I smiled. As if sensing that I enjoyed her sense of humor, she added, "I was born in very sorry circumstances. Both of my parents were sorry." This time I didn't smile, but again thought that I would have to watch out; she would certainly try to turn her analysis into a comedy show. Seeming almost prescient, she immediately became more serious. "My mother, Gladys Baker Mortenson, worked at the time as a lowly film cutter, splicing together films at Consolidated Film Industries, a processing lab for the Hollywood studios. I began life with two significant strikes against me: a crazy mother, and no father to help raise me, to love me, or to protect me from my mother's nuttiness. Not only was she batty, but I never felt she even liked me, let alone loved me," Marilyn said. "She was always cold and unaffectionate. I don't remember her ever holding me in her arms or kissing me. In fact, she never seemed interested in me at all. Once, when I was still trying to impress her, I said that I wanted to grow up to be a movie star. She just looked through me with eyes cold as steel and said nothing."

Poor little kid, I thought.

Marilyn went on to talk about her father, which was perhaps an even sadder subject than her mother. "Though my birth certificate identifies my father as Gladys's second husband, Edward Mortenson, she always said my father actually was C. Stanley Gifford, a man who also worked at Consolidated Film Industries. He abandoned Gladys after she told him she was pregnant. No wonder I always have trouble with the men in my life," she noted cynically. "When my own father ran away from me before he even met me, what can I expect from men who are strangers?

"When I was very little," she continued, "I noticed a photograph of a man hanging on the kitchen wall. The photo was of a handsome man wearing a pencil-thin moustache, like the one Clark Gable always wears. I asked my mother who he was. She said the photo was of my father. In that instant, my life changed forever. 'I have a father, I have a father, I have a father!' I screamed to anyone who'd listen. 'He's the great Clark Gable! It's not true that I'm different from everyone else! None of the other girls have a movie star for a father. That makes me better than any of them!'

"I dreamt about him at night, hugging my pillow and pretending it was Clark Gable, and told my classmates I was the daughter of a movie star. Even today, it would be one of the greatest thrills of my life if I could act with him in a movie. That's one of the reasons I work so hard to improve my acting. When we get to work together, I want him to think I'm a great actress. Maybe he'll even marry me. Or adopt me!"

I could not help smiling again. I, too, had always loved Clark Gable, and married a man I thought looked like him, mustache and all. "Did you ever meet Gifford?" I asked, hoping to bring her back to reality.

"No," she answered sadly. "When I was a teenager, I got up the nerve to speak with him on the phone. A strange woman answered. I said, 'I'm Norma Jeane, Gladys Baker's daughter, and I'd like to speak with Mr. Gifford please.' The woman said, 'Feel free to call his lawyer,' and hung up.

"After I became a famous movie star, I got a call from a man who said he was Gifford. He said, 'I'm dying, Norma Jeane. I'd like to meet you before I pass on.' I said, 'Feel free to call my lawyer,' and hung up."

I hoped I would never get to know sweet Marilyn Monroe's vengeful side firsthand. I rose and said, "You're doing very well, Marilyn, and I'm sorry to stop you, but our time is up. I will see you again the next time, if you care to make another appointment."

Marilyn was offended at the disruption. She glared at me ferociously and took her time getting her things together and rising from the couch. *It's a good thing looks don't kill*, I thought.

FEBRUARY 3, 1959

Marilyn indeed put herself down for another session—for the very next day—and she immediately picked up where she had left off in telling me about her mother, her fit of pique seemingly forgotten.

"Two weeks after I was born in the charity ward, my dear mother, unable to get *her* mother to take on my care, turned me over to a foster family."

I gasped, and hoped she had not heard me. *Rejected at two weeks of age! The poor baby never had a chance.* I noticed Marilyn's stutter emerging once again as she spoke to me haltingly. "I was a mistake. My mother never wanted me. I still wish—wish every d-day that she had wanted me." She shook her head, recovering a little. "But when I said my mother was a nut, I wasn't kidding. When I was seven years old, she was diagnosed as a paranoid schizophrenic and placed in a state mental institution, where she remained for much of her life. In fact, she's still there."

Marilyn may have heard my earlier gasp, for she added, "But she didn't reject me altogether. Before she went into the institution, she came and stayed weekends with me at the foster home and took me out to the beach or the movies. We both loved movies. Although I hate to remember it, when I was little, I looked forward to her visits like nothing else. What else does a child living in an orphanage have to look forward to? I desperately waited for her visit each week.

"Gladys always said she was going to buy us a house and we'd live together like other families. As the years passed and I realized we were never going to live in that house, I stopped looking forward to her visits. What good were they, if she never was going to be a mother to me? They just made me blue when she left. I think that's when I realized she was a liar and stopped loving her, and haven't really trusted anyone since. I determined then that if I ever have a little girl, I'll always tell her the truth, no matter how painful it is. I can live with anything as long as it's the truth.

"A publicity man at Fox said he'd never heard me tell a lie. I was happy to hear that, because if I'm not myself, who am I? But my reputation for being frank isn't always good for me and has sometimes gotten me into trouble. When I've upset someone with what I honestly think, then try to pull back, they think I'm being coy. I'm supposed to have said that I don't like being interviewed by women reporters. I never said such a thing. I might be dumb, but I'm not as dumb as all that. What I did say is that I honestly prefer men reporters, because I find them more stimulating.

"Fortunately or unfortunately, I have a kind of sincere stupidity. In interviews, I don't want to tell every reporter the same thing. I want to give each one something fresh, so my fans don't feel cheated and say, 'I know that! Why is she saying the same thing over and over again?'

"But I never will allow an article to be published in my name in a movie magazine. When I was a little girl, I used to follow fan magazines religiously, and often based my conduct on what the movie stars said. Well, what do you know, but that editors make enormous changes to such interviews. I wouldn't want to have that kind of influence on young girls unless I was sure it was really my words being passed onto them.

"The same thing is true about being funny. People say I have a great sense of humor. They don't realize that I'm simply telling the truth. George Bernard Shaw said it better: 'My way of joking is to tell the truth. It's the funniest joke in the world.'"

She was right. When I went over her published remarks in my mind, I saw that they simply represented her innocent way of telling the truth. For example, a reporter asked her, "What do you wear when you're sleeping?" Her answer was, "Chanel No. 5." As the whole world knew, Marilyn Monroe slept in the nude.

When I looked at my watch, I saw that the end of the hour had long passed. That was most unusual for me. Patients said they could set their clocks by how punctually I began and ended their sessions. I realized that I had been so fascinated by Marilyn's words, I had not noticed the passage of time. I thought, *I'll have to watch that. A psychoanalyst must be objective at all times!*

I stood up and said, "We will have to stop now." She remained seated for a few long moments, a bewildered expression on her face. Then the most beautiful woman in the world silently rose and tied the babushka around her head. Again, an amazing transformation occurred. It was as if a light inside of her suddenly was turned off. And the drab little woman I first met in the waiting room silently shuffled out the door.

FEBRUARY 6, 1959

Which Marilyn will come in today? I wondered, as I walked to the waiting room to welcome her to her third session. Would she be the effervescent, glowing, incredibly beautiful woman the world knew, or the dingy little creature one might suspect was homeless? *At least this patient isn't boring!* I thought.

Marilyn this time was someone in-between. "Hi, Doc," she said, plopping herself down on the couch. "I'm really getting off on this analysis stuff. I wanna go on with the story of my life, if it's OK with you."

"Of course," I answered. "I want to know as much about you as you want to tell me."

Was I correct in thinking her face lit up a bit?

"Where was I?" she asked. "I think I stopped where I was disillusioned with my dear mother. Oh yes, I told you I was placed with foster families, maybe ten or twelve of them. Some kept me longer, others got tired of me in a short time. I guess I made them nervous."

Ye gods, I thought. Ten or twelve foster homes? *It is amazing she is not in the asylum with her mother!*

"My first and most important foster home," she continued, "was with the Wayne Bolenders, where my mother placed me for the first seven years of my life."

I breathed a sigh of relief. *At least she had a family for seven years.* But my relief wasn't to last long.

"My mother boarded me out to Ida and Wayne Bolender in Hawthorne, California two weeks after I was born. No, wait a minute. If I remember correctly, she placed me with them when I was all of twelve days old." She said reminiscently, "They had a comfortable six-room bungalow I remember very well. Although they didn't have a great deal of money, they increased their income by taking in foster children."

Marilyn digressed a little at this point, not quite ready yet to move on from thoughts of her mother. "I must admit that life had dealt Gladys a rotten set of cards. Her S.O.B. husband not only left her, but kidnapped her first two children, and she never was able to recover them. That would drive me crazy, too." She sighed, returning to the topic of her foster parents. "She had no choice but to board me out. She had financial problems, too. She had to go back to work at Consolidated Film Industries in order to support us, working from 8 a.m. to 8 p.m., and there was no one to take care of me. She paid the Bolenders five dollars a week, probably half her salary, to look after me.

"Every Saturday, Gladys took the trolley to Hawthorne to visit me. In the early years, I desperately waited for her visit each week. One week, she didn't show up, and I stood waiting by the front window until bedtime. Ida tried to pull me away, and said, 'Norma Jeane, your mother isn't coming today. You have to come eat your dinner.'

"'No, no!' I screamed. 'She'll come. Just you wait and see.'

"She kept yanking me by the shoulder. But I held onto the wall with my nails until a huge chunk of the plaster fell off into my hands. 'You're a bad girl, Norma Jeane,' Ida said, and slapped me in the face." Marilyn raised her hand to her cheek, which was wet with tears. She winced, and added, "It still hurts."

Marilyn said that the Bolenders were a deeply religious couple who lived a comfortable lower middle-class life in an unstylish Los Angeles suburb.

"The house was still standing when I took my first husband Jim there to see it, although the name of the street had been changed from Rhode Island Avenue to West Hawthorne."

Ida Bolender, it turned out, was a rigid, conscience-driven woman who forcefully pounded her beliefs into Norma Jeane. Ida made the little girl promise never to smoke, drink, or swear, and insisted that she attend church several times a week or she would go to Hell. She was not even allowed to go to the movies. "We are a churchgoing family, not a movie-going one," Ida repeatedly said. "Do you know what would happen if the world came to an end while you were sitting in the movies? You would burn in Hell with all the rest of the bad people."

Marilyn began to laugh. "I was a smart little kid and, after a while, I asked myself, *If Ida's right, will there be enough room in Hell for all the ashes from all the movie theaters in all the world?*

"There wasn't much I could do to please my foster mother. I could never measure up to her standards of cleanliness and behavior, and was always in some kind of trouble. Like many children, I loved to play in the dirt. Ida would dress me up in pretty, clean clothes and send me out to play. Twenty minutes later, I would bounce back into the house with my dress caked in mud. Ida wasn't happy about it and gave me a wallop or two to punish me for my 'bad behavior.'

"I don't think that is such a terrible thing for a little girl to do, Doctor. Do you?"

"Absolutely not, Marilyn," I answered. "It is perfectly normal behavior for a little child." The inner light turned on again, as Marilyn's face lit up in an enchanting smile.

One of her foster sisters, Nancy Jeffrey, believed that despite Ida's severity, she was a good influence on Marilyn in many ways and a sta-bilizing influence in her life. Ida taught her foster children to love the Lord and each other, and gave Norma Jeane the only foundation she ever had, which served her well in her career. Without it, Marilyn Monroe might never have become the star she was. Ida told Nancy, at least as Marilyn recalled it: "I know I was hard on Norma Jeane, but it was for her own good. I was sure she would have a hard life, and I wanted to prepare her for it. I know in my heart I raised her the right way."

Norma Jeane soon learned how to live with Ida's strictness. "When she reprimanded me, I nodded, but I kept my fingers crossed behind me," Marilyn said with a smile.

In order to avoid punishment, this highly intelligent little girl learned to conceal her desire to sing, dance, and act out a fantasy life. She attended the movies surreptitiously whenever she could and also found her own unique ways of handling boredom in church—sexual fantasies.

"I'll tell you about them after I get to know you better," Marilyn laughingly said. "After all, how do I know you don't think like Ida Bolender?"

"Hmm," I said. Marilyn's comment signaled to me that she might be developing negative transference, conflating me with Ida Boldender and the negative associations Marilyn had with her. (Transference is the name for the patient's tendency to project, on the analyst, qualities belonging to early important figures in his or her life. This process keeps analysis from becoming too painful.) I would need to resolve this issue and allow Marilyn to develop positive transference instead, making our sessions a place of trust and eventually growth for her.

FEBRUARY 9, 1959

When Marilyn next came to see me, she started off on a decidedly negative note. "That was a long weekend, Doc! It seemed like a whole week."

Then she told me more about the Bolenders. In the days before the expression "stay-at-home mom" even existed, Ida took care of the house and several foster children, along with her and Wayne's natural son. Wayne was the breadwinner, a postman fortunate enough to keep his job throughout the Depression. He added to their low income by printing religious pamphlets for distribution to the members of their church.

Marilyn was aware that though the Bolenders shared many of the same beliefs, they didn't have much of a relationship. They rarely spoke to each other, and when they did, it was usually because Ida was chastising Wayne or chivvying him out of his reluctance to perform work around the house.

I thought it unfortunate that Marilyn missed the early chance to see a married couple getting along well with each other—a couple who could have served as a model for a union she could look forward to experiencing someday.

Nevertheless, she cared about Wayne, who usually was a pleasant, friendly fellow. "I can just see his big shoulders bulging with huge mailbags," she recalled. "He used to carry candy in his pocket to throw to the dogs so they wouldn't bite him. Sometimes he would give me a piece," Marilyn said wistfully.

"He also could be terribly frightening. When I became what he considered boisterous, down came my pants and off came his leather belt, huge silver buckle and all. I'll never forget the lash of his leather and the welts it caused on my bare buttocks as he pressed me against his genitals. I had to eat standing up for days. I have a sensitivity on my ass to the present day.

"But I loved Wayne at the time. What did I know? I thought that was how fathers were supposed to act—that they punished their children to teach them a lesson. You know the old story, 'This hurts me more than it hurts you.'"

No wonder she wiggles her behind when she walks, I thought. *Strange as it is to contemplate, the world has Wayne Bolender to thank for his part in giving us the sexiest behind in the history of the cinema.*

Then I thought angrily, *How could he? Didn't the man have a heart?* How, for some imagined transgression, could he possibly tear into the flesh of the helpless little orphan girl he was supposed to be taking care of? The man should be investigated even now and sentenced to prison. I also could not help but wonder if little Norma Jeane was already attractive, and if Wayne Bolender derived sexual pleasure while beating her. Then I felt ashamed of the thought. Whether she was seductive or not had nothing to do with Wayne's abuse. He was paid to be her guardian, and nothing gave him the right to mistreat her.

With the five dollars a week given them by Marilyn's mother, the Bolenders managed to avoid the devastation suffered by most Americans during the Great Depression. I suspected that Norma Jeane remained a part of their household largely because of the income she brought in, if not for the sexual gratification she provided her foster father; this was probably the reason she was kept by the couple much longer than by any of her other foster parents.

Still, that wasn't the whole story. It seemed that, in their own harsh way, the Bolenders loved Norma Jeane and wanted to adopt her. But in a rare show of motherly love, Gladys refused to allow it, because her persistent dream was that she would buy a home and take Norma Jeane to live with her in it.

"Ida Bolender thought I was beautiful," Marilyn said, "and enjoyed brushing my hair, making me pretty clothes, and giving me moral 'training.' She believed in protecting a child's spiritual, physical, and emotional health, in that order, although I believe her heart was largely in enforcing the first. One of the great disappointments of my life was when I asked if I could call her 'Mother,' so I could feel like a normal child. She wouldn't allow it, insisting that I call her 'Aunt Ida.' She said she didn't want to teach a charge of hers to lie! Also, she said that Gladys was terribly upset when she heard me call Ida 'Mother.'

"I did call Wayne 'Daddy,' and nobody seemed to object. I got along better with him anyway, even with the beatings. He gave me a dog I treasured, both because I loved the dog and because my 'Daddy' had given him to me. I named him Tippy. I hope someday to make a film with a dog in it named Tippy. That'll pay my debt to the best friend of my childhood.

"A few years ago, I phoned Wayne, and he said, 'Norma Jeane, I'll always love you and be there for you.' Although years had passed since we had seen each other, a thrill ran down my body from the top of my head to the tip of my toes, just as it had when I was a little girl. Yes,

Doctor, even in my ass."

In my professional opinion, despite the terrible drawbacks of being raised by the God-fearing Bolenders and the traumatic, sexually-tinged beatings by her foster father, Marilyn was better off with their somewhat steady parenting than she would have been without any parents at all. They gave her a little emotional security and a consistent home, and built her a conscience, no matter how distorted.

Marilyn continued, "I told you that I lived with them until I was seven. By then, I never expected to live with my mother, no matter what she promised. But to my great surprise," she smiled, "Gladys came through after all on her pledge to buy a house for herself and me. In August 1933, when I was seven years old, she signed a contract with the California Title Mortgage Company, which, when added to her savings, gave her enough of a down payment to buy a small white bungalow at 6812 Arbol Drive in Hollywood. Money was still scarce, but Gladys was resourceful. She said to me, 'It's all on time, so don't worry.' I wasn't worried. It never entered my mind. 'I'm working a double shift at the studio,' she said, 'and soon I'll be able to pay it off.'

"I guess Gladys wasn't kidding when she said she really wanted me to live with her. I was ecstatic! For the first time in my life, I was able to live with my mother like any normal girl.

"The house even had a yard and a white fence around it," Marilyn said with wide open eyes, as though she still couldn't believe it. "At the time, Gladys was working as a film cutter at Columbia Pictures, but to supplement her low paycheck, she rented the whole house, except for the two rooms she saved for us, to an English couple who had minor film jobs. The husband was a stand-in for George Arliss, the character actor, and the wife worked as an extra.

"I was *very* impressed with them," Marilyn said, sounding as enthralled as she must have been at the time. "They were the first people I'd ever known who actually acted in movies. They had easygoing natures and, unlike the Bolenders, enjoyed smoking, drinking, and card-playing—in fact, all the things the Bolenders had taught me were sinful. But they seemed very nice and didn't appear to be overly worried about spending eternity in Hell.

"'Movie stars live in my house!' I bragged to my classmates. Of course, they didn't believe me. 'That Norma Jeane is always making up stories,' they said behind my back.

"I didn't care. I was happier than I'd ever been with the Bolenders. I was delighted to be living— finally—with my real mother, despite all her peculiarities. The ambience in the household was much less strict than it had been at the Bolenders, and I was allowed to do many more things. Gladys and I often went to the movies at Grauman's Egyptian Theatre and Grauman's Chinese Theatre. I can picture us sitting side by side, gorging on chocolate Kisses, spellbound by the fantasies we saw on the screen.

"'Someday, you'll be up there,' Gladys said to me, at a time when she was still well. I listened and believed her. I even wrote out her prediction and held it to my breast at night.

"Gladys also took me to the famous cement forecourt of Grauman's Chinese Theatre, where I proudly placed my little feet in the footprints of Clara Bow and Gloria Swanson, and dreamt that someday, mine would be next to theirs. Gladys didn't disillusion me. She said, 'Of course they will be! We'll come back and look at them together.' Too bad we never did.

"To my utter despair, our reunion was only too brief. She really wasn't well, and I guess I knew it even then. Actually, I knew it when I was three and still living with the Bolenders. One day, Gladys came to see me and insisted that the Bolenders turn me over to her. Ida refused, because she knew how unstable Gladys was and was frightened for my welfare. Gladys pushed Ida into the yard, bolted into the house, and locked the door. A few minutes later, she rushed back out with one of Wayne Bolender's military duffel bags zipped up and slung over her shoulder. Guess what was inside? Me! I screamed and screamed when she stuffed me inside.

"Ida rushed at her and tried to yank the bag away from her. It split open and dumped me to the ground. As Ida grabbed me and pulled me back into the house, I was still screaming.

"Just now, telling you this, I'm wondering why Gladys needed to stick me in the duffel bag. Why didn't she just pick me up and carry me? I was only three years old. Could it have been because I was scared of her and started screaming when she came near me? Like lots of things about my dear mother, I guess we'll never know."

Marilyn returned to the latest point in her story—herself at seven years old, losing her mother once again. Marilyn had lived with Gladys for around two years when things began to deteriorate. As the months went by, Gladys became increasingly depressed until, one morning in January 1935, she lost control and came at her friend Grace with a kitchen knife. The English boarders called an ambulance.

"I remember my mother laughing and screaming as she was forcibly removed to Los Angeles General Hospital, and later to the state hospital in Norwalk. I knew once again that my mother would never be able to take care of me the way I wanted her to."

Except for very brief periods, Gladys was institutionalized for the rest of her life. Thus ended the only significant amount of time Marilyn ever lived a normal life with her mother.

"I have always felt guilty," Marilyn said pensively, "that my love for her wasn't great enough to keep her sane.

"Years later, I drove by the house to show it to Jim, my first husband. 'I lived there once with my mother,' I said nostalgically to him, 'before she got ill and was taken away to the asylum. It was very beautiful. We had lovely furniture and even a white baby grand piano. I had my own room.' It all seems like an exquisite dream now. The way you wake up in the morning sometimes and half-remember a seductive dream that you try and try to recapture but cannot quite get hold of.

"The English couple, whose names I can't remember for the life of me, kept me for nearly a year, although we moved to a small apartment when they were unable to keep up the payments on our house. I was enrolled at the Selma Avenue School. I'll never forget my first day there, when all the children except me were accompanied by their parents. The couple had dropped me off at school and gone about their business. I stood there forlornly in line. One little girl pointed to me and said loudly to her mother, 'That little girl must be an orphan. Nobody brought her to school.' Her mother said, 'Shhhh, Susan! She'll hear you!' I ran out of the line, hid in a corner, and sobbed. Nobody noticed. After a while, feeling abandoned and alone, I crept to the end of the line, where I turned my face to the wall.

"Eventually, the English couple returned to England, and I was moved into the home of our neighbors, Harvey Giffen and his wife. Harvey Giffen was quite taken with me. He thought I was beautiful and charming and even offered to adopt me, just like the Bolenders had— and a colleague of Gladys's from Consolidated Film Industries, whom I haven't mentioned yet, Doctor—but Gladys again refused."

How selfish of her! I thought indignantly. *When she knew she could not take care of Norma Jeane herself, Gladys should have let a kind and willing family adopt her.* But I quickly amended my thinking. *She was psychotic, and always expected she would get well enough to take care of the child herself.*

It was perhaps even more of a tragedy for her than for her daughter.

FEBRUARY 10, 1959

"The Giffens moved away, too," Marilyn began, picking up the story of her life where she had left off, "and Gladys's best friend, Grace McKee, was named my legal guardian and took over my care. Grace and Gladys were good-time girls of the Roaring Twenties, and had no trouble finding men, who would often supply them with illegal liquor. These were my role models, Doctor.

"I remember overhearing a conversation between Grace and a friend of hers, who tried to convince her not to take me on. She said I would be a 'mental case,' like my mother, and Grace would be stuck with the responsibility of my care for life. I lay there shivering in the dark as I listened to their conversation. I had no idea what a mental case was, but I was sure it wasn't good. Fortunately, Grace didn't listen to her friend, and filed the necessary papers to become my legal guardian.

"She quickly became a key figure in my life. She was around thirty-nine at the time, and had already been divorced twice. A petite woman no more than five feet tall, she was around the same size as my mother, and the two of them often wore each other's clothes. Sometimes from the back, I couldn't tell which woman I was following. After a while, it didn't matter.

"Grace couldn't have children, so my mother encouraged her to share in the responsibility for me. Grace possessed a certain magnetism, and when she was in a room, all eyes were fastened on her. When I became a star, people said the same thing about me. Maybe I learned how to do it by copying her. She wasn't a beautiful woman, but her vitality and charm gave the impression of beauty. You can still see it in her photos. She had brown hair, which she dyed a peroxide blonde. Sound familiar? And, wait till you hear this, Doctor. She'd always wanted to be an actress, but never had the backbone to try. Guess who did it for her?

"After Gladys lost her mother, she needed someone to lean on, and became even more dependent on Grace for counseling and guidance. Grace lived her life through others, and the two women were a perfect combination. When they went shopping, Grace selected clothing for both of them. Grace thought nothing of correcting Gladys's grammar when they were with friends. My mother didn't seem to mind. Grace loved to advise, and Gladys was happy that Grace cared enough about her to give her advice.

"It was then the depths of the Depression, and despite the scarcity of money, the optimist Grace was convinced that their future could only get better. She loved and adored me so much that people who knew us then still tell me about it," Marilyn said. "My spirits were low, with my mother gone, and Grace did all she could to cheer me up. Like my mother, Grace fed my fantasies of becoming a great movie star. When I missed Gladys, Grace changed the subject. 'You're going to be very beautiful when you grow up,' she told me. 'You'll be a most important woman, a big movie star, as big as Jean Harlow.' Grace was much enamored of Jean Harlow, the platinum blonde superstar, so naturally Jean Harlow became my idol, too.

"Grace was really my first teacher. She knew how she wanted me to look, and conducted a charm school for one pupil—me. She taught me to look people directly in the eye when talking to them, to be polite, to speak and enunciate clearly, and to curtsey correctly, in case I ever met the Queen of England. When I did meet her years later, I curtseyed very properly and felt very grateful to Grace that I didn't fall flat on my ass.

"Grace really believed the things she said to me. 'There's just something about her. I feel it,' she'd say to anyone who would listen. I guess she felt I had something that today's called the 'X factor'—some indescribable quality that leads to stardom. Many people have used the term about me since Grace first described it. I don't know if Grace was prescient or just needed to believe it because she'd wanted to be an actress so badly herself.

"But I heard it so much from her that I believed it," Marilyn said. "I would go to bed at night sucking my thumb and dreaming of becoming another Jean Harlow. *I even have the same name*, I remember thinking. *What better proof that God wants me to be a movie star?*"

I smiled and thought that both Marilyn and Grace were guilty then of wishful thinking.

"Around that time, I had a dream that seemed to bear out our belief in my future," Marilyn said, as if she had listened in on my thoughts. "I call my dream 'The Blinding Light Dream.' I dreamt that I heard a knock on Grace's front door. When I opened it, there was a blinding light so powerful I could hardly see who was there. I put my hands over my eyes to shield them, and saw through my fingers that it was Jean Harlow. She said, 'Congratulations, Norma Jeane. You'll be a great star like me.' 'Thank you, Jean,' I said humbly. 'I know you're right.'

"I told Auntie Grace the dream, and she said, 'Yes, yes, Norma Jeane! Your dream's a message from Heaven. I always knew it! Jean Harlow has come down from the heavens to bring you the truth.' I only hoped Jean Harlow knew what she was talking about."

What a prescient dream little Norma Jeane had! I did not know about Jean Harlow, but the dream told me that in her unconscious, Marilyn always knew her destiny. As with many of us, her unconscious was more knowledgeable than her conscious mind.

"I still missed my mother," Marilyn continued. "Grace treated us to lunch at a coffee shop once, on a day's outing from the hospital, but Gladys was not interested in me. I told you about this, didn't I? All Gladys talked about was the poor quality of the coffee shop's food. 'I eat better at the asylum,' she said glumly.

"When I tried to get her attention, saying, 'Mother, someday I'm going to be a great movie star and make you proud of me,' she just looked at me with steely, unimpressed eyes and went right on eating her hamburger. I felt as bad as I ever had and could hardly finish my lunch, although it was my favorite—a rare hamburger and milkshake.

"I was quite gloomy overall," Marilyn recalled. "I knew I could be thrown out of Grace's place at any moment. I knew I had no real home. There was little in my life that gave me pleasure, so I dreamt up all kinds of make-believe to feel better. Fantasies of Clark Gable coming down the chimney like Santa Claus to carry away his long-lost daughter nourished me through many an endless, dreary night, and soothed the wounds inflicted by an absent mother.

"Come to think of it, isn't that what I'm still doing? Maybe there was something good about my daydreaming after all," she said insightfully. "Haven't the fantasies prepared me for my acting career, where every role involves the pretense of being someone else?"

FEBRUARY 11, 1959

"As I'd feared," Marilyn resumed, "Grace found herself in the late summer of 1935 without any money, unable to support me financially. So, on September 13th, she told me she had no choice but to take me to the Los Angeles Orphans Home Society, a dreary red brick building in the center of Hollywood. My admission to the orphanage was the all-time low of a short life which up until then had been little but a series of low points. Being moved out by Grace proved to me what I'd always felt—that I could be gotten rid of easily when it was no longer convenient to have me around. It felt like I was being sent to prison, and I wondered what I'd done to merit such punishment.

"When I saw the sign 'Orphanage' over the front door, I began to scream, 'Please, please don't make me go inside! I'm not an orphan! My mother isn't dead! I'm *not* an orphan! It's just that she's sick in the hospital and can't take care of me. Please don't make me live in an orphans' home!'

"It didn't help. I was dragged into the orphanage where, instead of being Norma Jeane, I suddenly became anonymous orphan number 3463. I was pulled, still screaming, into a grim gray dormitory with twenty-seven cots. My bed was right by the window, overlooking RKO Studios, where my mother had once worked. I stared at it every free moment I could find to reassure myself that I really did have a mother. I felt so wretched that every night, I lay in bed with a blanket over my head so nobody would hear me crying.

"The whole first year, I had nightmares practically every night. In one of them, which I call 'The Adrift at Sea Dream,' I was alone in a rowboat way out in a vast ocean. I looked far and wide, but saw nothing and nobody. I searched for an oar to start rowing, but there were none in the boat. I started to scream, 'Help me! Help me! I'm too little to find my way home by myself.' I woke up before I could see if any help came. The nightmares were so terrifying that I forced myself to stay awake by sleeping on pieces of gravel from the yard.

"I used to wake up some days and think I'd died. I couldn't feel anything, and it seemed like I wasn't part of my body anymore. I didn't mind. At least if I was dead, nothing could hurt me anymore. Then I would go into my fantasy world, where I would be so beautiful that everybody would turn around to look at me when I passed by. When that didn't work, I'd fill my pockets with sand to weigh me down so I wouldn't float away. I still do that sometimes."

"Does it help?" I asked.

"Well, I haven't floated away yet," she said.

FEBRUARY 12, 1959

The next session, Marilyn, who was rapidly becoming an old hand at the business of psychoanalysis, continued her lifestory . . . and her associations.

"I call it 'The Dying Baby Dream.' It wasn't as nice as the Jean Harlow dream, and it was mighty short, so even I know the meaning of this one. I dreamt that I saw a baby dying, and no one was helping.'"

I teared up. *If only I could have helped that dying baby!*

Marilyn returned to the topic of the orphanage as if there had been no break in her thoughts.

"Oh, how I hated the orphanage, Doctor! I snuggled under the covers as long as they let me. When I had to get up, I ran into the bathroom with all the other girls and brushed my teeth and my tongue. I made sure not to skip scrubbing my tongue, because the nurse checked all the children's tongues every day as we left to go to school, and if yours was even a tiny bit coated, you were forced to take castor oil. Believe me, I made sure to scour mine religiously every day!

"After the inspection was over, we went to the Vine Street School, which was a horrible ordeal from the moment I entered. All the girls wore lovely-colored gingham dresses, except for those of us from the orphanage. We had to wear the same faded blue uniforms every day. The other girls made fun of us, and would point and giggle, 'Tee-hee, they're from the orphanage! They look like they're all from the same scrap heap!' To the present day, I won't be caught dead wearing anything in that dismal blue color.

"At the home, I had to wash a hundred cups, a hundred plates, and a hundred knives, forks, and spoons three times a day, seven days a week. For my work, I was paid the huge sum of five cents a month, four of which I had to put in the collection plate at church. Boy, was I rich! I could keep one cent a month, which was more than I'd ever had before. I'd walk to the candy store and buy a red lollipop, and try to take only five licks a day to make it last. Sometimes, I'd think what would become my lifetime motto: 'Life is rough, so what the hell!,' and gobble down the whole lollipop at once. Then I was even sadder for the rest of the month."

Marilyn started to smile. "People are always trying to cheat me," she said, "starting way back then. I had a friend called Gennothy for a while. We would walk to the candy store together, where I'd buy my red lollipop and she'd buy an orange one. On the way home one day, I said, 'I'll give you a lick of my lolly if you'll give me a lick of yours.' She said, 'OK.' She then grabbed my lolly, put it in her mouth, and covered it with her hand. I said, 'Hey, wait a minute! I know what you're doing. You're taking a lot of licks!' That was the end of that friendship."

Marilyn returned to her memories of Grace. "Fortunately, Grace hadn't abandoned me completely. I don't know what would have become of me if she had. She visited me frequently and took me to the movies, bought me clothes, and taught me how to apply make-up at the youthful age of ten. I looked in the mirror and lit up. For the first time in my life, I loved my face, with my lips filled out with bright red lipstick and my eyelashes gleaming with black mascara.

"I thought, 'I *do* look like Jean Harlow. Maybe I *will* get to be a real movie star someday after all!' For that moment, I felt happy. None of the other girls my age had any make-up, or knew how to put it on, and I could tell they were jealous of me by the mean looks cast my way and the fact that they giggled whenever I came into a room. But I didn't care. I had Grace, whose visits were like shooting stars lighting up the black skies of night. For me, they were the only bright spots in an otherwise colorless existence.

"In the summer of 1937, Grace at last rescued me from the orphanage. Earlier that year, she had married Ervin 'Doc' Goddard, who had three children from a previous marriage. They were trying to establish some semblance of a normal family life in Doc's little home in Van Nuys.

"Unfortunately, it wasn't terribly normal. Like Wayne, Doc made sexual advances on me. He called me into his study when Grace was out shopping and said, 'Come here, Norma Jeane.' He put his arms around me and held me close. It felt so good I didn't want him to ever stop. Then he said, 'Norma Jeane, take down your panties. I want to see what you look like.' I didn't want him to stop holding me, so I did as he said. It was exciting having him look at me, but I experienced a funny feeling down there I'd never felt before and wondered if it really was all right. He gave me a nickel and said, 'Let's keep this our little secret, shall we?' I nodded and backed out of the room.

"But I felt funny about 'our little secret.' I was worried that I would go to Hell, as my first foster parents, the Bolenders, had predicted, so, despite Doc's request that I keep it between us, I decided to ask Grace about it.

"'Auntie Grace,' I said, 'is it all right if Doc makes me pull down my panties?' To my surprise, my beloved Auntie Grace, who'd always believed me when I told her something, refused to listen, shouting, 'Don't you dare say such things about my beloved husband! You must have provoked him!'"

Marilyn paused to collect herself. Her voice shaking, she said, "The trauma left me with a stutter I have to the present day. It only comes out when I'm feeling nervous. I try my darndest to stop it, but the more I try, the worse it gets. Fortunately, nobody but me usually notices, or if they do, they don't tell me about it.

"Which reminds me of a time a director did notice. I was stuttering badly in a scene he was trying to shoot, and he began to yell at me, 'What's the matter, Marilyn? You don't stutter!' I answered, 'That's w-w-what you th-th-think!'"

Even I had to smile.

FEBRUARY 13, 1959

Marilyn returned to her story about Aunt Grace and her pedophile husband. "Blaming me for the assault, my dear Auntie Grace threw me out of the house again and placed me in another foster home. But it was a case of jumping out of the frying pan into the fire. There came a succession of foster homes, each one worse than the one before.

"In one of them, they gave me empty whiskey bottles to play with. I played 'store' with them. I'll bet I had the finest collection of whiskey bottles of any little girl in history. I filled them up with water and lined them up beside the road. When cars drove up, I'd ask, 'Would you like to buy some whiskey today?' Nobody bought any, but I remember one sour-faced old lady muttering, 'How terrible! What is this world coming to when a little girl like that is selling whiskey?! What kind of parents must she have?'"

Good question, lady!

"I was so miserable in the foster homes they placed me in. So many of the fathers sexually abused me that I actually pleaded with Grace to send me back to the orphanage. These fathers weren't as kind as Doc had been, and I thought anything was better than having those dirty old men poking at me. One boarder even raped me in his room, but by then I knew better than to tell the foster mother about it. I knew she wouldn't believe me, because that would have meant throwing the boarder out of the house and losing much-needed income.

"It was right after the rape that my," and here Marilyn struggled to get the word out, "my stutter got worse, and still returns when I'm in a difficult situation, such as having to speak in front of a group. Grace noticed my speech impediment, and I suppose some part of her was forced to admit I was telling the truth, or that I had faced some kind of trauma. Either way, she invited me to live with them again.

"For some time after I moved back in with the Goddards, I was nicknamed 'the Mouse.' I would come into a room where people were talking and listen intently to their conversation, but rarely joined in. Like many children from an orphanage, I felt my opinions were of little value, and that no one was interested in hearing them. I still feel that way sometimes, and often don't speak unless I am spoken to. However, I always kept a picture of Clark Gable on my wall, and often spoke to him, so I didn't feel completely alone. *If he were my real father*, I thought, *he would be happy to hear what I have to say.*

"I didn't stay long this time at the Goddards, however, again because of Doc's continued attempts to sexually abuse me. Grace sent me to live with my great-aunt, Olive Brunings, in Compton, California. Would you believe this was also a short stay ended by a sexual assault, this time by one of Olive's sons? It didn't seem to bother him that I was his second cousin."

She sounded puzzled. "Why did men keep assaulting me, Doctor? Was Grace right? Did I provoke them? Was it my fault?"

"No, Marilyn," I said, indignant at the very thought. "Absolutely not! You were a little girl and they were grown men who presumably had you in their care. Whatever you did or did not do, they had no right to lay a hand on you. What they did was criminal, and they deserve to be prosecuted for it."

Marilyn burst into tears.

Surely most of Marilyn's symptoms—among them her hypersexuality—were the result of the sexual abuse she suffered during childhood, as well as her relationships with her supposed caregivers: an absent father, a psychotic mother, and a series of abusers. Who among us could have escaped unharmed from so many traumatic incidents? Her beauty, which later brought her great fame and glory, was at the time a true curse. Surely, ordinary-looking women like me, who often envied that beauty, were better off without it.

FEBRUARY 16, 1959

"In early 1938, when I was twelve years old," Marilyn said, beginning her next session, "Grace sent me to live with her aunt, Ana Lower, whose home was in Van Nuys in Los Angeles County. When I first set foot on her doorstep, I trembled. I was terrified that this placement would be a repeat of my experiences in the endless line of foster homes I had known.

"But the moment I entered Auntie Ana's home, I sensed a different, more positive atmosphere. Ana was a nice-looking, grandmotherly widow of fifty-eight when I moved in with her, and the sweetest, dearest, least selfish woman I have ever known. She gave me the love and kindness I rarely had received before, and I gloried in her attention. She was divorced, and received a small income as a Christian Science lay counselor. And a good one she was, according to many of her clients, who kept returning to her for advice year after year.

"She tried to pass on her knowledge to me, but I didn't find it helpful at the time. I regret that, because it would have made her very happy. It did at least one good thing for me, however, which greatly contributes to my fame. Auntie Ana always said, 'Evil is the awful deception and unreality of existence.' That philosophy is the basis of my lifelong ability to seem innocent, to never see evil in anything, and to avoid feelings of guilt about anything I do. It's a pretty important gift she bequeathed to me. I wish I could be a believer in Christian Science. It might help me with my zillions of problems. No offense, Doctor, but I could use someone like Auntie Ana now." Marilyn stopped to wipe away a tear.

"Why don't *you* adopt me, Doctor? No, it wouldn't help if you did. You're too cold and unfeeling, like Gladys. Auntie Ana didn't have much, but unlike you, she shared whatever she had with others. She was a true mother to me, and the only one I've ever known. I loved her dearly, and knew she loved me, too. She was the one human being who taught me what love is. She never hurt me or said a mean thing to me—not once. She didn't have it in her even to kill a fly, but would cup it in her hands like Dr. Albert Schweitzer and carry it outside, where she would happily watch it fly off.

"Unlike my other placements, this one was a huge success. Thank goodness I had her to love me. I hesitate to think what my life would have become without her to show me that there are good and loving people in the world. Thank goodness, too, that there were no men in the house to abuse me sexually, or heaven knows what would have happened to me. Had there been yet another one, I would probably be a stark raving lunatic like my mother.

"I spent four straight years with Auntie Ana, and it was one of the few periods in my life when I felt I had a home." Marilyn's smile faded unexpectedly. "At first, though, I had trouble getting along with the other students at school." Her voice began to shake. "They all seemed to know the latest slang and current jokes, and I stood around like a dummy, not knowing how to join in their conversation. I was heart-broken when I overheard one nasty boy say I was a dumb girl with no personality."

This memory, it seemed, was too much for her. To my surprise, Marilyn dashed out the door without saying goodbye.

FEBRUARY 17, 1959

The next day, Marilyn came in looking at the floor and handed me a piece of paper.

"This is for you," she said. "I wrote it. It's a poem. A parody of Robert Browning's 'My Last Duchess.' You won't like it."

That's my last Analyst painted on the wall,
Looking as if she were alive. My Shrinker's head
Works busily all day, and there she sits,
A true Shrinker by design.
It was not this patient's presence alone that called a spot
Of joy into the Analyst's cheek.
She had a heart—how shall I say?—too soon made glad,
Too easily impressed; she liked whate'er
She looked on, and her looks went everywhere.
My favor at her breast,

The dropping of the daylight in the West,
The book of Freud (Jung would do)
All would draw from her alike the approving speech.
Oh, yes, she smiled, no doubt,
Whene'er I passed her; but who passed without
Much the same smile?
There she sits
As if alive.

I was secretly delighted at her cleverness, though not very pleased at the continuing signs of negative transference. I just hoped it would not last too long.

FEBRUARY 18, 1959

She came in for her next session still looking glum.

I said, "Are you still mad at me, Marilyn?"

"Nah," she said. "You're not so bad, though the last session reminded me of an awful experience I had in junior high school."

"I'm sorry about that, Marilyn. Please tell me about it."

"It was Valentine's Day, and we were told to make cards for our classmates. I diligently designed and drew thirty of them, staying up late at night to get them finished on time for the big day. I made a beautiful colored Valentine for every student in the class, and waited impatiently to see the cards I'd get in return. When the teacher distributed the cards, I was devastated to find that I didn't get a single one, and in fact was the only one in the classroom who hadn't received any at all. One popular girl named Marie Louise got fifteen. When she asked me, 'How many cards did you get, Norma Jeane?' I answered, 'Three.' In my heart, that's how I'll always see myself—the only person in my class who didn't receive a single Valentine.

"To make matters worse, because I was tall and skinny, they nicknamed me 'Norma Jeane, the Human Bean.' When I first heard it, I felt so bad that I decided to play hooky from school the next day. But for the first time in my life, I had a sympathetic ear when I came home from school. Auntie Ana listened to my tale of woe and reassured me. 'Norma Jeane,' she said, 'you're new to the school. It's hard for all children to be accepted into a new school. I promise you that you'll learn to get along with the other children. It just takes time.' So great was my trust in her that I completely accepted what she said and returned to school the next day. I was glad I listened to her. She turned out to be right.

"Then something important happened which was to change my life forever. I began to develop sexually, and to see myself in a different light. For the first time, I recognized the value of my beauty and began to do all I could to enhance it. To show off my figure, I started to wear sweaters and tighter clothing. The other girls admired my new flair and began to imitate me.

"Even more important, Emerson Junior High School was two and a half miles away from Auntie Ana's and I had a long walk to and from school. Suddenly, every guy who drove by began to honk his car horn at me, and I felt more self-confident. Soon, the whole world became a friendlier place.

"I just remembered a dream I had when I was about thirteen years old. I was walking by the ocean enjoying the fresh sea air and watching the swells of water. All of a sudden, a wave as large as a mountain came rolling toward me. I was terrified that I was going to drown. I tried to run inland, but my legs were paralyzed—all I could do was stand there and watch in horror as the wave came closer and closer. But just as the water began rising over my head, a miracle happened. The terrible wall of water fell away and I began happily skipping along the oceanside."

"Wonderful, Marilyn," I said. "The dream corroborates everything you said about the way you felt when boys began to notice you. We can see from your dream how well you mastered the tremendous surge of feelings adolescents experience. Some people's lives end at adolescence; yours was just beginning."

She seemed pleased, and was quiet for a few moments, as if she wanted to mull over what I had said.

Then she continued, "At the time, I loved Ginger Rogers. I thought she was a beautiful, sexy woman. I wanted to grow up to be just like her. I confessed my desire to Auntie Ana, expecting her to say, 'Don't be silly, Norma Jeane. Who do you think you are? You're just a poor orphan girl who'll be lucky to grow up to be a cutter like your mother.'

"But to my delight, she said nothing of the sort. Instead, she encouraged me to practice reading Ginger's lines out loud to her. She said, 'You have talent, Norma Jeane. If you work hard, I believe you can grow up to be a famous actress like Ginger.'

"Things were going so well, I knew they couldn't last. This time it was Auntie Ana. To my great distress, Aunt Ana developed serious health problems as she grew older, became more and more fragile, and was eventually unable to take care of me. This upset her very much, and she worried about me all the time, which made her health deteriorate even further. So back to Grace and Doc Goddard's house I had to go. I was about sixteen at the time.

"One of the great regrets of my life is that Auntie Ana will never know she was right about my becoming a successful actress. It would have made her so happy." Marilyn's voice choked and her stutter reemerged. "She died—died before I got my first part. I—I felt I'd drown in grief. Even now, there isn't a day that goes by that my heart doesn't bleed for her."

FEBRUARY 19, 1959

The next day, Marilyn arrived a bit out of breath and said, "I'm late because I stopped to buy you this." She opened her purse and took out a huge, luscious peach. She plopped herself on the couch and laid the fruit on the table next to it. We both looked at it with awe. It was enormous, rosy-cheeked, and mouth-watering. Never had I seen such a glorious peach.

"Did you bring me a belated Valentine's Day present?" I asked.

She smiled but didn't answer my question. "I've brought you a peach," she said. "But it looks so good I might change my mind and eat it all myself."

"Why do you want to give it to me?"

"It's an apple for the teacher," she said smilingly, and then went on to other matters.

Poor Marilyn got short shrift of an analyst that session. The peach lay there invitingly all hour, and I couldn't tear my eyes away from it.

FEBRUARY 20, 1959

Marilyn's next session was odd indeed. Not because of Marilyn, but because of me. I found myself filled with a strange yearning I had never felt before in the presence of a patient. I felt a strong pull to take Marilyn in my arms and comfort her. When an analyst has such strong feelings, it is usually because the patient is doing something to induce them. In the jargon of the trade, such a reaction is called "counter-transference." I looked at Marilyn carefully.

Marilyn began to cry, and she said to me in a pleading voice, stuttering brokenly, "Why won't you ever hold me, like Auntie Ana did? What a m-mean woman you are! I don't know why you're so stingy with your affections. Would it hurt you to hold a girl for a few minutes?"

Holding her arms around herself, she had thrown back her head, thrust her breasts forward, and was looking at me with those haunting blue eyes. I knew she was pleading with me to love her. I felt overwhelmed by one of the most powerful emotions I had ever known.

What is it with this woman? I thought. *What is this strange power she has that makes her the sweetheart of the world? Here I am, a woman who is 100 percent heterosexual, but this . . . this child-woman is exuding something that makes me ache to cuddle her in my arms. The feeling is so strong I can barely resist it. It is as if she is silently beseeching me, "If you come and comfort me, all my problems will go away."*

After all, what harm possibly could be done simply by holding her in my arms? For a long moment, I considered going to her. I knew very well it was against the rules of psychoanalysis to have physical contact with a patient. Giving in to such a wish is called, in analytic jargon, "acting out." But a little voice inside me said: *Surely Marilyn is not like other patients. She was terribly deprived as a child, and she has never recovered from it. Isn't it possible that giving her affection now will make up for what she never received?* Besides, I would have loved to hold her.

It was this thought that gave me away. It was not only that *she* wanted to be held, but that *I* wanted to hold *her*! Where did this temptation come from? What need did Marilyn's desperation awaken in me in return?

I remembered a story told to me by the great psychologist Harry Harlow, about a game he played at a party. Records of crying infants were played to guests. When the cries of a brain-damaged infant were heard, no one responded. But when the record of a normal infant's cries was played, all the guests were uncomfortable. "The cry of a normal infant," Harlow said, "causes an instinctual response in a normal adult."

Like Marilyn, schizophrenics often are notoriously appealing, attracting surrogate parents like stray kittens. To my knowledge, no one had questioned the reason for their appeal. Could it be that they were simply telegraphing the signals of an infant?

Marilyn was crying. Should I answer the cries of a normal infant who had never grown up? I knew, deep down, that I absolutely should not.

Your indulgence, I rebuked myself, *would just add your name to the list of her exploiters. Your job is to resist the impulse to gratify her—and yourself!—and find out why she needs to be held so strongly at this moment, and what she is doing to make you and the whole world fall in love with her—not to discover the secret of her screen genius, but to help her take one more step along the path to emotional health.*

"I know very well why you won't do it, and so do you," Marilyn said, crying and tripping over her words as she so often did in our sessions. "Despite your pretty words, in your heart of hearts, you don't like me. That's why! When it comes right down to it, you're just like everyone else. I wonder how long you'd see me if I didn't pay you enough to take care of your rent!" She wound her arms tightly around herself and began to rock back and forth.

Then, seemingly out of the blue, vindicating me and the dictates of psychoanalysis, Marilyn verbalized a memory. Sniffing, she said, "My Aunt Ana never would be so mean. She always took me on her lap and rocked me when I was upset. You look just like her, but you're far from being the kind woman she was." She cried, "Auntie Ana, Auntie Ana, why did you abandon me?" She sobbed, "I love you. I need you. Come back to me now."

Marilyn cried for perhaps ten minutes before she was ready to again recount her memories of her beloved aunt.

"I can feel what it was like when she held me as clearly as if it were happening now. We rocked together on her brown wooden rocking chair. I can hear the sweet sound of her chair creaking, and I can feel the heat of her body against mine, rising and falling as the chair rocked. Her skin smelled of lilac soap, which I love, and her long brown braids fell over my back and tickled me. I didn't want to move them even though they tickled. I didn't want to lose a single sensation of being in her arms.

"I once wrote a poem about her and showed it to somebody and they cried when I read it to them. It was called, 'I Love Her.' It was about how I felt when she died.

"She was the only person who loved and understood me. She showed me the path to the higher things of life and gave me confidence in myself. She was not mean like you. She never hurt me—not once. She couldn't. She was all kindness and all love. *She* was good to me. She taught me how to love."

Freud was right, I thought, as Marilyn continued crying and rocking herself. *An analyst should not indulge patients in their deepest desires.* "Acting out" keeps memories away from consciousness. Hard as it was to resist the pull that had millions of people all over the world in its grasp, I breathed a sigh of relief that I hadn't gone to Marilyn in her moment of need. If I had, the wonderful memory of being held and loved by her beloved Aunt Ana never would have returned to her. She needed to remember that even in the midst of a hostile world, she once was loved. She needed that far more than she needed to be indulged by her analyst.

FEBRUARY 22, 1959

"Thanks for seeing me on Washington's Birthday," Marilyn said. "Come to think of it, why *should* I miss my session to celebrate his birthday? He may've been the father of our country, but he wasn't *my* father."

Then she went on to chat about inessential matters, which is known in analysis as "resistance."

FEBRUARY 24, 1959

Apparently, Marilyn did not support my not holding her, despite the wonderful memories my decision had brought out in her. The next day, I received this poem in the mail.

"The Healer"
(With apologies to my good friend, Robert Frost)

Something there is that doesn't love a Shrink
That makes the frozen-ground swell, whatever I think.
And makes gaps we two can't pass abreast
You, mighty Shrink, remain the boss
And my soul to you will ne'er get across
The sturdy unbreakable Maginot Line
Of the wall between us that stands just fine.

Spring makes me mischievous, and I wonder
Will it also crack your head asunder?
Before building a wall like yours, I'd want to see
What was walled up inside of me,
And to whom I was likely to give offense,
And if what I was doing made any sense.
Something there is that doesn't love a Shrink
When what she needs is one stiff drink.

Something there is in a Shrink I don't love,
Get out of my head or I'll give you a shove.
What you are thinking would I could gather
But you certainly know I would much rather
You said it yourself, as you sit there
Half asleep in your Shrinker's chair.
You hide in darkness, and one can see
That is exactly the place you need to be.

I wrote her back a short, admiring note. "Wow, Marilyn! That's wonderful! Your friend Robert Frost would be impressed, too. I am properly chastised."

Reading my response to her poem, she probably beamed.

FEBRUARY 25, 1959

Forgetting all about out last exchange, Marilyn rushed happily into my office and shouted, "My sister's coming to see me today!"

I said, "Your sister? I did not know you had a sister."

"Neither did I until I was twelve years old. She's my half-sister, actually, the one my father stole away from my mother before I was born. Her name is Berniece Baker Miracle, and she *is* a miracle, if anyone ever is. She's seven years older than me, but you wouldn't think it to look at her. She's very pretty, and has the same figure as I do, but she isn't as blonde. I'm taller than she is, but not all that much."

"How did you find out about her?"

"My mother, in one of her saner moments, asked my Aunt Grace to tell me about her. Gladys wouldn't let her tell me before because she didn't think I was ready to hear it. Who wouldn't want to know she has a sister? If you need any more proof that my mother is nuts, that's it!"

"Tell me about Berniece. Is she important in your life?"

"God, yes! Imagine how thrilled I was to hear that I had a living relative, that I wasn't a lonely only child after all. I loved her before I ever met her, and she feels the same about me. She's been my best friend since I first heard she existed. As soon as Auntie Grace told me about her, we started corresponding. We exchanged photos and letters in which we told each other all about our lives during the years before we got to meet. She lived in Kentucky, and there was no way a twelve year old in an orphanage could get the money to pay her a visit. I used to daydream that we would meet and fall into each other's arms. That's exactly what happened, too. It's one of the few times in my life when the reality of something turned out to be better than the fantasy.

"Our meeting, in 1944, was one of the most exciting days of my life. Jim—that's Jim Dougherty, whom I married in 1942—was on sea duty with the Merchant Marines. I was lonely and decided to blow all my service-wife allotment money to visit my big sister in Detroit, where the Miracles had moved to improve their financial status.

"I was eighteen years old and trembling with so much anticipation it was as if I were about to meet a new lover. I was terrified that we wouldn't recognize each other or that nobody would be at the station to meet me and I would have to turn around and go right back home. I stood waiting at the exit doors for a half hour before the train was due to pull into the station. Would Berniece like me or send me back on the next train? It wouldn't be the first rejection I'd known.

"Would I like her? I doubted very much that I wouldn't. In my position, I couldn't afford to be picky, and I thought any sister would be better than none. What would it be like having a big sister? Would she behave like a mother to me, or would I feel we were the same age? Would she boss me around? After all, she was twenty-five years old, and might consider a little sister a pest.

"Would we look alike? We did in our photographs. Was she prettier than me? I wouldn't like that. But then again I wouldn't like it if I were prettier than her. Then she'd be jealous and dislike me, like some of the girls at school. Could we ever make up for the long years we hadn't known about each other's existence and be real sisters? All these questions and more raced through my brain as I waited for the train to crawl into the station.

"But I needn't have worried. I got off the train, and before I could look around, a beautiful young woman rushed up to me and threw her arms around me. We hugged each other for a long, long time, until our tears soaked each other.

"When she took me home, we just sat there looking at each other like two people who'd recently fallen in love. Then we stood in front of the mirror, side by side, examining and comparing our faces. We had very similar hair, even though hers was a little darker even before I began to bleach mine. The strands curled off our foreheads in identical widows' peaks. I breathed a sigh of relief when I saw that we were equally pretty. We had exactly the same mouth and large, very white front teeth, which some people might think are slightly protruding, although the studio fixed mine later on."

She turned around, bared her teeth in a grimace, and asked, "Do you think they still protrude, Doctor?"

I shook my head. "No," I said, "they are the most perfect teeth I have ever seen."

She looked relieved and continued. "Our eyes were different colors, though. Berniece's were brown like her father's, and mine were a cobalt blue, like my mother's. If you covered up our eyes in a photo, you might think we were the same person.

"Berniece had seen pictures of our mother Gladys, and knew she'd been very beautiful when she was young, but wondered what she looked like now. I said that she was still pretty, but never, ever smiled. I also said that our mother was almost as much a stranger to me as she was to Berniece. My feeling was that my sister was not missing very much.

"If I envy Berniece at all, it's because she has a father," Marilyn said wistfully. "When Berniece said that Jasper Baker wasn't all that close to her and always had a drinking problem, I said, 'At least you have a father.' My newfound sister said, 'I'm sorry you don't have a father, Norma Jeane. I know how you must feel. I'd gladly share mine with you if I could.' Then she took me in her arms again and we wept together for the fatherless child I was. I never envied her again. How can you envy someone so loving and so dear?

"But the comparison that made us roll on the floor with laughter was when we stretched out our feet and compared them. They were exactly the same. We both had middle toes that were longer than the others. When we put our feet next to each other, you'd have thought we were a four-footed person." She began to laugh. "The funniest thing was that her five-year-old daughter, Mona Rae, also had the same feet. If anyone doubted that the three of us were related, we'd all fling off our shoes and say, 'Here, take a look, and believe!'

"Berniece is coming to visit me here in New York because I invited her. I'm having a little problem with Arthur—my husband Arthur Miller—and I want her advice. It's nice to have a big sister to go to. If only I'd had her around when I was little, my life would have been very different. She's been happily married to Paris Miracle for years. If anybody knows how to have a happy marriage, she does. I have a successful career and she has a successful marriage. If I had a choice, I'd trade with her any day."

I wondered about Marilyn's marriage to Jim Dougherty, which she had so far mentioned only in passing. Had he been her chance at happiness and health? Would she have stayed well if she had given up her career for him and followed a more mundane path, more like her sister's? Marilyn was deeply troubled, but perhaps she need not have been. There are people who live with the seeds of insanity—seeds that never sprout because the individuals concerned live comfortable, stress-free lives, with perhaps a loving parent or mate protecting them from "the slings and arrows of outrageous fortune." These people manage to function fairly well in the world, and no one doubts their sanity, thinking, if anything, that they are perhaps a bit more sensitive than the average person. They never have to live through the stresses, strains, and humiliations that Marilyn said she had to endure every day of her professional life.

FEBRUARY 27, 1959

In the next session, Marilyn picked up where she had left off before speaking of her excitement about her sister.

"When I was in the tenth grade at Van Nuys High School, Doc Goddard received a good job offer in Virginia, and the couple decided to accept it and move there. Perhaps for financial reasons, they decided not to take me with them."

Or maybe Grace was afraid that Doc's lustful feelings toward the blossoming young Marilyn would pop out again, I thought. They had run out of foster homes for her. She was still only fifteen years old, and there seemed no other option but to return her to the orphanage.

"I was very upset about this, of course," Marilyn said. "When Grace took me out of the orphanage the last time, she promised I'd never have to return there again. I felt she'd now gone back on her word. Knowing how upset I was at what I considered her betrayal, Grace was frantic to find another solution. Ever resourceful, she found one. 'You can get married,' she said to me.

"'Get married?' I protested. 'But Auntie Grace, I'm only fifteen years old!'

"'As my father used to say,' Grace cheerfully responded, 'if they're big enough, they're old enough!'

"'Who would I marry?' I said. 'I don't know anybody who wants to marry me.'

"'How about our neighbor's son, that nice Dougherty boy? You know, the one whose mother and I are always talking over the back fence,' she said, as if it hadn't already been prearranged by the two of them. 'He's tall and athletic, and he looks like a movie star. I know you like him, and I'll bet he'd be thrilled to have you for a wife. As a married woman, you'd never have to go back to an orphanage.'

"I dragged my heels for a few minutes, to Grace's irritation, and then thought, *Anything is better than going back to the orphanage.*

"I reluctantly agreed. I was two years under the California legal age. What a reason to get married!

"Later, Jim told me of his own uncertainty about marrying me," Marilyn said. "'Gosh, Mom,' he said, 'I never thought about getting married. I'm only twenty-one years old!' He asked his best friend Christopher for advice.

"Chris answered, 'She'd marry you? Wow! I'd love to get her between the sheets. Just think, you can have sex with her every night of the year! If you don't want her, just turn her over to me! I'll be happy to marry her!' That was all Jim needed to relent and agree to marry me.

"Grace was very relieved. She'd no longer have to care for me, and her conscience wouldn't bother her anymore.

"My feelings about the marriage were quite different from hers.

Living in so many foster homes had given me some interesting ideas about marriage, especially as a young girl of only fifteen. I didn't like what I'd seen of it. I guess you can say I was ahead of my time. All the husbands dominated their wives in matters of money and careers, and I was determined not to follow in their footsteps. But I had to get married. I had nowhere else to go.

"I felt betrayed and abandoned by Grace, who, it seemed, was shoving me into a loveless marriage. I thought, *If she really loved me, she'd take me with her to Virginia*.

"Despite her poor health, Auntie Ana made all the arrangements for the wedding, including sending out the invitations. A real mother couldn't have been more helpful. The wedding was three weeks after my sixteenth birthday, and took place at the home of our friends, Chester and Doris Howell, which I chose because it had a lovely winding staircase, and I could picture myself dramatically gliding down it to the lovely strains of 'Here Comes the Bride.'

"The actual experience was a bit different, however. I nearly tripped on my long train and almost broke my neck. But somehow I managed to regain my balance before any serious harm was done.

"At the bottom of the stairs, I was given away by Auntie Ana, because I had no father to do the job. People still say how lovely I looked in my hand-embroidered lace gown with its full skirt, long billowing sleeves, sweetheart neck, and white veil, while carrying a bouquet of white gardenias. Neither my mother nor the Goddards were there, but I was happy that Ida Bolender attended. My maid of honor was Lorraine Allen, a high school friend I never saw again, and Jim's best man was his brother Marion. I went through the ceremony as if I were floating above it all. And try as I might, I can't remember Jim's kiss after we were declared man and wife."

MARCH 2, 1959

Freud said that over the weekend, a "Monday morning crust" begins to develop, in which the analytic patient develops a resistance to treatment. This certainly did not seem to be true of Marilyn, who, at this next appointment, continued associating as if no weekend had interrupted her sessions.

"I was fairly happy with Jim for a while. I didn't know any better. I'd have liked to finish high school instead of dropping out in the middle of my sophomore year, but I was afraid that being a student and a housewife didn't mix, so I quit school on an impulse I've regretted ever since. I enjoyed playing housewife in our pretty little house in the bungalow court, every night making one of the two dishes I knew how to cook—macaroni and cheese from the package, and hamburgers. I also packed Jim a cold egg sandwich every day for lunch.

"We were quite poor, so I had to keep house on a small budget. We were always looking for bargains, and even stood in line to buy day-old bread. For a quarter, you could get enough to eat for a week. I remember wondering, *Will I ever have enough money that I don't have to stand in line for stale bread?*

"I was a bride, a woman on the outside, but really I was still a child. I actually took several of my dolls with me into the new house. One of Jim's brothers taught me how to play craps, and I bet my best doll on one roll of the dice. I lost and burst out crying. Jim asked me what was wrong and I said through my tears, 'I lost Esmerelda at crappies.' I didn't stop sobbing until he made his brother give me back my doll.

"The major effect the marriage had on me was to decrease any interest I may have had in sex. I was terrified at the idea, and asked Aunt Grace if it were possible to have a platonic marriage and be 'just friends.' She gave me a book on sex education. It wasn't very helpful. In fact, after looking at the illustrations, I was even more scared. I thought, 'Jim would do *that* to me? I won't allow it!' On our wedding night, I spent a lot of time in the bathroom and became very creative at finding ways to avoid my marital obligations."

I had to smile at the idea of Marilyn Monroe, often portrayed as a sex-happy woman if not a nymphomaniac, in a "platonic" marriage. Marilyn apparently didn't think I should find the idea even remotely funny. Although she was not looking at me at the time, she suddenly asked me, "Are you laughing at me?"

"Do I sound like I am laughing?" I said.

"No, but I bet you're laughing inside. That's the worst kind of being laughed at, because the person who's laughing refuses to admit it. Well, I'll give you the benefit of the doubt this time, but if I ever hear you laughing at me, I'll walk out of this office and never come back!"

By this time, I understood Marilyn well enough to know that when she said something, she meant it. Now, I would have to say something, but what? How do you prove that you have not been laughing? Or never would? I took a deep breath and said, "Many people have laughed at you in your lifetime, Marilyn. They were cruel and too limited themselves to be able to see the depth of your personality and talents. But you have accomplished the dreams they laughed at, and now you are the one who should be laughing at them."

My words seemed to reassure her. Although I believed every word of what I had just said, I sighed with relief that she had not seen me smiling.

MARCH 3, 1959

"When we got married, both Jim and I were virgins," she began, "and had little idea what we were doing. Jim wasn't particularly skillful at knowing what would please me, but just jumped into bed and got his own rocks off. He was usually in a hurry to get to sleep or go to work. I couldn't understand what all the fuss concerning sex was about. It seemed to me like getting all excited about shoe polish.

"Jim loved the sex, and I usually put up with it because I wanted to be a good wife. I'd just lay on my back and think of becoming a movie star. Later, he wrote a book in which he said I loved sex with him and was very passionate in bed. That was news to me! After sex with Jim, I often just rolled over and went to sleep. Sometimes, he worried that I would be unfaithful to him. He needn't have been. At that time, I had a complete lack of interest in sex.

"That first year, we spent a lot of time together and had fun doing many things. Unfortunately, more often than not, the 'fun' centered around Jim's interests rather than mine. We went fishing at Sherwood Lake, and skiing at Big Bear Lodge, and as a special treat once in a while, we went to the movies or out dancing.

"I loved it when we kicked off our shoes and walked by the ocean in the moonlight. I've always loved the ocean. Do you know, it reminds me of a wonderful story the Bolenders used to tell about me. When I was two years old, they took me to Manhattan Beach, where I saw the ocean for the first time. I jumped up and down and clapped my hands and shouted with delight, 'It's a big wet!'

"I like this story, too: When I was three years old, I first saw snow. I picked some up and watched it melt in my hand, and said with wonder, 'Snow makes juice!' I guess I've always had an original way of looking at things, even when I was two or three years old.

"Jim thought we were leading a great, fun-loving life, but I'm not so sure I was. Living someone else's idea of fun is not my cup of tea. I made my first suicide attempt that year by swallowing a bottle of pills, but I guess I wasn't very serious. Jim rushed in, stuck my head in the toilet bowl, and made me vomit up the pills right away.

"After that, I slept around the clock, and when I awoke to the light of day, I wasn't sure whether to be glad or sorry to be alive. Suicide is a person's privilege. Ending one's own life is neither a sin nor a crime. It's my right to kill myself if I want to, although, in retrospect, I'm just as glad I didn't succeed that time.

"Jim turned out to be a typical, old-fashioned chauvinist, who treated me like his private property," Marilyn continued. "When I confided my secret dreams of becoming a movie actress to him, he laughed. In high school, it turns out, he had won a Shakespeare contest for reciting Shylock's 'revenge' speech from *The Merchant of Venice*, and so he said, 'I used to be the ham around here. How come all of a sudden you want to be the performer? Well, dream on, little wifey, if it makes you happy. But I assure you that you'll never make it.' He didn't know it, but he had just rung the death knell of our marriage.

"Poor Jim," Marilyn mused. "He wasn't a bad guy. I'm sure he was disappointed that I wanted more out of life than washing dishes, scrubbing floors, and cooking meals. But if that was to be my lot, I might as well have been back in the orphanage.

"I might still be married to him," she said, "if it hadn't been for the war. In 1943, Jim enlisted in the Merchant Marines as a physical training instructor and was stationed on glorious Santa Catalina Island off the west coast of California, where we had a pretty little thirty-five-dollar-a-month hillside apartment. I was a compulsive housekeeper then, and cleaned house thoroughly every single day.

"We also had a collie called Muggsie, whom I bathed twice a week and kept immaculately groomed. I treated him as if he were my own beloved baby, and felt very proud whenever anybody commented on how beautifully I took care of him.

"Telling you that makes me wonder who I am," she mused. "I've changed so much, I don't know myself anymore. Am I a compulsive housecleaner or a slob? If you saw my bedroom this morning, Doctor, you could easily answer that question.

"Island life was idyllic in many ways," she continued. "I would stand on a hilltop, my hair blowing in the breeze, and gaze for long stretches at the foaming waves. I remember thinking that marriage was not so bad after all. Of course, Jim wasn't with me at the moment I had that thought.

"The island was the most beautiful place I'd ever lived, and it brought back one of the few good memories I had of my mother, because she had brought me there one weekend when I was little. I'll never forget how we wandered hand in hand on the beach and ate ice cream cones like any normal girl and her mother. Little did I know it would never happen again. Shortly after that weekend, she was hospitalized, and I hardly saw her at all after that.

"Well, enough of that, or I'll never finish telling you about my first marriage. Jim was the breadwinner and I cooked and cleaned house. We went to the beach and swim and dive or just lie around in the sun. At night, we sat on the porch and looked out at the starry skies. Sometimes Jim played the guitar and sang to me.

"It was mostly pleasant, as long as I didn't talk about becoming a film star. I soon learned to keep my ambitions to myself—shades of what I did when I boarded with the Bolenders—and I lived contentedly with Jim for several months in the lovely town of Avalon before they shipped him out to the Pacific.

"I was terrified that he wouldn't come back, and I wanted a baby desperately. 'Please, please, Jim,' I begged." Marilyn's stutter surfaced as she relived her anxiety. "'If—if God forbid, anything bad—happens to you, I'll—have something left to live for.'

"'No, Norma Jeane,' he kept insisting, 'you're too young to have a baby. What do you know about taking care of a child?'

"I never forgave him for that," she said grimly. "I was a strong and healthy nineteen-year-old girl, and surely could have gotten pregnant easily at that time. If a woman wants to have a baby and the man she loves won't allow it, it greatly hurts her deep down inside. Just think, I would have had a fourteen-year-old child by now!"

Tears ran down her cheeks as she mourned that never-to-be child. As was so often the case when Marilyn openly grieved, I was surprised to find that my cheeks were wet, too.

"After Jim shipped out, I moved in with his mother, Ethel," Marilyn explained, "so I could pocket our usual rent payment. But I hated being bossed around by that bitch and moved out as soon as I could. I didn't need anyone to tell me when to get up, when to go to bed, when to get washed, and when I should write to her son!

"Sometimes she wasn't so bad, to be fair. After Jim received an overseas assignment, Ethel got me a job at the defense plant at the Radio Plane Company in Burbank where she worked as a nurse. I enjoyed making my own money for the first time since getting paid a nickel at the orphanage for washing dishes. This time I didn't buy lollipops, but saved my money with the idea of renting my own apartment.

"At first, I inspected parachutes at the plant, but soon was promoted to another job where I stood on my feet for ten hours a day and sprayed sharp, tangy liquid plastic over target plane fuselages. It wasn't bad work, if you didn't mind coughing all day. Ethel, who had her nice moments, said, 'Honey, you'll ruin your beautiful hair with all those dreadful paint fumes.'

"But I wanted the money and persisted anyway. Despite the drudgery of the task—workers called the area the 'dope room,' supposedly because of the pungent vapors, but I think it was because you had to be a dope to keep working there—I was a conscientious employee who was awarded an 'E' certificate for my superior work. I even was crowned queen of the Radio Plane Picnic, where I won a gold button for making a useful suggestion about plant operations. For the first time in my life, I thought maybe I wasn't so dumb after all.

"During one of Jim's leaves, we went together to visit Gladys at the state mental hospital. 'Good morning, Mother,' I said. 'This is my husband, Jim, whom I'd like you to meet.' She ignored him and acted as if she hadn't heard me. The woman before us seemed like a stranger, and an unstable and peculiar one at that. She stood there rigidly, her arms held straight down by her sides, and showed no feelings at all.

"I badly needed some kind of emotional reaction from her, but it became apparent I was not going to get it. Tears streamed down my cheeks as we silently stood there waiting for a word from her that never came. 'Goodbye, Mother,' I finally said. 'We have to go now. But I'm leaving you my address and phone number so you can call me whenever you like.' I bent down and kissed her on the cheek. She had no more reaction than if I had kissed the Sphinx. I knew she wouldn't miss me, and it broke my heart.

"Something very exciting happened that spring, however, which made me feel better. I made my first appearance in a nationally circulated magazine—*Family Circle*—although I went unnamed and uncredited. An unknown admirer had publicized my company award, and I somehow ended up on the cover. I looked like a little girl of about thirteen years old, wearing an apron and playing with a tiny lamb. A worse picture of me you have never seen! It looked as if a retarded kindergartner had taken a red crayon and smeared it all over my mouth. Nevertheless, I was thrilled to be pictured on the cover of a national magazine, and somehow sensed it would be the first of many."

MARCH 4, 1959

Marilyn plopped herself down on the couch and began speaking as if no time at all had elapsed between sessions.

"Within a few months, I was recognized for something infinitely more exciting than the *Family Circle* cover. David Conover, an Army photographer, was assigned to visit the plant to shoot photos of women working to help the war effort. He was looking for a beautiful woman who would boost the morale of soldiers overseas. He came upon me, diligently at work in the 'dope' room, and thought I looked quite charming in my baggy company overalls. He also said he liked my 'fresh-faced look.' *Fresh-faced*? I wash my face fifteen times a day!

"When Conover found out I had a sweater in my locker, he asked me to model it for his series of photos for *Yank* magazine."

Marilyn raised her head from the couch and turned around and looked at me. "Hey, Doc," she said, "are you awake back there? Can you guess how he 'found out' I had a sweater? I told him, of course."

I smiled and said nothing, because I did not want to interrupt her flow of associations.

"He was a great photographer," she went on without waiting for a response, "and his stunning shots of me resulted in my first credited magazine cover and led directly to my career as a model. I'll always be grateful to him for discovering me, or I might still be Jim's 'itsy bitsy wifey.'

"I found out I was in my element as a photographer's model. Conover said he had never seen a model who took so naturally to the camera. Would you believe," she continued, "he said that I—little Norma Jeane, orphan number 3463, whom nobody ever looked at twice—was 'extraordinarily beautiful and exuded an incredible light'? At first, I couldn't believe he said that about me and wondered if he'd mixed me up with someone else.

"From the first photo on, I loved every second of posing. 'You mean I get paid for doing this?' I asked, when he took that first photo of me on the beach. I would have happily posed for nothing. I was very curious about the whole process and extremely critical of how I photographed. I constantly asked Conover questions about lighting, the difference between various lenses, how he got models to do their best work, and most important of all, what I had done wrong if I didn't like a shot. He was amazed at how quickly I seemed to grasp the principles of modeling. I really was a perfectionist about it."

"Your compulsiveness about housekeeping found a new home," I said. "And a much more productive one."

"Very good, Doc!" she said, turning her head and looking at me. "I never would have thought of that. For me to be happy with it, every shot had to be perfect. Although I wasn't consciously aware of it, I was learning the art of communicating human emotion through photographs. As Conover said, I had a love affair with the camera.

"*Finally*, I thought, *I have a love affair in which the affection is mutual. I love the camera, and the camera loves me.* It was like finding a fulfilling lover you never have to leave. I love it and it loves me back, and always will. For the first time in my life, I knew exactly where I belonged, and I no longer felt like Norma Jeane, the poor little orphan girl—at least not all the time. I've never really been the same since.

"Unlike the eyes of men, who see a luscious sexpot ripe for the picking, the camera's eye dives beneath the surface. Even in my early days of modeling, someone said the photographer 'uncovered in me a haunting combination of sweetness, vulnerability, sensitivity, and unselfconscious sexuality.'

"Wow! All that in one twenty-year-old girl! Men's eyes saw only the superficial covering. The camera's eye exposed the fears, anxiety, and courage behind my mask. The camera looks behind people's blinders and sees life like it is. Just put me in front of a camera and I'm in love with the world!

"Men are jealous, resentful, possessive, demanding, and vengeful; they're driven by feelings they don't know they have. Too many men in my life have turned nasty and cruel. But the camera? Never! Whatever I do, the camera worships me. Unlike the rest of my lovers, the camera has never failed me. It's the all-adoring mother I never had, my missing father, and the one lover who always leaves me feeling satisfied, beautiful, and loved. Why wouldn't I love it back?

"From my earliest intercourse with the little black box, the undercover message I sent to the world was, 'Love me! Love me, everybody! Make me famous. Please!'

"Conover encouraged me to apply to the Blue Book Modeling Agency, where Emmeline Snively, the owner, signed me up immediately, saying excitedly to her secretary, 'Remember this gal! She's a natural-born model.' I thought, *How nice that I've found someone who agrees with my feelings about myself!*

"Don't worry, Doc! I'm only kidding!

"She said they were looking for models with light hair, because unlike brunettes, blondes can be photographed in any light or wardrobe, so I bleached my dull, dull brown hair a golden blonde. I looked in the mirror and crowed, '*Ooh la la!* Could that beautiful sexy blonde be mousy little Norma Jeane?'

"I've made sure that my hair has never been brown again, though once in a while, if I get lazy, a dark fringe appears at the part. I'm pretty good, though, at preventing that from happening.

"Snively recommended me for a three-month, one hundred-dollar modeling course, which she let me pay off with compensation from modeling jobs. I was thrilled, and filled out the application form. I put down that I had blonde curly hair and was five feet six inches tall. Actually, I was five feet five and a half inches, but that only counts as a little white lie, right?

"I had only one bad moment in the class. When I walked in, I saw I was the only student who had come without her mother. It was like being the new girl at school all over again!

"I was working nonstop, so much so that my friend Sheila Sovern, who was also a model, wanted to know if I was sleeping with the photographers. I was indignant. 'Of course not!' I said. 'What do you think I am? You hurt my feelings even suggesting it. Men who try to buy me disgust me!' I'm not a forgiving person. That was the end of my friendship with Sheila Sovern.

"Which reminds me of how I feel about women friends in general. I don't do too well with members of my own sex. I don't trust them. Maybe it's a carryover from when I was in the orphanage. All the matrons, teachers, nurses, and foster mothers were mean women. But I guess the real reason is that I'm angry with my own mother for bringing me into the world and then leaving me to cope with it myself. If she's representative of women, forget it!"

Marilyn returned to the story of her modeling career. "Even though I was working an awful lot, I still got down in the dumps sometimes. The black moods seemed to come out of nowhere. I felt there was something unusual about me, that I was the kind of girl found dead in a sleazy bedroom with an empty bottle of pills clutched in her hand."

"But I was young and healthy," she continued, "and unlike now, my dark moods usually lightened the following day. One of the things that depressed me the most was my indecision about having a child.

On some days, I thought my life would be incomplete if I never had a baby, and there was nothing I wanted more.

"We would be mother and daughter—I always imagined having a daughter—and I'd finally be part of a loving mother-daughter relationship. Sometimes, I thought I shouldn't ever have a child anyway, as it might inherit my mother's emotional problems. To complicate matters, I had a bad case of endometriosis, which the gynecologist said would make it difficult for me to have a child.

"Also, I wasn't sure if I would know how to take care of a baby. Sometimes I worried that I'd turn out to be as bad a mother as my own. Heaven forbid my daughter end up in an orphanage like me. Other times, I thought I'd be a wonderful mother, because I knew exactly what a child needed—everything I didn't get.

"I decided to go see the Bolenders and ask their opinion. It so happened that Ida wasn't home, and I talked to Wayne. 'Uncle Wayne,' I said. 'I'm thinking about having a baby, which would be the most wonderful thing in my life. But I'm worried that the child would turn out to be crazy like my mother. What do you think?'

"He said, 'Marilyn, you're not at all like your mother. You're kind and generous and I think you'd make a fine mother.'

"'Thanks, Uncle Wayne,' I said, crying in his arms. 'You're very comforting. Now all I need to do is find a father for my baby and my troubles'll be over.'"

MARCH 5, 1959

"I soon became one of Blue Book's most successful models, and appeared on dozens of magazine covers," Marilyn said, continuing to recount the beginning of her career. "But most important of all, my successful modeling experiences brought me to the attention of Ben Lyon, a Twentieth Century Fox executive, who arranged a screen test for me. It seemed like a miracle! My lifelong dream was about to come true.

"When he told me about arranging the test, I broke down and sobbed convulsively. I remember an article in the newspaper a long time ago by a poet called Anne Mary Lawler, which I carried around in my wallet until the clipping fell apart. It said, 'Yes, dreams do come true, if you dream them long and hard and earnestly, and never, never give them up.' Right on, Anne Mary! You and I are on the same wavelength.

"At the time my new career was unfolding, Jim was still overseas. When I wrote him about my success, he wasn't at all happy about it. 'It's nice for a hobby,' he wrote, 'but when I come home, I'd like you to settle down, get pregnant, and be a good mother and housewife.' Funny, isn't it? Now that I'd found something I enjoyed doing, he wanted to have a child?

"My mother-in-law also disapproved of my new career. She said it was unseemly for a wife to be photographed by strange men, and that doing so would cause strains in my marriage. She made sure to keep Jim up to date on my activities, which served to pour oil on the rapidly spreading fire.

"Nobody was going to tell me what to do, especially my mother-in-law," Marilyn said indignantly. "I responded by packing up my few belongings and moving back to Auntie Ana's house. When Jim returned, I found that I had no more need for him. He didn't like that at all, but there was nothing he could do about it. I was a grown woman who knew what she wanted to do, and I was going to do it. Besides, I'd never forgiven him for saying that I'd never make it professionally.

"'Nyaaa nyaa, Jim!' I said, sticking my tongue out at him. 'So there! You were wrong about me. I'm not just a daydreaming kid after all.'"

MARCH 7, 1959

"On September 13, 1946," Marilyn began, "Jim and I stood before a judge in Reno, Nevada and applied for a divorce. Although Jim was unhappy about it, he didn't contest it. I told the judge that Jim had inflicted mental cruelty on me, had impaired my health, hadn't supported me, had criticized my working, had embarrassed me in front of my friends, and would often fly into rages that terrified me. That, and I saw no possibility that the situation would ever improve or result in a reconciliation.

"The judge merely nodded and granted the divorce. It took all of about five minutes, and it was the best of my three divorces. 'I'm a free woman!' I shouted to Berniece, who'd come to Reno to support me in my decision. She threw her arms around me and said, 'Hooray! Let's go celebrate!'"

MARCH 8, 1959

"The divorce brought me good luck," Marilyn continued the next day. "To my everlasting delight, the studio offered me a standard six-month contract with a starting salary of $125 a week. 'Wow,' I sang out. "One hundred and twenty-five dollars! I'm rich! I'm rich! The kids at the orphanage should see me now!

"Lyon thought my name, Norma Jeane, didn't sound professional enough, so I began to look for a new one. I decided on my mother's maiden name of Monroe, which I'd always liked. After all, I was related to President Monroe—yes, it was a thousand times removed, but it was close enough for me. Lyon suggested 'Marilyn' for my first name, because I reminded him of Marilyn Miller. According to him, 'Marilyn Monroe' was a sexy name, had a nice ambience, and was charming because of the double "M" sound. *Well*, I thought, *I guess I'm Marilyn Monroe!* Thus Norma Jeane Baker became Marilyn Monroe forevermore.

"The name was so strange to me that the first time a person asked for my autograph, I had to ask her how to spell Marilyn. I didn't know where to put the 'l.' But I must confess to you, Doctor, that despite its success, I've never liked the name Marilyn. I've often wished I had held out that day for Jean Monroe. But I guess it's too late now to do anything about it.

"Then came a trickle of publicity that indicated I might be getting somewhere. I was actually mentioned by a gossip columnist for the first time. Was it Hedda Hopper or Louella Parsons? I don't remember, but I do remember the column saying, 'Keep your eye on the Twentieth Century Fox beauty, Marilyn Monroe. That dame is going places.' Whoever it was apparently knew something I didn't.

"My first movie role, for which I got no credit, was as a telephone operator in *The Shocking Miss Pilgrim*. We shot it in 1946. It came out in 1947. It starred Betty Grable. Don't tell anyone, but in my heart of hearts, I thought I was sexier. Unfortunately, if anybody agreed, they neglected to tell me. Right after that, in 1947, I won a small role in *Dangerous Years* and worked as an extra in two films, *Green Grass of Wyoming* and the musical *You Were Meant for Me*, all of which which got me exactly nowhere.

"Then I was very excited about being cast in a three-scene role as Betty in *Scudda Hoo! Scudda Hay!*, but wouldn't you know it? Before the film was released, my part was cut to only one line! The last three films were not distributed until 1948. So far, my brilliant screen career was zipping along at a snail's pace.

"But I decided I wasn't going to let the slow progress discourage me. When Ben Lyon told me not to get depressed, that things would get better, I responded, 'Righto, Ben. Only gravity will get me down!'

"But it was hard to keep up my spirits when I couldn't pay the rent. I'd done everything the studio had asked me to do, but still nothing was happening. According to my contract, they could either renew it or drop me. After a few months, I was so tense I couldn't eat, which was fine because I didn't have money to pay for food anyway.

"That didn't stop me from buying a gold charm to try to make myself feel better. It said, 'Don't be bitter—glitter!' I wore it once, and then stuck it in the back of a drawer, where I suspect it remains to this day. Would you like a 'Don't be bitter—glitter' charm, Doctor? It's real gold, and you can have it for half the price of this session. A quarter the price? Hmmm, silence. Can I deduce, 'No sale'?

"I told Ben at the time, 'Life is so shitty! It makes me wonder why I go on. I'm miserable. I hate being alive because I always hurt. I'd rather be dead. At least if I'm dead, I wouldn't be in pain all the time.'

"'True, sweetie,' he said. 'But then you wouldn't get to be a star, either.'

"I said, 'Ben, you have a point there.'"

"The studio terminated my contract in late 1947."

MARCH 9, 1959

"Something very fortunate happened shortly thereafter, which was to change the course of my life. In 1947, I was walking on the Twentieth Century Fox lot when Joe Schenck, the head of production, happened to be driving by. He saw me, asked his chauffeur to stop, called me over, and asked my name. I recognized that he was a studio big shot and said, 'M-M-Marilyn Monroe.'

"He mustn't have been turned off by my stuttering, because he invited me to his house that evening for dinner. I was twenty-one years old, and Schenck was nearly seventy. But since when would I let a man's age stop me from having a nice dinner?

"I had many dinners after that at his mansion— he had a great cook—and soon I was known around town as 'Joe Schenck's girl.' I kept denying it, but nobody believed me."

"What were you, then?" I asked.

"Let's say we had a friendship with sexual favors. I can't say that I enjoyed the sex, but I felt I had no choice but to make the old guy happy. How could I do less? Joe was crazy about me. He said to anyone who would listen, 'She has an electric quality. She sparkles and bubbles like a fountain.' Who could resist that description? Certainly not a fatherless little girl from an orphanage. He did all he could to make my career a success, and got me my first Columbia contract from Harry Cohn, which led to my first co-starring role, in *Ladies of the Chorus.*

"Eventually, I became very fond of him, and we remained friends for the rest of his life. I was a lucky girl to have had Joe Schenck in my life, although there are plenty of folks—mostly men!—who think an old guy of seventy was lucky to have had me. I guess you can say it was one of those rare mutually beneficial relationships you stumble on once in a while. We both were lucky to have found each other."

MARCH 10, 1959

"So, because of Joe," she began in her next session, "things started to look up for me, as Ben had suspected they would. When I stood before the movie camera for my first screen test for Columbia, something strange happened that I haven't gotten over yet. I transformed from the nervous and embarrassed girl I usually was into a poised, self-assured woman. Cohen said to me, 'You stood there and glowed with radiance. I think you'll be another Jean Harlow. I haven't seen such a luminescent actress since Gloria Swanson walked the boards.'

"When I heard that, I thought, 'Who, me? They must have mixed up the screen tests.'

"Columbia Pictures then signed me to a six-month contract and increased my salary from what I'd been getting at Fox. I now was paid one hundred fifty dollars a week. Hurray! I was rich, so I went out and bought five hundred dollars' worth of clothing. It all still hangs in my closet, hardly ever worn. I go on wearing my checkered black-and-white pants and white sweater." She looked down at her legs and laughed. I laughed too. That was exactly what she had on that day.

"After Columbia signed me, they sent me to study with their head drama coach, Natasha Lytess. Ah, Natasha! She became one of the great teachers of my life. When I was cast in the low-budget musical *Ladies of the Chorus*, I put what I'd learned from Natasha to good use. I was promoted as one of the film's bright spots, although the movie was only fairly successful financially.

"During my short stay at Columbia, Harry Cohn, who was the studio head at the time, sent me to a plastic surgeon to correct my slight overbite. I was terrified, but if he'd said to jump off the Brooklyn Bridge, I wouldn't have hesitated. Cohn was pleased when I followed his advice, and gave me a rare compliment. He said, 'This makes you more beautiful. Your face now matches the faultlessness of your body.' I turned around to see who he was talking to. The surgery turned out to be one of the most important things I ever did to advance my career. Even *I* could see that it contributed to the beauty for which I later became known.

"I know you're interested, Doc, in hearing about my career—everybody is—but I'll have to disappoint you. I have to digress for a while to tell you about my relationship with Natasha."

Marilyn was right. As a lifelong movie fan, I *was* fascinated to learn about the development of her career. But it was the end of the hour, and another patient was waiting.

I said, "I am sorry, Marilyn but we will have to stop now. Please tell me more about Natasha in your next session."

She groaned and muttered, "You're just like everyone else. I get what I pay for and nothing more," and then slowly got up from the couch.

I felt so bad I could hardly pay attention to my next patient.

MARCH 12, 1959

"I have to tell you about Natasha Lytess," Marilyn began the next session, "because she was an important part of my life, and because the ending of our relationship still weighs heavily on me. Endings are always terribly hard for me, and I'm not proud of the way I cast her out of my life."

A flag went up in my head. *Uh-oh*, I thought. *People's relationships tend to run in patterns. I'll have to watch out that she doesn't try to walk out of her analysis with me in the same way.*

"She was my first acting teacher," Marilyn continued, "and probably the best friend I ever had. Believe me, I wouldn't be the star I am today had she not tutored me, encouraged me, and taught me the basics of acting. I was a young, completely uneducated girl from an orphanage. I knew nothing of the world of art, music, and books. She taught me about all of them. A closet lesbian, she fell in love with me the first moment she laid eyes on me, and entrusted me with her very soul. She kept wanting me to make love with her. I wasn't at all interested, but she wouldn't take no for an answer. Natasha Lytess went right on pleading with me to the very end."

"Tell me a little more about her, Marilyn," I said.

"Natasha was a character! She had dark, fierce, brooding eyes and was so thin people thought she was anorexic. She was the kind of person who smiled so rarely that people were taken aback when she did. She was rather pompous, and pronounced everything she said as if it were of great importance. Of course, it usually was. I must add that she was considered by many in the field, including me, to be a brilliant teacher. She owned an impressive library of theater books, and I was free to browse or borrow them to my heart's content, which I did for years.

"She was born in Austria, studied in Europe with the great Max Reinhardt, and had taught theater in Hollywood since 1941. Although she was cast in a few small film parts, she couldn't earn a living as an actress, and to support herself and her daughter Barbara, she accepted an offer from Samuel Goldwyn to coach actors under contract with his studio, MGM. She was, thank goodness, a much better teacher than an actress."

Marilyn's voice warmed up a bit as she continued. "In 1948, she was sent by Columbia to train me for my role in *Ladies of the Chorus*. That was how," and here Marilyn's voice broke, "one of the longest and most important relationships of my life began. She kept on supporting me for the next twenty movies, until 1955, when I made *The Seven Year Itch*.

"You heard me right. She stuck with me through twenty movies!"

Tears filled her eyes. "She was like a mother to me and provided me the most stability I've ever known. She invested her heart and soul in my career at a time when nobody else showed any interest in me. She had the courage to take a chance on an unknown, clumsy, stuttering would-be actress. She helped me to develop and express my talents, my curiosity about the theater world, and my intelligence." Marilyn was openly crying now but continued speaking through her tears.

"Professionally, she taught me gesture, elocution, diction, graceful movement, and how to breathe. She encouraged me to speak more naturally. She always said, 'The voice register expresses the variations of human feelings, and each feeling requires a different voice modulation.' Starting with our first collaboration, she gave me intensive courses before each audition. We worked together for three whole days and nights to prepare me for my callback audition for *The Asphalt Jungle*, which was the real beginning of my career. When I was cast in that part, Natasha actually left Columbia Studios to tutor me full-time. She risked her daughter's and her own livelihood to bring about my success.

"But," she continued, "we never solved the problem of her being *in love* with me. She never let up on propositioning me, and it really irritated me. She was equally determined not to take 'no' for an answer.

"Can you imagine what it's like to be propositioned night and day to sleep with someone you have no desire to have sex with? For a while, I thought I could just put up with it. But eventually, I'd had as much of it as I could take and decided to be direct once and for all, whatever the consequences.

"Soon enough, she grabbed me and said, 'Marilyn, I want to love you.' So I rudely pulled her arms off me and said, 'Natasha, you don't have to love me. Just teach me.' I told her about a dream I'd had, in which a wise woman—who, incidentally, looked like you, Doctor—said to me, 'To love is to teach.' I told Natasha the dream, and said, 'I'm honored that you love me, Natasha, but please demonstrate your love in the way my dream dictates.'

"Natasha hardly ever laughed, but she laughed at that. I grew even angrier and said, 'People don't always get what they want in life, Natasha. Just ask *me*. I've wanted many things, not gotten them, and survived. You're a spoiled woman! You've always received what you wanted in life and don't know how to cope when you don't. There's nothing I can do about that. If, under the circumstances, that means you don't want to work with me anymore, I'm sorry, but so be it!'

"Do you think that changed anything, Doctor? Of course not! She continued to be my teacher, and she kept right on pestering me about sex for six more years!"

MARCH 13, 1959

In 1948, right around the release of *Ladies of the Chorus*, Marilyn suffered a terrible loss. Her beloved Auntie Ana died of heart disease. Marilyn was brokenhearted. She sobbed even telling me about it a decade later.

"Auntie Ana was the kindest, warmest, most generous person on earth. I didn't want to live in a world without her. I had no one nearby to take my troubles and hopes to. Without her, 'love' would have just been a word in the dictionary.

"I remember looking at the cars roaring past on the highway and thinking, *How come traffic doesn't stop? Don't they know Auntie Ana died?* Everything grew dark, and I thought, *A storm must be brewing.* Then I realized the blackness was inside my head.

"She left me an ancient book called *Palissey the Potter*, which I'll treasure forever. I only let myself read a page at a time, to make it last as long as possible. When I came across the potter's quotation in it, I knew why she had left it to me. It said: 'If I have freedom in my love and in my soul (I) am free.'

"Typical of Auntie Ana, she had placed a note in the book: 'My sweet, dearest Norma Jeane: When you miss me, read this book and remember how much I love you. I'm so sorry I can't leave you much else besides my love, but know that it will always be there for you and not even death can take it away.'

"Grace, Doc Goddard, and I had a private viewing of Auntie Ana's body. She looked so lifelike it was hard to believe she was dead. When I went to her coffin and leaned down to kiss her goodbye on her icy cold forehead, I cried out, 'Don't leave me, Auntie Ana! How can you do this to me?' and slumped to the floor, momentarily passing out.

"When I came to, I ducked out of the chapel, not wanting to talk to the other mourners. I had enough pain of my own without having to comfort them. After that, I cried for a week nonstop. It is good that I had to go to work in *Ladies of the Chorus*, or I probably would still be crying. Come to think of it, I am," she said, wiping away a tear.

In *Ladies of the Chorus*, Marilyn sang solo numbers in a film for the first time: "Every Baby Needs a Da Da Daddy" and "Anyone Can Tell I Love You."

"I sure could sing 'Every Baby Needs a Da Da Daddy' with feeling," she said. "Nobody knows as well as I how true that is."

She did extraordinarily well in the film, and got wonderful reviews. Unfortunately, perhaps because of a lack of sufficient publicity, the film did not do as much business as the studio executives had hoped, and Marilyn was shocked when she was fired by Columbia.

"What stupid people, Marilyn!" I said angrily. "I'm sure they regretted it many times over."

"Being fired after Auntie Ana's death,' Marilyn continued, 'was just too much for me to bear. I went to my room and cried for another week. I didn't talk to anyone, or even eat or comb my hair. I felt I was burying Marilyn Monroe, along with Auntie Ana and my so-called career. I considered myself a fool for thinking I was attractive. When I dared to look in the mirror, I didn't see Jean Harlow's heir, but a coarse, cheap-looking bleached blonde.

"'What do you have? Nothing!' I told myself. 'Your so-called beauty is a joke. And your talent? What talent? You have a talent for killing people—that's what you have. Do yourself and the world a favor: Take a page from Auntie Ana's book and follow her into the grave!' Then I fell asleep for two whole days. When I awoke, the sun was high in the sky. I sniffed the fresh air, which smelled like Auntie Ana's lilac perfume. I decided to give myself a little more time to see if I would recover."

MARCH 17, 1959

In her next session, Marilyn returned to her discussion of Natasha Lytess. Marilyn said that John Huston was the first director confronted with her complete dependency on Natasha. He didn't like it one bit. I didn't blame him. I wouldn't either. I would hate it if a patient of mine checked out every interpretation of mine with someone else. After each scene was shot, Marilyn looked to her teacher for approval or disapproval. You can actually see her looking off to the right after the first scene of *The Asphalt Jungle*.

Before finally signing a long-term contract with Twentieth Century Fox in 1950, Marilyn requested just one change: that Natasha Lytess be employed by the studio as her personal drama teacher. For tutoring her, Natasha earned five hundred dollars a week from the studio, plus two hundred and fifty dollars from Marilyn's own pocket. Unlike most actors and their coaches, Marilyn came away with less money than her coach her first year at Fox. She said, "She was worth every nickel I paid her. If I had more, I gladly would've given it to her."

Natasha perfected a series of hand signs like those used by people who are hard of hearing, which she displayed behind the director's back. This allowed Marilyn to see how she was doing in the eyes of her teacher. Natasha's continuous interventions made her extremely unpopular with all of Marilyn's directors.

But it did not matter. In the fall of 1950, their relationship deepened when Marilyn moved into Natasha's house on Harper Avenue in West Hollywood. She slept on the sofa, studied, read, and looked after Natasha's daughter and the Chihuahua which Joe Schenck, Marilyn's mentor and close friend, had given her for her twenty-fourth birthday.

MARCH 20, 1959

Marilyn informed me during her next session that Natasha had done more than teach her and give her a home: She had saved her life. Whether Marilyn appreciated it or not was another story.

Marilyn was extremely close to her agent, Johnny Hyde. She said she'd tell me about him another time. Johnny died in 1950, while Marilyn was living with Natasha. Shortly afterward, Natasha found Marilyn unconscious, with puffed-out cheeks, white foam bubbling out of her mouth, and an empty pill bottle from Schwab's beside her bed. Natasha stuck her hand into Marilyn's mouth and pulled out fistfuls of half-dissolved pills.

Marilyn said, "When I woke up the next day and saw that I was still around, I said, 'Alive. Bad luck!' Then I wrote this poem:

Help help Help
I feel life coming closer
When all I want to do is die.

Oh Marilyn, I thought in despair, *what a sad woman you are! You have the strongest death instinct of any person I know. Night and day, I wonder how I can get the life force, which is also very powerful in you, to balance out your wish to die. There is no one I can ask for advice because all the great analysts are gone by now, and there is no one I know of in a better position than I to know how to deal with you.*

My colleagues, who had by then found out that Marilyn was my patient, were envious. How wonderful, many said, to be counseling the most beautiful and talented woman in the world. Well, they could have her! They had no idea how much anxiety she caused me. I worried about her all the time, and I knew that I would never forgive myself if she took her own life while under my care.

She even slipped into my dreams. One night, I dreamt that she was standing at the edge of a cliff, ready to jump. I was leaning back against the wind, and, with all my strength, holding onto the bottom of her dress to keep her from jumping. I woke up before I knew whether or not I had succeeded.

I would not really have given her up. I would have missed Marilyn: her charm, her wit, her unique character, the strangest combination of strength and weakness I had ever seen in one human being.

Marilyn was also a very kind-hearted woman. In 1951, Natasha bought a house. She needed a thousand dollars for her down payment and Marilyn, who lived at the time at the Beverly Carlton Hotel, sold a mink stole her agent, Johnny Hyde, had given her and presented the proceeds to Natasha. She explained, "That was the least I could do for someone who'd been so good to me."

At the end of 1951, during the shooting of *Don't Bother to Knock*, Marilyn came back to live at Natasha's house at 611 North Crescent Drive. She needed Natasha around the clock, and thought nothing of barging into her bedroom at 3 a.m. to say, "Natasha, what do you think of this idea for the second scene?" Natasha was always available and never complained about the interruptions. Marilyn's success was as important to Natasha as it was to Marilyn.

Don't Bother to Knock was Marilyn's most important part to date. And it was different from any she had had before. In it, she was cast as Nell Forbes, who recently had been released from a mental institution following a suicide attempt.

"Imagine how I felt about that," Marilyn said, "having tried suicide myself, and with a mother in a loony bin! On the other hand, there *was* something good that came out of my mother's institutionalization. I sure knew what it was like to be mentally ill!

"In the movie, Nell is hired as a babysitter in a hotel," Marilyn continued. "She quickly gags the child and ties her to her bed. No wonder I'm afraid to have a baby! Is that what I might do, if the kid was bothering me? She then tries on all the mother's sexy lingerie and jewelry, and flirts at the window with Jed, an airline pilot—Richard Widmark— who occupies a room directly across the courtyard.

"He soon knocks on her door, and Nell lets him in, but confuses him with her former lover, also a WW2 pilot, who'd been killed in the line of duty. I needed this, after losing Johnny Hyde? Anyway, Nell's strange behavior soon makes Jed aware she's the last person on earth to be entrusted with the care of a child. When he tries to leave the room, she threatens to throw herself out the window—does this sound familiar?—or kill her young charge. In the lobby, Nell steals some razor blades and is about to slash her wrists. Jed persuades her to give him the blades. He says that if she goes to a hospital, he won't abandon her. Nell submits to the police and is taken away.

"I got great reviews," Marilyn continued. "No wonder! I was playing a suicidal young woman from a mental institution who'd lost a man she loved! The man who advised creative people to 'just open a vein and bleed' must've been watching me prepare for the part!"

Many have claimed that Natasha encouraged Marilyn's quivering, almost childlike, yet sexy, acting. Knowing Marilyn as I did, I doubted that she needed encouragement for this self-presentation.

Natasha was not a popular person in Marilyn's small social circle. She was terribly jealous of other people Marilyn was close to, like Johnny Hyde, which greatly annoyed Marilyn. Directors hated seeing Natasha on the set, and winced when they saw her coming.

Marilyn hesitated before she said, haltingly, "I'm ashamed to say that I cut her off when I came here to New York to study with Lee Strasberg at the Actors Studio a few years ago. I was sick of acting in dumb blonde roles, and I felt I'd learned all she had to teach me. It was time for me to move on, and that was the only way I could muster the strength to leave her.

"Despite how it looked to Natasha and the world, I never really forgot that she was a real friend to me and helped me through the dark struggle of becoming a success. She was there for me when I needed her. There was no way I could have done it without her.

"She knew me well, too. Once, when a reporter told her that I was childlike, Natasha indignantly responded, 'A child she is not! Children are open and trusting. Marilyn is shrewd as can be. I wish I had her business ability and half the knack she has for promoting what's right for her and discarding what isn't.' Yeah, Natasha! I wish the men in my life knew me as well."

When Marilyn returned from New York in 1956, Natasha was eager to see her. Although she had been told by Marilyn's attorney not to contact her, Natasha arrived unannounced at Marilyn's home. Lew Wasserman, the MCA talent agency president, was there with Milton Greene to meet with Marilyn. Wasserman barred the door and said to Natasha, "Go away, lady! Don't you know when you're not wanted?"

Marilyn was sobbing now. "I've never told her I loved her. I've never told her how much I appreciate all she did for me."

Marilyn remained inconsolable. Contrary to my usual habits, I found myself unable to let her leave in that shape, and allowed her to stay ten minutes beyond the hour.

MARCH 23, 1959

Marilyn returned from her weekend in a completely different mood. She bounced into my office, obviously delighted to see me. Her warm "Hello, shrink!" rang cheerily in my ears, with her breathless emphasis on the "lo," her sparkling blue eyes peering deeply into mine, and her face lighting up in a radiant smile. She happily ran to the window and said, "Come and look down there."

From my third floor office, I searched the street, and other than trucks, cars, buses, and a few pedestrians, saw nothing unusual.

"What do you want me to see?" I said.

She pointed across the street, where a youngster, sitting on the steps, was looking upward at my window. He saw Marilyn and waved. She waved back and blew him a kiss.

"That's Jimmy—Jimmy Haspiel," she said.

"Jimmy?"

"Yes. He's my number one fan. He waits for me every day and walks me wherever I'm going. Sometimes, if I take a cab, I let him ride with me. Where I go, he goes, and then he walks home." She sat down on the couch. "He's twenty-one years old. He's my alter ego."

"Your *alter ego*?"

"Yes. He's an orphan, like me. His mother left his father the week Jim was born, and like me, he grew up without a father. He, too, was 'farmed out,' and spent his first seven years in the homes of people who treated him like an outsider and often punished him violently. We recognized each other right away. I can go into a room of strangers and immediately pick out the people raised in orphanages. They have that certain pleading look in their eyes."

"Doesn't he work or go to school?"

"He works as a messenger. He makes twenty-eight dollars a week and hardly has enough to eat. But he finds the money to take the most wonderful snapshots of me, and always gives me a copy. I try to slip him a few bucks now and again, but he won't take it. I fight with him, but he's never taken a penny yet.

"He once took out a crumpled dollar bill and tried to pay for one of our taxi rides. I stuck the bill down the front of his shirt and said, 'If you try that again, Jimmy, I'll never let you ride with me again!' That was the last time he ever tried to pay my taxi fare. I've never had anyone so devoted to me. He works his job around the hours he knows I'm in town."

"How did you meet him?"

"He was waiting for me outside of a Broadway show I went to. I guess he read in Earl Wilson's column or somewhere that I was going to be there. He came up to me and tapped his cheek, and said, 'Kiss me. Right there.' I was so taken aback by his gall—and his cuteness—that I did! He's been in love with me ever since."

I shook my head. "Doesn't it bother you to be trailed by someone all the time?"

"Not by Jimmy. He adores me. He's kind of like the little brother I never had. He's often with a group of fans who call themselves 'the Monroe Six.' They're sort of like a family to me. They wait for me after rehearsals and meet me at the airport when I come in from Hollywood. I can depend on them to always be there." She added, "It's kinda nice.

Other than Auntie Ana, I never had anyone I could depend on to always be there for me."

MARCH 24, 1959

After mulling over her sense of loneliness, I said the next day, "Marilyn, do you think it might be therapeutic for you to write your autobiography? I believe it would be as interesting to read as *War and Peace*. You would be reliving your life, and unlike the first time around, you would be sharing it with a great many people."

Marilyn had her doubts. "I don't think so," she said. "It would be mostly *War*."

I grimaced.

MARCH 25, 1959

During the next session, Marilyn returned to the subject of her oscillating career. This meant that we returned to her brief stint with Columbia Pictures, her initial meeting with Natasha, and the passing of her Aunt Anna at the end of 1948.

After the release of the poorly received *Ladies of the Chorus*, Marilyn was dropped by the studio. She, like thousands of actors making the Hollywood rounds, had to struggle to find work. Although she badly wanted to be cast in films, no offers came, and she had no choice but to return to modeling.

In 1949, the photographer Tom Kelley invited her to pose nude. At first, she worried about what people would think of her and refused, saying, "Nice girls don't pose naked, Tom!" But the weeks dragged on, and soon she could not even afford to get her car out of hock in order to look for work.

Marilyn accepted the job. With "Begin the Beguine" playing on the record player, she removed her clothes and laid down on a large fabric of red velvet. Agreeing to be paid fifty dollars for the job, she signed the model release form as "Mona Monroe." It was the only time in her life she was paid for posing nude.

"What did it feel like to pose naked?" I asked.

"It was very simple . . . and drafty! I just did what he told me and listened to the music."

"Did you mind posing in the buff?"

"Not at all," she said. "I hate shoes. I hate underwear. In fact, I hate clothes, and never wear any at all if I don't have to. I guess you can say I'm a rebel against society's double standard on sex, and live by my own moral rules. Believe me, I'm no Joan Crawford. I refuse to wear bras and girdles. There's actually a photograph of her wearing only a girdle under her blouse that I saw in some magazine. You'd think she'd be embarrassed to be seen like that! I want to feel free, like a bird flying through the sky, or a dolphin diving in the sea. Besides, I'm proud of my body. No naked woman in the world looks quite like me."

She mused silently for a moment. When I asked what she was thinking, she replied, "Doesn't that make a good poem?

I want to be free,
I want to be free
With nothing at all between God and me
Just the way we are meant to be.

"It does," I said.

"I still don't understand what all the fuss is about," she continued. "Everyone has a body, and why they should be ashamed to show it, I'll never understand. It's not like anything was missing or something. I know you Freudians are all gung-ho about castration. Maybe that's true for you folks, but it's never been a particular worry of mine. I'm too busy enjoying what I've got.

"A few years later, Tom asked me if he could put the photos on a calendar. I said OK, little dreaming what the reaction would be. After the calendar was published, it seemed as if every garage owner wanted one, and the calendars sold like hot tamales. I understand they still are making lots of mullah. I got fifty bucks for posing, and they're making millions. They never thanked me for my part in making them a fortune. I even had to buy a copy of the magazine at the newsstand to see my picture on the calendar. You'd think I'd be angrier about it, but I'm not. I guess I take pleasure in knowing that millions of men look at my body and find it beautiful.

"Everybody thought my career would be ruined when it was plastered all over the newspapers that I'd posed nude. You understand, by this time, I'd had a string of successes with Fox and some high profile magazine covers, and presented at the Academy Awards, too. The studio insisted that I deny having been the model. But I don't like to lie, and so I decided to tell the truth—that when I posed for the pictures, I was broke and needed the money to get my car out of the shop. To everyone's surprise, the public rushed to my defense, identifying with the poor waif who didn't have enough money to get her car repaired. As a result, I become more successful than ever.

"I autographed a few calendars. I wrote on one, 'This one may not be my best angle,' and on another, 'Do I look better with long hair?'

"I don't go in for false modesty. A woman who behaves that way only hurts herself. A coy woman denies herself a wonderful part of life."

I was filled with admiration for this uniquely moral woman who always told the truth, whatever the consequences. Marilyn was routinely criticized for having posed in the nude. What was rarely commented upon, or indeed noticed, was that she dared to stand up against the all-male power of Twentieth Century Fox, who insisted she deny having posed for the calendar. Similarly, no publications I knew of mentioned her courage in defying a convention she did not believe in and refused to lie about.

Back in 1949, however, Marilyn was still in need of a break after posing for Tom Kelley. A friend told her that RKO Studios was producing the Marx Brothers film *Love Happy*, and suggested that she telephone Lester Cowan, who was doing the casting. Marilyn called and said to him, "I understand you're looking for a blonde. I'm blonde." He answered, "But are you a sexy blonde?" She answered, "I haven't had any complaints yet."

The film has a famous scene in which Marilyn remarks to detective Groucho that men are always following her. Groucho looks at her undulating hips as she walks away. Chewing on his cigar, he says,

"Really? I can't imagine why!" This single scene led to her first big break.

"The producers were very impressed with me and featured me in the promotional campaign for *Love Happy* in New York," Marilyn said. "That publicity led to my first mention in Earl Wilson's column on July 24, 1949, in connection with the promotion tour. Wilson wrote, 'Over the years, Hollywood has given us its `It Girl,' its `Oomph Girl,' its `Sweater Girl,' and even 'The Body.' Now we get the `Mmmmmmm Girl.' Aw gee! All this time, I thought I was Norma Jeane!"

It was at this point that Marilyn met Johnny Hyde, whose death had already come up in our conversations about Natasha Lytess. Johnny Hyde died in 1950, but in 1949 he was vice president of the most powerful talent agency in Hollywood, the William Morris Agency. On first meeting Marilyn, Hyde was struck like a bolt of lightning by Marilyn's beauty. "You're going to be a great movie star," the aging but influential agent said right away. "It's there—I can feel it. I see a hundred actresses a week. None of them have what you have. I insist on representing you."

"At the time, agents weren't standing in line to represent me," Marilyn said, "so I didn't argue with him. When I met Johnny, I was twenty-two years old, in glowing good health, without a nickel to my name, and not under a contract to any studio or agent. With Johnny so wildly behind me, how could I refuse? The least I could do to thank him was to sleep with him. So I became 'Johnny Hyde's girl.'"

According to Marilyn, Hyde was a short, unattractive, married man who at the age of fifty-three was already deathly ill with heart disease. Whether he unconsciously felt that a beautiful young woman would rejuvenate his failing health, we will never know, but he fell madly in love with Marilyn and worked night and day to get her good roles. He became her agent, advisor, manager, teacher, mentor, confidant, lover, and friend.

He practically shoved Marilyn down the throats of every studio in Hollywood. They all thought she lacked "star quality," and was "just another dumb broad sleeping with her agent," or, as Dean Martin observed, "a creature who happened to be blessed with the beauty of a goddess and the brain of a peacock." Johnny only laughed, and told them, "You have to be pretty smart to play such a dumb blonde."

"The first three roles he finagled for me," Marilyn said, "were *A Ticket to Tomahawk*, in 1950, a stupid stagecoach western in which I had a bit part as a pretty blonde chorus girl; *Right Cross*, also in 1950, where I had a tiny role as Dick Powell's girlfriend; and *The Fireball*, yet another 1950 film, in which I played a roller-skating groupie. None of these movies did anything whatsoever to advance my career. I thought I never was going to get anywhere, but Johnny reassured me, 'This is only the beginning, my love. Just you wait and see!'

"I said to him, 'Don't laugh, Johnny, but I want to become a great actress. I want to be an artist, not a pinup. I don't want to be sold to the public like a celluloid aphrodisiac.'

"'Laugh? Of course I won't laugh, sweetheart,' he answered. 'You'll become the greatest movie star Hollywood has ever known, if you'll only give me a little time to work things out.'

"I threw myself into his arms and kissed him smack on the lips."

MARCH 26, 1959

Working night and day for Marilyn despite his life-threatening illness, Hyde arranged for her to audition for John Huston, whose eyes lit up when he saw her screen test. He said, "What an enchanting woman! Her beauty . . . contributes largely to our fascination with her because it is so unique."

Marilyn did superbly at the audition. She quoted Huston to me as saying, "Marilyn's audition was unique because the scene was supposed to be shot on a couch. But there wasn't a single couch on the set, so with her customary creativity, she simply laid down on the floor for the scene."

Although Huston thought she was terrific, Marilyn wasn't happy with her initial reading and asked if she could do another. Huston said, 'Sure, do it as many times as you want.' What I didn't tell her was that she was so perfect for the part that we'd given her the role before she even read."

Marilyn said, "I don't know what I finally did in the scene, but it felt wonderful! But would you believe the nerve of the man?! Letting me knock myself out time after time when he knew all the while I had the role! That's a man for you!"

Huston cast her as Angela Phinlay, the sexually exciting mistress of an elderly, married, white-collar criminal played by the then-famous actor Louis Calhern, in a short, memorable cameo in the classic MGM black noir film *The Asphalt Jungle*. "I must admit," Marilyn said, "that role was not too hard for me to play!"

I remembered seeing the movie at the time of its 1950 release and being very impressed with the beauty and talent of the young actress in it. I even nudged my husband and said, "I wonder who that gorgeous young woman is. I'm sure she's headed for stardom." Like all men, he couldn't have agreed more.

Apparently we were not alone in our reaction to her. Marilyn's performance brought her wonderful reviews, and was seen by Joseph Mankiewicz, the famous director and writer. He cast Marilyn in a small but crucial comedic role in *All About Eve* as the aspiring actress Miss Caswell, whom George Sanders described in the film as a student of "the Copacabana School of Dramatic Art." Mankiewicz later told the press he had immediately seen an innocence and vulnerability in the young actress he found delectable. The calculating quality he discerned beneath her sweetness confirmed his feeling that she was exactly right for the role.

In the story, a malevolent, manipulative young woman (Anne Baxter), who is all sweetness and helpfulness on the surface, insinuates herself into the life of the aging star, Margo Channing (Bette Davis). The sweet-seeming ingénue manages to wreck the lives of everyone she is close to, subtly clawing her way to the peak of stardom. By the end of the film, the innocent Marilyn has become just such a conniving ingénue. Marilyn's star shone brilliantly in the film, and even when she was seated among some of the greatest stars of the screen, it was impossible to take your eyes off her. Thanks largely to the labors of Johnny Hyde, the gifted Marilyn Monroe was on her way to stardom.

MARCH 28, 1959

In our next session, Marilyn rewound slightly to early 1949, when Johnny Hyde helped get her cast in *The Asphalt Jungle*.

"Natasha was coaching me for the role, and we were working on a scene in which I was supposed to be happy and chatty. In the script, there is a knock on the door, and a bunch of men charge in and threaten me with going to jail if I don't confess lying about something or other. When Natasha arrived at my apartment to work on the scene, I was so scared that I wouldn't open the door. I guess I was so into the role that I thought the frightening men were real.

"Natasha first thought I was just acting, but when my terror continued, she got scared that I was having a nervous breakdown. So what did she do but call Johnny Hyde. She told him that she thought he was putting too much pressure on me, and that I was cracking up. She said I was hearing voices.

"Johnny wasn't too concerned, because I'd already told him about the voices. But he wanted to do something to help. In those days, if an actor was having problems with a script, the first person the studio called was a doctor. Whatever the cause of the difficulty, be it physical or emotional, barbiturates were prescribed, to the point where they had become a staple in the movie-making world. Johnny believed they would calm my anxiety. At the time, nobody knew of any downside to taking the pills. After all, Judy Garland and many other important actors used them daily. So Johnny had the studio doctors prescribe drugs to me on a regular basis. I loved them, because they considerably eased my anxiety and made me feel happy. Little did I know the terrible problems they would cause me later in my life."

MARCH 29, 1959

At some time during this 1949–1950 period, Johnny also arranged for Marilyn to have a slight bump of cartilage removed from her nose. Marilyn felt that this improved her appearance greatly.

Disregarding the state of his own health, Johnny continued to work to advance Marilyn's career. In December 1950, while practically on his deathbed, he negotiated a seven-year contract for her with Twentieth Century Fox.

"He was the only man in my life who never disappointed me. Nobody has ever been nicer to me than Johnny Hyde," Marilyn said, interrupting the flow of her words to turn her head and ask, "How come I never fall in love with anybody like him, Doc? Life would be so much easier!" To my relief, she continued speaking without waiting for an answer.

"One of the nicest things he ever did for me happened shortly after I signed with him as my agent. As usual, I was broke, and behind in my rent at the Studio Club, a huge, block-long apartment complex that housed more than a hundred girls. You'd think they would have had room for one more. But apparently they were sick and tired of extending the deadline for me to pay the monthly tab. I was only fifteen dollars and thirty days late, for God's sake! Well, one day, I came home to find the lock changed and my suitcases all packed up outside my door. I carried them down to the sidewalk, sat on one, my head drooping like a dying swan, and cried nonstop.

"It was probably the lowest point in my life. I had thirty cents in my purse and didn't know where to go or what to do. I felt even worse than I had in the orphanage—at least there I had a roof over my head and a full stomach. My roommate must have seen me and called Johnny. Quicker than the flash of a rat's tail, he was there, picked me up, and held me in his arms.

"'There, there, little one. Don't cry,' he said. 'Johnny Hyde is here. I'll take care of you.' He found me a room near him and paid the first month's rent. I was so relieved that night, I again slept with him. It was the least I could do.

"He was as financially generous to me as he was emotionally supportive. I never had money problems when I was with Johnny. Finally, I could focus on my career instead of worrying about having enough money to pay the rent. Nevertheless, I wouldn't allow him to support me. One thing in my life I'm very proud of is that I've always supported myself, and never was a 'kept' woman. Of course, a little gift now and then, like my mink stole, didn't hurt."

Johnny left his wife for Marilyn, and kept pestering her to marry him. He made a constant play for her sympathy, saying, "Marilyn, I'm a dying man. My heart could give out any minute. Marry me and you will be a rich widow." But Marilyn could not be bought. With her typical integrity, she refused his offer. She said, "No, Johnny. I love you, but I'm not in love with you. I can't marry a person I'm not in love with. It wouldn't be fair to you."

"We did move in together on North Palm Drive in Beverly Hills, which made him very happy. I'm glad I could do that much for him before his death. After his funeral, I remained at the grave site—at Forest Lawn Memorial Park—for many hours to be alone with my thoughts and memories. In fact, I stayed so long that an attendant suggested that I leave. I screamed at him, 'I'm not going! I want to be with Johnny. How could he do this to me? What kind of friend would go off and die without taking me with him?'

I kept thinking, *It's my fault he died. My fault! My fault! I killed him. If he hadn't cared for me so much, he wouldn't have worked so hard to make me a success and he would still be alive for his wife and family and me.* The feeling that I'd killed the man I loved was so terrible. I couldn't cope with it.

"After he died, I went into one of the deepest depressions of my life. No one knows the depth of the intimacy we shared. I understood him as no one else did. When a man's heart beats for you, then you really know him. I thought, 'My life is over. I'll never find anyone else like Johnny again.' I was right. I haven't. I decided that life was not worth living without him, so I swallowed the whole bottle of pills I told you about, when Natasha unfortunately found me and dug them out of my mouth.

"Johnny Hyde was a kind, gentle, brilliant man, who gave me much more than compassion and love. He was the first man I ever met who understood me. Most people thought I was conniving, calculating, and two-faced. No matter how truthfully I spoke to them, that's what they chose to believe. Johnny knew and loved the real person under the Marilyn Monroe make-up. When I was with him, I felt at peace." Marilyn's stutter became pronounced as she grew more emotional. "Although—he didn't l-live to see his prediction come true—the one about my becoming a star—he was around long enough to ensure my future, a f-future I owe mainly to him.

"But that wasn't all he did for me. He f-furthered my education in every way he could. Before I met Johnny," she continued, "my definition of an intellectual was someone who could listen to the *William Tell Overture* without thinking of the Lone Ranger. He taught me about music, art, the theater, literature, and the world. He had me read authors like Turgenev, Tolstoy, Thomas Wolfe, Marcel Proust, and both volumes of *The Autobiography of Lincoln Steffens*. After I finished each book, we would talk about it together. My world expanded a bit further with each discussion.

"He gave me Stanislavski's *An Actor Prepares*, which was to become my bible. I didn't truly understand anything about the art of acting until I began to study that book. A loving father couldn't have been any nicer or more helpful. He was determined to make me a great star and urged me to devote every waking minute to furthering my career.

"His influence will last all my life. Shakespeare had that famous line, 'The evil that men do lives after them; the good is oft interred with their bones.' With Johnny, it's just the opposite. The good he did lives after him, at least for me.

"One night, when I was in the deepest part of my depression, I had a dream. Johnny came to me as clear as in life and said, 'Don't despair, Marilyn dear. I'll always be with you. You'll feel better soon and go on to become a great star.' He was as right in death as he had been in life. After the dream, I felt better."

Hearing this, a line from one of the great early psychoanalysts—Karl Abraham, I thought—expressed my sentiments perfectly: "My loved one is not gone, for I carry him around inside of me and now I can never lose him."

MARCH 30, 1959

"In 1951, I started taking classes at UCLA. Besides going to school at the time," Marilyn began her session, "I played minor roles in two comedies and the low-budget drama *Home Town Story*, an industrial film in which I played another boring secretary.

"And I had to play a secretary again right away in *As Young as You Feel*, the first film I did at Twentieth Century Fox. To me, that movie is only notable for being the first time in my life that all thirteen letters of my name—I counted them to make sure—were placed on a theater marquee in electric lights six feet high! I thought surely they had made a mistake and stood in front of the theater for quite some time, gawking at the marquee, until a policeman came along and said, 'No loitering, lady!' I'll bet he'd have been surprised if he'd known who that 'lady' was. I won't tell him if you don't.

"After that, there was *Love Nest*, in which I played a former Women's Army Corps enlistee who wreaked havoc on the June Haver-Bill Lundigan marriage. The movie was so bad that having to play in it wreaked havoc on me as much as the public," Marilyn quipped. Then she sighed. "I could only hope that the films weren't as bad as I thought they were."

She was then hired to play the role of Joyce, a lascivious gold digger who hunts for a husband at a posh hotel in *Let's Make It Legal*, starring Claudette Colbert and Macdonald Carey.

Marilyn said, "Oh my god! I screamed when I heard I was to be in a film with Claudette Colbert. I leapt up and down on my bed until feathers floated through the air. I'd always loved Claudette when I was a little girl. Many is the time I stood in her footsteps at Grauman's Chinese Theatre and pretended I was Claudette Colbert, and here I was, playing in a movie with her! To make matters even more wonderful, she liked me and said we should get together for lunch sometime after the movie was finished. Of course, we never did, but I was still thrilled that she offered. I looked up to the heavens and said, 'Thank you, Johnny!'

"Unfortunately, all these films were made on moderate budgets and became only modestly successful. I was very disappointed. If a movie with Claudette Colbert brought only a ho-hum reaction from the critics, and people didn't fall all over each other at the box office, what could a greenhorn like me expect?"

But it didn't take long until Marilyn began to feel really famous. In March 1951, she was invited to appear as a presenter at the twenty-third Academy Awards ceremony. "I felt really puffed up about getting the invitation."

MARCH 31, 1959

"I didn't feel so great when I read Joan Crawford's attack on me the next day in the morning trades," Marilyn continued in the next session. "I haven't saved the clippings—who needs them?—but I remember them very well.

"I first met Joan Crawford at Joe Schenck's house. She impressed me very much. I can only hope that if and when I reach her age, I'll keep my looks as well as she has.

"Some movie stars don't seem anything like stars when you meet them, but appear to be normal human beings, while others appear more like stars off the screen than on. Joan Crawford is definitely the second type. She was as much the queenly movie star in Mr. Schenck's home as in any of her dramas, if not a little bit more so. I couldn't help giggling when she leaned her head back and extended her arm like an empress and said, 'Champagne, please' to the lowly waiter." With her chin held sky high, Miss Crawford said, 'My dear, I think I can help you a great deal with your wardrobe. For instance, the white-knit dress you are wearing is absolutely out of place for this kind of dinner.' I should have responded, 'Too bad they neglected to teach formal dressing at the orphanage.' I cleaned the dress myself every day. It was the only good dress I owned. I wore it evenings as well as daytimes when I was going anyplace important. But when I looked at Miss Crawford's elegant evening gown, I could see what she meant."

(I had to smile as Marilyn spoke. She still wore the same white dress. In fact, she was wearing it right then.)

"'Taste is every bit as important as looks and figure,' Miss Crawford said as she looked me up and down with a steely eye. Then she smiled and asked, 'Won't you let me help you, *dear*?'

"I said I was flattered by her offer. We made a date to meet the next Sunday morning after church. It turned out we went to the same church.

"After the service, Miss Crawford continued her unsolicited lecture on my wardrobe. She said, 'My dear, you mustn't come to church in flat heels and a gray suit with black trimming. If you wear gray, you must wear different gray tones, but never black.'

"It was the only suit I had, but I wasn't about to tell her that."

"'Would you like to come to my house with me?' Miss Crawford asked. I said I'd like to very much. I had a fantasy she might offer me some of her old ball gowns and ensembles that she'd grown tired of.

"Her house was very beautiful and elegant, of course. We had lunch in the kitchen—in the *kitchen*!—with Miss Crawford's four adopted children and a beautiful white poodle. After lunch, Miss Crawford asked me to come upstairs to her bedroom.

"'Brown would look good on you,' she said. 'It will bring out the gold of your hair. The main thing about dressing well is that everything you wear must be just right'—implying, of course, that what I usually wore was far from right. 'Your shoes, stockings, gloves, and bags must all fit the suit you're wearing. Now, what I want you to do is to make a list of all the clothes in your wardrobe. And I'll make another list of all the things you need to buy, and then make sure you get the correct accessories.'

"I didn't say anything. I usually didn't mind telling people I was broke, and didn't even mind trying to borrow a few dollars from them to tide me over. But for some reason, I couldn't tell the great Joan Crawford that she had seen my wardrobe in full—the 'incorrect' white-knit dress and the wrong gray suit. I also neglected to mention that I refused to become known for the way I dressed, and found the very idea insulting. Unlike her, I go barefoot or without clothes altogether whenever I can. I like the way I look most when I'm standing on the top of a hill, with my hair blowing in the wind, not wearing any clothes at all.

"'It's so easy not to look vulgar,' Miss Crawford said, as if I were worried about it. 'Do make out a list of all your things and let me guide you. You'll be pleased at the results, as will everyone else.'

"I don't know why I called her again, except that I'd said I would and I pride myself on keeping my promises. Also, I was still hoping she'd present me with some of her discarded ball gowns. She didn't. I think, also, that I wanted to see the look on her face when I told her I couldn't afford to buy any fancy clothes, and maybe, if I had enough nerve, what she could do with her list. But, in the end, I couldn't quite carry that off.

"'Have you made out the list of your wardrobe?' she asked before even saying hello.

"'Well, no, as a matter of fact, I haven't. That was very lazy of me. I'll make out the list in a few days and call you again.' I didn't mention that my 'list' would take up all of two lines.

"'Good,' she said. 'I'll be looking forward to hearing from you.'

"Well, I never did call her again. Maybe I felt like I was back in grammar school and the teacher had given me an unwelcome assignment. I didn't always comply then, so why should I now?

"As I told you before, I was to present an Oscar to a winner at the Academy's annual awards ceremony in 1951. A bit of a Marilyn Monroe boomlet had begun. I was all over the magazines and movie columns, and the fan mail at the studio was beginning to arrive in large quantities. Trembling so much I was afraid I'd drop the Oscar statuette—and I didn't even know if they were breakable—I prayed I wouldn't trip and fall and that my voice would still belong to me when I said my obligatory two lines. Fortunately, I managed to reach the platform, say my part, and gracefully return to my table without breaking my neck.

"I thought I'd done well, at least until I read Joan Crawford's remarks about me in the morning papers. She said. 'Marilyn Monroe's vulgar performance at the Academy affair was a disgrace to all of Hollywood.' The vulgarity, she said, consisted of my wearing a dress too tight for me and wiggling my rear end when I walked up with the Oscar in hand. I was so shocked I could hardly believe what I was reading. I immediately called some people who'd been at the presentation and asked them if what she'd said was true. They laughed and said, 'Of course not! She's just jealous. Try and forgive a lady who used to be young and seductive herself.'

"The truth is, my tight dress and my wiggling ass were all in Miss Crawford's mind. She obviously had been reading too much about me. Or maybe she was just annoyed because I'd never brought her the wardrobe list she requested.

"Another story made the rounds about what precipitated Joan's nasty remarks—that she made a pass at me and I turned her down. I'm not about to say one way or the other. I'll be nicer to her than she was to me, and the truth will remain a secret between the lady and myself forevermore."

In 1952, Marilyn was photographed on the cover of *Look* magazine wearing a Georgia Tech sweater, as part of an article celebrating female enrollment in the school's main campus. "To change the subject, it was about that time that I first took up jogging," Marilyn said. "Every morning before breakfast, I ran through the Hollywood alleyways for a half hour or so. The air was fresh, and nobody was around. It felt great and kept me in shape. It also made me ravenously hungry, so I enjoyed my breakfasts all the more.

"Nobody else I knew ran, in the mornings or any other time. Well, I always was ahead of my time! I'm proud to say I never do things because they're 'in' or 'out,' or because that's what we're supposed to do. If I'd observed all the rules, I'd never have gotten anywhere. I didn't run because it was the 'in' thing, but because it made me feel good. Too bad I stopped jogging a few years ago. These days, it's hard enough just to climb out of bed."

APRIL 1, 1959

"Guess what?" Marilyn said, rushing into my office. "I'm pregnant!"

My heart gave a lurch. *Pregnant*? Many different thoughts flashed through my head. Could Marilyn handle it? Could she carry through a pregnancy this time? It seemed highly unlikely. What would it mean for her career? For her analysis?

"Congratulations, Marilyn," I said, feigning pleasure. "And the lucky father is—?"

"Abraham Lincoln, of course!" she said, bursting out laughing. "April Fool!"

"Oh, Marilyn!" I said, breathing a sigh of relief and trying to be a good sport about her little joke. "You really got me that time. Now please, *please*, can we get to work?"

"Hmmm," she said. "Some people just have no sense of humor. *They* need to be analyzed."

Marilyn returned to the year when she and *Life* magazine began their lifelong love affair.

"It was 1952, Doc!" she exclaimed, thrusting a copy of the actual magazine at me. "Norma Jeane, number 3463 at the orphanage, was on the cover of *Life* magazine! And that's not all. Look inside! Look inside!"

I quickly opened up the issue. The cover story was indeed a story entitled "Marilyn Monroe: The Talk of Hollywood." It began:

Every so often, more in hope than conviction, Hollywood announces the advent of a sensational glamour girl, guaranteed to entice people from all lands to the box office. Usually the sensation fizzles. But today the most respected studio seers, in a crescendo of talk unparalleled since the debut of Rita Hayworth, are saying that the genuine article is here at last: a sturdy blonde named Marilyn Monroe.

APRIL 3, 1959

"*Clash by Night*," Marilyn began, "which was released around the same time, is a black-and-white drama with some film noir aspects. It was directed by Fritz Lang and starred Barbara Stanwyck, who was as sweet as could be to me, Paul Douglas, Robert Ryan, and Keith Andes. The film was based on the Broadway play by Clifford Odets, in which Tallulah Bankhead played the leading role. It felt funny to be in a movie which had been on Broadway with some of the same people I used to daydream about.

"When I first met the cast, I felt like the only kindergartener at a party of schoolteachers. I was sure I'd wake up one day and find out it all had been a dream. But I got wonderful reviews, like the one in *The New York World Telegram*, which said: 'Marilyn Monroe, the ingénue, has a refreshing effervescence about her, a predominance of youthful animation.' I must have been manic during the filming. 'She also is a powerhouse of an actress who has all the earmarks of a gifted new star.'

"One reviewer even said I was better than Barbara Stanwyck, which upset me because she had been so nice to me. I thought she'd be mad, but to my surprise, she expressed only kind words about the review.

She's truly a Hollywood queen, in character as well as talent, and I hoped I could be as generous under similar circumstances. Did I know that I had 'a refreshing effervescence'? I didn't. I was delighted at my success. So was Twentieth Century Fox, who finally set about looking for new scripts that would show off my newly recognized talents."

But despite the sensational publicity she was receiving, Marilyn's career still was not 100 percent successful. In the early 1950s, she auditioned for the role of Daisy Mae in a proposed Li'l Abner television series based on the Al Capp comic strip, but nothing ever materialized, at least for her.

"I was very unhappy about that," Marilyn said. "As a child, I always adored the character of Li'l Abner and would have loved to play Daisy Mae, his girlfriend. Who knows? He and I might even have had a real-life romance. But it probably wouldn't have worked out," she mused. "Do you know the song, 'After You Get What You Want, You Don't Want It'? That's the story of my life."

True to character, her mood suddenly changed. "A funny thing happened to me today on my way to you, shrinker," she said. "I got in a cab to come here and the driver looked at me in the mirror. He said, 'You know what, lady? You're prettier than Jayne Mansfield. I'll bet you could be in the movies like her if you wanted to.'

"'Aw gee, thanks,' I responded. 'Do you really think so? Maybe I should give it a try.'"

APRIL 6, 1959

"I got the best birthday present ever on my twenty-sixth birthday!" Marilyn sang out as she sailed into my office. I mentally placed whatever she was about to tell me as occurring during this popularity surge she had been telling me about—not long after her series of films with Fox, the release of the calendar featuring her nude photo, the subsequent controversy, and then the Life magazine cover.

"I learned," Marilyn said, "that I was to be cast as Lorelei Lee in *Gentlemen Prefer Blondes*. The publicity said it would introduce 'the singing, dancing, irresistibly and comedically appealing Marilyn Monroe.'"

She turned around and asked, "Do you find me irresistible, Doc? If you do, I haven't noticed."

I found it hard to keep a poker face.

"The screenplay was based on a novel by Anita Loos," she went on. "It was first produced as a silent film and then readapted into a smash Broadway musical starring Carol Channing. Columbia planned on buying it for Judy Holliday, who'd just won an Oscar for *Born Yesterday*, but the foolish girl turned the part down. Fox wanted it for Betty Grable, who would have liked to do the picture, but her career, fortunately for me, was on the wane.

"Besides, I was cheaper. Grable would have cost them $150,000. My co-star, Jane Russell, got paid anywhere from $100,000 to $200,000— she wouldn't tell me how much—while the notoriously stingy Twentieth Century Fox got away with paying me the niggardly sum of $1,500 a week. It turned out that Jane got the bigger share of the money and I got the glory, which was fine with both of us.

"I said haughtily to Twentieth Century Fox—I thought I had them over a barrel—'I'll agree to play the part for that salary if you'll give me my own dressing room. May I remind you that *I* am the blonde, and the film *is* called *Gentlemen Prefer Blondes*!' After putting me through a hard time, they installed me in Betty Grable's old dressing room.

"Betty was lovely about it. She said, 'I've had mine, kid. It's your turn now.' Sometimes the biggest stars are the nicest. I won't mention a few exceptions!

"The film turned out to be a terrific success. It got great reviews, did absolutely great business at the box office, and established me as a talented comedic actress. I also love the movie because I sang some of my favorite songs in it, including '*Diamonds Are a Girl's Best Friend*.' Funny, I love the song, but I personally don't care at all about diamonds.

"*Gentlemen Prefer Blondes* was the most fun I've ever had making a movie, mainly because of Jane Russell. We 'two little girls from Little Rock' were like giggling schoolgirls. We seemed to bring out the child in each other. It was like having a sister to grow up with. We just naturally fell into step with each other, and hardly needed direction at all. When we sang 'Diamonds Are a Girl's Best Friend' in rehearsals, I spontaneously sang, 'Janie is a girl's best friend' at the same moment she came out with, 'Marilyn is a girl's best friend.'

"We got so bent over with laughter they had to stop the rehearsal. I've never seen such funny, friendly camaraderie between any two women on the screen, nor did I ever again find such a perfect co-star— or friend, for that matter. I always loved the scene at the end where we got married as twin brides," she mused. "Every time I see the film, it comes as a surprise to me. I wish I had such a close friend in real life," she said wistfully. "Will you be my friend, Doctor?"

"I *am* your friend, Marilyn," I answered, with tears in my eyes.

She was silent for a few moments, and then resumed where she had left off describing her brief friendship with Jane Russell. "In June 1953, not long after *Blondes* opened, we were invited to dip our hands and feet into the wet cement at Grauman's Chinese Theatre. I suggested that Jane imprint her boobs in the concrete, and said I'd do likewise with my ass, but the owners wouldn't allow it. Some people have no sense of humor. Like you," she added, delighted as always to be teasing me.

"Although we were close friends, our attitudes were very different. Jane, who is a deeply religious woman, tried to get me to join the Hollywood Christian Group, a gospel quartet and weekly Bible study group which met in her home. I went—once. I tried to introduce her to Freud, but," Marilyn added wryly, "Freud lost. Also, Jane was a staunch Republican, while my sympathies are with the Democratic Party. The differences didn't bother me, but just made our conversations more interesting, and if they bothered her, she never said so.

"What a true friend Jane was! She learned from Allan 'Whitey' Snyder, my make-up artist, a secret I'd kept from most everyone—that I suffered from extreme stage fright, and that's the reason I was always late for shoots and scenes. From then on, she called me each morning on her way to the set, and I was able to be on time. I never even told her that I agreed with Igor Stravinsky, who said, 'Hurry? I never hurry. I have no time to hurry.' Jane understood me, as no other friend ever has.

"After the film was finished, we stayed friends for a few years. Jane's husband was Bob Waterfield, a UCLA All-American quarterback for the Cleveland Rams. After I married Joe—Joe DiMaggio, my second husband—the four of us often double-dated. This was in 1954, I think. Anyway, the *men* got along great. In fact, I think they would have been just as happy if Jane and I had dined at another restaurant. I suspect we'd have been happy, too.

"Then, you know how things happen, Doctor. We saw each other less and less, until now we only exchange Christmas cards. It's too bad. I could use some fun in my life. Which reminds me, Doctor, sometimes I actually have fun here with you."

"I'm pleased," I answered.

"Me, too."

APRIL 8, 1959

"Speaking of having fun," she began, "as I did at the last session, I had quite a bit of it in September 1952, when I served as the grand marshal of the Miss America Parade in Atlantic City, New Jersey. I was the first woman in history to be appointed the event's grand marshal. It was a promotional event arranged by Twentieth Century Fox to publicize my new film, *Monkey Business*.

"I loved riding on the boardwalk, standing up in one of those carriages pushed by a man, with my *décolletage* down to my you-know-what, waving to cheering crowds. Everybody stared at me all day long, but I thought they were looking at my grand marshal's badge. I don't know if they knew who I was, or just cheered anybody who happened to pass by.

"It didn't really matter. I enjoyed it either way. I had to pose separately with each of the forty-eight pageant contestants. *Whew!* By the time I finished with the forty-eighth, Miss Alabama, who ended up winning, I was ready to pull a Greta Garbo and say, 'I tink I go home now.'

"We had only one real problem—my backless and almost frontless black dress, in which I was photographed between four service women: a WAC, a WAVE, a WAF, and a lady Marine. A photographer took our photo from a balcony, where he could see all the way down to my navel. Unfortunately, the prissy United States government wouldn't allow the photo to be published. Too bad! It was a great picture of my navel.

"It seems to me that the Johnston Office—you know, the enforcers of the Motion Picture Production Code—does an awful lot of worrying about whether a woman has cleavage or not. You'd think they would worry more if she didn't have any. Maybe they'd like girls to look more like boys. Personally, I prefer looking like a girl."

APRIL 10, 1959

"Did you ever see my film, *Niagara*, Doc?" she said at the beginning of her next session.

"No, I'm sorry," I said. "I somehow missed that one."

"That's too bad. The tide really turned for me with the release of that film, along with *How to Marry a Millionaire* and *Gentlemen Prefer Blondes*. They all came out the same year, you know.

"I'll tell you a little about *Niagara*, because it was a defining moment in my life. Since then, the credits have always listed my name above the title, and most often in the top position. My work in the movie launched me to fifth place in 1953's list of top ten box office stars.

"*Niagara* is a thriller-film noir, produced by Twentieth Century Fox, directed by Henry Hathaway, and starring Joseph Cotten, Jean Peters, and me. Unlike other film noirs of the time, *Niagara* was photographed in Technicolor, which showed off my blonde hair in a way black-and-white film never could. I'm happy to tell you that it became one of Fox's biggest box office hits of the year. I was given first billing in *Niagara*, and the critics said I stole the show from my co-stars. If you'll excuse my lack of humility, the film catapulted me to superstar status. One critic wrote that I wasn't just a sex symbol, but *the* sex symbol, displaying a certain kind of sex appeal I'd originated and perfected. Now that's the kind of criticism I like to hear!

"People said that when I walked in that film, I wiggled and wobbled. I don't know what they're talking about. I just walk to get places. I've never deliberately wiggled in my life, but people always say I do it on purpose. I always ask what they mean. I first walked when I was ten months old and haven't had a lesson since. I defy any girl to walk down a street made of cobblestone wearing high heels and not wiggle at least a little bit.

"Which reminds me of another phony claim people make about me. One catty actress—and I imagine you can guess who I'm referring to—announced to the press that I wear falsies. I responded, 'Those who know me better know better.'

"My *Niagara* reviews were superb. *The New York Times* wrote something like: 'Seen from all angles, both the exquisite Falls and the equally stunning Marilyn Monroe leave nothing to be desired.'

"Here's a little about the plot of *Niagara*, so you can see why I was good in it. George and Rose—me—have a troubled marriage. She's younger than him and very attractive. He's recently been discharged from an Army mental hospital, and is jealous, depressed, and irritable. As I'm sure you understand, I know exactly what it feels like to live with a man like that, so I was quite believable. In the film, I have to do something to preserve my own sanity, so naturally I take a lover. While touring the falls the next day, the camera catches me passionately kissing Patrick.

"That evening, sensing something's in the air, George goes into a terrifying rage, which becomes, for my character, the straw that breaks the camel's back. Patrick and I plan to murder George. The next day, I lure George into following me into the dark tourist tunnel underneath the falls.

"Patrick is there, against the awesome beauty of the falls, waiting to kill George and run off with me. There's a bell tower nearby, and Patrick is supposed to request that the operator play a specific song to let me know that the murder has been successfully accomplished. The tune is played by chance, though, and I happily conclude that George is dead and I'm free to flee with my lover.

"But as often happens in life, things do not go as planned. George kills Patrick, instead of the other way around. He throws his body into the falls, and collects Patrick's shoes at the exit instead of his own. This causes the police to believe that George is the victim. The body is retrieved and the police bring me in to identify what they tell my character is George's body. When the cover is lifted from his face and I see Patrick instead of George, I faint and have to be admitted to a hospital.

"Thank goodness for 'the Method,' which I'd already begun to study with Michael Chekhov, or I'd not have been able to access my murderous feelings. I knew exactly how Rose felt, and what motivated her to kill her husband, because I've felt the same way many times. Maybe I can play Lady Macbeth after all!"

Freud, I recalled, had written that all of us should be capable of experiencing every emotion known to mankind, and so I admired the courage of this extraordinary woman who seemed to do just that.

APRIL 13, 1959

Marilyn came into our next session sounding most thoughtful. "Around the time of *Niagara*," she said, "I had a very beautiful dream which I've never forgotten, although it feels dangerous to tell it to you. In it, I was lying on the grass in a lush green forest, looking up at a magnificent tree. Suddenly, the tree burst forth with multicolored blossoms, and each one turned into a vividly colored bird. I don't know what the dream meant, but I know it made me very happy."

"Why is it dangerous to tell it to me?"

"Because it's tempting the fates! If I'm feeling happy, they'll be jealous of me."

"Oh no, Marilyn!" I said. "That is pure superstition. It is a wonderful dream! Your tree is the tree of life, blossoming with creativity in all the wonderful movies you made at the time. Each bird stands for another one of your films. You can allow yourself to be happy. Heaven knows, you deserve it."

"I hope you're right," she said, sounding less than convinced. "Whenever anybody is jealous of me, they try to do me harm."

APRIL 14, 1959

"There were no more blossoms or birds in 1953," she went on during the next session. "You'd think the studio would have learned. Instead, I was tossed into another dumb blonde film, *How to Marry a Millionaire*, to capitalize on the terrific success of *Gentlemen Prefer Blondes*. The plot, if you can call it that, concerned three beautiful models who rent an expensive New York apartment as part of a plan designed to find each of them a millionaire husband.

"The movie was just so stupid! I played a half-blind dumb blonde who's too vain to wear glasses and is always bumping into furniture and doors and knocking things over. I'll never understand why anyone thinks having impaired vision is a joke. The writers should try it for a while and see if they think it's funny. Maybe in grammar school I would have laughed at it, but now I just think it's sad.

"I'm not a feminist, but I do object to the film's philosophy that the only way for women to get money is to marry it. Why didn't the three women just work to be successful at a job, as you and I do? In any event, most of us know there isn't much of a market for beautiful young women seeking rich husbands. Rich men pick rich women as mates. Now, why doesn't somebody write a movie built around *that* fact? I wouldn't mind playing a role in such a film. But in this ignorant environment of ours, with its lack of interest in culture, probably nobody would go to see it.

"I originally objected to my casting because I'm as vain as that character and didn't want to wear glasses either. I really wanted to play Betty Grable's role of Loco Dempsey, but Jean Negulesco, the director, convinced me that the part of Pola was better-suited to me. Much as I hate to admit it, he turned out to be right, and the film was a smash hit. Nevertheless, I'm sick to the gills of playing dumb blondes, and have to do something soon to play more serious roles, or I'll end up joining my mother.

"Incidentally, I thought Lauren Bacall was wonderful in *Millionaire* as the wise-cracking Schatze Page, and it was a pleasure to work with a real, trained actress—she was then a student of the Actors Studio.

"But for the life of me, although I personally like Betty Grable very much, I cannot understand how she became so great a star. I thought she was stiff and completely charmless in the movie, and not a bit sexy. In my perhaps biased opinion, she isn't even beautiful, although she does have a great figure. Maybe you have to be a man to appreciate her appeal. Or maybe it's just that she's getting old. I better take better care of myself, or I'll find myself in her shoes soon. After all, I'm thirty-three years old, and Betty is only ten years older! I just might have to kill myself first."

My ears perked up. I hoped she was joking. But as Chaucer first said in *"The Monk's Tale,"* "Many a true word is spoken in jest."

Marilyn continued, "On the other hand, I remember what Lee Strasberg always says, that the actor's art grows richer with age, not less. That puts a whole other face on aging, doesn't it?"

Marilyn returned to her discussion of *How to Marry a Millionaire*. "There's something else I detest about that movie. I'm very proud of the fact that I've always supported myself and have never been a 'kept woman,' although I've had many offers that would've given me a far larger bank account than the one I have now. I'm told that I'm a role model for many women all over the world. I don't relish the idea of being a role model for dependent women. You work, too, Doctor, so you must agree with me."

"Indeed I do, Marilyn. I suspect that you and I are women ahead of our times."

APRIL 15, 1959

"In the summer of 1953," she began at her next session with me, "I arrived at Jasper in the Canadian Rockies. Have you ever heard of Jasper? I hadn't either, and hope I never do again. I was deeply resentful at being shipped off to such a distant location to play in a western. A western! Me, Marilyn Monroe? Who were they kidding? I'm no more a woman of the west than the queen of Romania. We were to film *River of No Return*, with Robert Mitchum, who played the roughneck lover to my saloon singer.

"They say life is stranger than fiction, and here's perfect proof that the old adage is true. Would you believe that Mitchum had been an old friend of my first husband, WhatsHisName, and that we saw each other all the time way back when I was seventeen years old and he and Jim worked together on a factory line before World War II?

"When we first met on location, we stood and looked at each other, and we both said at the exact same moment, 'You? You?' I said, 'I had no idea you would be *that* Robert Mitchum!' Then we threw our arms around each other and sobbed. We cried for our lost youth and for our continuing belief it was possible to live happily ever after. But mostly we sobbed because we were thrilled to see each other again. He reintroduced me to his hard-drinking, boisterous self, and brought me out of myself for a time.

"In bygone days, he had teased me about my intellectual pretensions. Turned out he hadn't changed much. One story he told the stage hands on location was that I was reading a psychology book at the age of seventeen and innocently asked him, 'What is anal eroticism, Bob?' I prefer not to remember his answer.

"Once, I refused to read a line in the soft-slurred way Otto Preminger, the director, insisted on, preferring to enunciate it clearly á la Natasha Lytess's instructions. Bob slapped me on the rear end and said, 'Stop that nonsense! Play it like a human being!' So, Natasha notwithstanding, I did.

"I'll always remember *River of No Return*, not for its artistry, but because I want to make sure I never return there. That's a pun, Doc! You know, a pun on the word 'return.' How come you aren't laughing? OK, *don't* laugh. I'll tell my joke to someone with a sense of humor!

"Anyway, I barely escaped with my life. There were terrifying scenes on a raft ricocheting down the raging river that Preminger insisted be shot with the actual actors—us!—and not stuntmen. I had a number of very real accidents which I've been accused of faking, but believe me, I didn't.

"The worst one was when I slipped into the stormy river while wearing high waders. My boots filled with water and dragged me down under. As I drew what I was sure would be my last breath, they hauled me out of the river with ropes pulled by Mitchum and some crew members. I didn't know whether to be glad or sorry. I thought I'd just as soon stay under the swirling, deadly, white water of the river as climb back onto that decrepit old raft, only to be tossed back later into the treacherous river rapids. Newspaper headlines all over the world screamed, 'Marilyn Monroe Nearly Drowns.' They weren't kidding!

"Another time, Bob and I were out on that corroded old raft when it got stuck on a rock. The raft wobbled from side to side for over an hour, nearly tipping over each time a gargantuan new wave hit it, terrifying and drenching us until finally a crew member found a lifeboat and rescued us. Dripping wet, with chattering teeth, out of sorts, and out of breath, I considered getting a job as a supermarket clerk.

"You think that was all? Well, it wasn't. The worst was yet to come. I slipped on a rock and broke my ankle, again causing worldwide headlines, 'Marilyn Monroe Hurts Leg in Canada.' Next morning, a posse of private doctors arrived by plane and x-rayed my leg. I was fitted with a plaster cast and had to walk on crutches for several weeks, causing expensive delays in the shooting. The film overran its budget so much that Mitchum, a man after my own heart, called it 'The Picture of No Return.'

"Did I like anything about the movie? Well, yes. I liked some of the songs I sang, like 'River of No Return,' and I thought I did some of my best singing ever. I liked the blue jeans I wore. I'd bought the tightest ones I could find in the Army and Navy store, and wore them into the Pacific Ocean until they dried to the point where they seemed molded onto me. I never had a pair of jeans I liked as much, and held it against the producers that I wore them out while making the film. They owe me! I enjoyed seeing Bob Mitchum again and working with him. He was great fun to be with. I can hear you wondering if there was anything else I liked about the movie, Doc. Not much, I must say. I wouldn't go down the river on that raft again for all the opium in China.

"Shortly after that, Twentieth Century Fox decided to produce *The Egyptian*. I fancied myself playing the glorious, bejeweled Queen Cleopatra floating down the Nile, and asked the studio to cast me in it. Fox responded by optioning Elizabeth Taylor for the role and instead giving me the lead in *The Girl in Pink Tights*. The so-called plot of that great work of art revolves around a schoolteacher who becomes a saloon dancer.

"I was outraged. I asked to at least be allowed to read the script of the *Pink Tights* before agreeing to do the film. Darryl Zanuck, then the production head, flat-out refused. He said I was under contract to Twentieth Century Fox and therefore had to do whatever I was told. I don't take well to being ordered around, especially when I don't like the order. So I didn't show up for the first day of shooting and simply disappeared. Fox responded by suspending me and my salary.

"I'd made up my mind that *The Girl in Pink Tights* was just not good enough for me, and I'd not do the role, no matter the consequences.

"Well, my life wasn't all fun and games at the time. I was still in bad shape after Johnny died, even after a few years passed. The pain was so bad, I didn't know how I could go on living. I've had many terrible losses in my short lifetime, but there was something about this one that shattered me in the place where I live. Friends tried to fix me up with men they thought I'd like, saying, 'There are plenty of other fish in the sea,' but none of the fish interested me.

"I had a terrible dream last night. I dreamt I had a dead baby. At first, I thought the dream meant that I was worried I'd get pregnant again and the baby would be born dead. But then I remembered what you always say—that everything in a dream represents the dreamer. So I guess it means that you, shrinker, have a dead baby instead of a live patient! Because part of my heart died along with Johnny Hyde, and it'll never come to life again."

Marilyn was right. That was exactly the meaning of her dream.

I silently wept when I heard it.

APRIL 17, 1959

Marilyn bounced into her next session in a completely different mood and started to talk before she even hit the couch. "I've told you all about the movies I made after Johnny died, but I haven't told you a thing about Joe! I met him before a lot of my really big movies from 1952 were even released. The *Life* cover had come out, though. I remember that. And probably the calendar, too.

"I had taken a few publicity photos standing alongside Gus Zernial, a power-hitting outfielder for the Philadelphia Athletics. A few days later, the ballplayer Joe DiMaggio—even you must know who he is—played in an exhibition game against Zernial, who said Joe looked at the picture and said, 'How come I never get to pose with a beautiful girl like that?'

"Zernial told me that Joe DiMaggio was an American hero all through the Depression, when the country needed heroes to boost its morale. I was very impressed and said, 'I'll meet him. My morale can stand some boosting, too.'

"What DiMaggio wants, DiMaggio goes after, in life and on the ball field. He had the press agent who set up the photo shoot arrange a date between us in March 1952. He called me and asked, 'Would you like to meet a nice guy?'

"I answered, 'I didn't know there were any.'

"Afterward, a gentleman of the press asked me, 'Are you planning to get married again?'

"I answered, 'I'm going to stay single forever . . . for now.' He scribbled down every word I said, with an expression on his face as serious as if I'd told him I'd just written the Declaration of Independence.

"Baseball has never been among my major enthusiasms. In fact, in my own mind, I was rather vague about the differences between football and baseball. Nonetheless, I agreed to meet DiMaggio at the Villa Nova Italian restaurant, thinking, if worse came to worst, I could always gulp down my spaghetti and go home.

"I expected Joe to be a coarse, gaudy, New York-type jock wearing a pink tie. Instead, I met this reserved guy wearing a white silk shirt, gray silk tie, with a gold baseball bat stick-pin on it, and black, well-cut trousers. He looked more like a tanned movie star than a famous jock. Surprise of surprises, he didn't make a pass at me right away, like every other hotshot does. Instead, he treated me as someone special. *Hmmm*, I thought, *could it be that there really is a gentleman in town?* He didn't have a car with him, so I surprised myself by offering to drive him home.

"He didn't say a word during the whole drive, so right before we got to his house, I said, 'I'm sorry, I don't know anything about baseball.' He replied, 'That's all right. I don't know anything about movies.'

"I thought he was a nice guy, but somehow nice guys never set my world on fire unless they had something else to offer, so I still wasn't terribly excited about him. He called as soon as I got home, though, and then every night for the next two weeks. Maybe I was just testing him, but I turned down every request for a date. Finally, he stopped calling.

"You know my favorite song, 'After You Get What You Want, You Don't Want It'? Well, it should have a second verse: 'When you *don't* get what you want, you start wanting it pretty quick.'"

Marilyn is pretty shrewd! I thought. I knew that she was unusually smart—she wrote on a patient questionnaire that she had an IQ of 169—but it was interesting to see that not only did Marilyn know things intuitively; she acted on them. (I was far from the only person in the world to have initially underestimated her intelligence.)

"A week later, I called *him*," she said. "And we began bi-coastal dating, which was to last a coupla years, until early 1954."

"What was the attraction?" I asked.

"What was the *attraction*? Come on, Doc. You're supposed to be a psychoanalyst. You should be able to figure that one out. I was twenty-five when we first started dating, and Joe was thirty-eight. You know I like older, successful men who are father-figure types. Joe liked blondes, though I turned out to be more than just another blonde trophy to hang on his belt. As for me, I never had been in love with Jim Dougherty, my first husband. Joe Schenck was a kind, influential man who never set me on fire. And much as I would have liked to, I never truly fell in love with Johnny Hyde, either.

"But it was a different story with Joe DiMaggio. We fell madly, passionately in love. I became the love of Joe's life. Despite what happened later, I guess you can say that he became the love of my life, too. The dead baby lives again!"

APRIL 20, 1959

Marilyn continued the saga of Joe DiMaggio. "Among baseball writers, Joe had a reputation for being a man of vigorous lust. They said, 'Joe is a hell of a hitter in that league, too.'

"I can vouch for the accuracy of those statements—I told my friends, 'He brings a great bat into the bedroom.' In fact, Joe had the finest male body I'd ever seen, and reminds me of Michelangelo's statue of David. I was so in awe of Joe's physical beauty that sometimes I just wanted to look at him instead of making love. I found him a compassionate, thoughtful, and completely satisfactory lover, who was as interested in my pleasure as in his own. He could knock out as many home runs in the bedroom as he did on the ball field. If that were all it took, believe me, I'd still be Mrs. Joe DiMaggio. I still love him. He's for real.

"But I must say that, although he was the best lover I ever had, he was not as good as he thought he was. Once, when he was bragging about the size of his sexual equipment, I sent him a mirror and a ruler. As it turned out, Doc, Joe is like you," she said, turning around to see if her arrow had hit the mark. "He doesn't have much of a sense of humor, either. He didn't think the mirror-ruler prank was at all funny.

"In the early months of our marriage, I really appreciated Joe. I felt he'd given me some roots, and admired his vitality, strength, and stability. When he was standing beside me, I wasn't afraid of anything. I once wrote him this note and pinned it to his pillow:

Dear Joe:

If I can make you happy, I will have succeeded in the biggest and most challenging thing in the world—making one person happy! Your happiness means my happiness.

Love,

Marilyn

"As I told you, I'd refused to do *The Girl in Pink Tights*, which was to shoot at the end of 1953. And I wasn't doing anything else professionally. So Joe said, 'Since you're having all this trouble with Fox and aren't working, why don't we just get married? I have to go to Japan on baseball business, and it would make a great honeymoon trip.'

"So we got married. From such little acorns great decisions are made!

"It was January 14, 1954, and we had a small, private civil ceremony. Joe's best friend, Reno Barsocchini, arranged for the wedding to take place at San Francisco City Hall and was Joe's best man. I had no maid of honor because I had no girlfriend I liked well enough to ask. Joe and Barsocchini's former San Francisco Seals manager, Lefty O'Doul, and his wife were the only others who attended, besides the judge, of course.

"I may have lacked friends at the ceremony, but there was no scarcity of paparazzi. Over one hundred photographers, reporters, and fans congregated outside the judge's chambers. Did I say the ceremony was supposed to be private? Maybe the gang was all there because I just happened to mention that morning to Harry Brand, the head publicity man at Twentieth Century Fox, that Joe and I were getting married in San Francisco.

"As we tried to duck the barrage of questions, a reporter asked, 'How many kids do you want?'

"I'd like to have six," I said.

"At least one," Joe corrected, in the first of what would turn out to be countless disagreements in our brief marriage.

"I expect to continue my career," I added. "But I'm looking forward to being a housewife and cooking for my husband." And I did cook for him—twice!

APRIL 21, 1959

"One of the greatest experiences of my life came during our honeymoon in Japan, although it had nothing to do with Joe. In Tokyo, we had to be smuggled out of the plane through a baggage hatch. A huge crowd was screaming, 'Mon-chan! Mon-chan,' which means 'sweet little girl' in Japanese. They didn't stop yelling until I appeared on a balcony to thank them for coming. My head was in a whirl with all the shouting in my honor. I felt like some dictator being saluted in a wartime newsreel.

"The journalists bombarded me with questions like, 'Are you wearing underwear?' Always the diplomat—ha!—I answered, 'I am buying a kimono.' The newspapers came out with the statement, 'The Japanese probably will not discard their underwear as a result of the visit of the honorable, buttocks-swinging actress. It is much too cold.'

"I have another good Japan story for you. I flew to the plane in one of those new, see-through plastic helicopters. As I climbed into my bucket seat, I thought, *Maybe this is the one time I should've worn underwear!*

Even I couldn't help laughing.

"Joe seemed very unhappy," she continued. "I think he was jealous that I was getting much more attention than he was. Sorry about that, Joe! I wish they'd been as interested in your underwear as in mine.

"Then came the experience I'll never forget if I live to be one hundred, which, incidentally, I'm not planning to do. I went to entertain the soldiers in Korea—without Joe.

"A few weeks before our wedding, I'd spoken with a marine who knocked at my door specifically to tell me he had just returned from Korea, and wanted me to know how much my photos had meant to the servicemen there. I took what he said to heart.

"In a makeshift tent in Korea, in whirling snow and below-freezing weather, I changed into my costume—a low-cut purple gown—and lo and behold, shy little Norma Jeane became *the* Marilyn Monroe for the First Marine Division of thirteen thousand men. They shrieked for ten minutes when I said, 'You fellows down here are always whistling at girls wearing sweaters. Well, take off their sweaters and what have you got?' They roared thunderous approval, as I sang 'Diamonds Are a Girl's Best Friend,' 'Do It Again,' and 'Bye Bye Baby.'

"Unfortunately, a prissy brass officer had told me the military considered the song 'Do It Again' too suggestive, so I had to change the lyrics to "Kiss Me Again.' As if the boys who were old enough to give their lives for their country had to be protected from learning about the evils of sex!

"What I want to stress to you, Doc, is that this was one of the high points of my life. Can you imagine being the object of lust of thirteen thousand men all at the same time, in person, for three whole days?"

I couldn't—not even before *thirteen* men.

"I'd never truly felt like a star before," she continued with stars in her eyes, "but after Korea, I thought I never again would feel unloved. In fact, I never thought I had an effect on people at all until I was in Korea. I didn't even mind that performing practically naked in freezing weather gave me pneumonia, and I had to be hospitalized for two weeks afterward. It was worth every minute.

"Nevertheless, I was so sick, I thought I was going to die, so I asked Joe to promise that after I died, he would put roses on my grave every week, as William Powell had once romantically promised to do for Jean Harlow. Joe agreed, but I noticed that he didn't say what you would expect a husband to say in such a case, such as, 'Come off it, Marilyn! You're too young to think about dying.'

"I came back to Japan to a sullen husband, annoyed about all the ruckus in the newspapers about my Korean trip, and he wouldn't let me tell him anything about it. He just sat and sulked whenever I tried to bring it up, which was often. I wanted to share my joy with him, but to no avail. It reminded me of when I was a little girl who came home from school and had no one but a cat to tell I'd gotten an A on a test. I looked at Joe and wished I had a cat.

"Joe turned out to be a delightful suitor, an exquisite lover, and a marvelous friend. Unfortunately, he was a lousy husband."

APRIL 22, 1959

"I hate to say this about Joe, for he's a wonderful guy, but he was quite boring. And, frankly, I don't think he was smart enough for me. I suspected this even before we were married. When he was a teenager, his own beloved sister Maria thought he was no great brain, and maybe even a little backward mentally. 'Not quick,' she said. 'Marilyn's smarter than he is.'

"Joe has a limited vocabulary, no intellectual interests, doesn't know what abstract art is, and spends most of his time looking at television. He thinks a *cuisine* is his cousin. The only book I ever saw him read was a comic book. Oh, I forgot. He also reads the sports pages.

"You might be wondering how Joe gets away with it. Everybody adores him, male or female, truck driver, waiter, or scholar. Nobody I know of is aware of his intellectual shortcomings except me and his sister. Joe DiMaggio doesn't have to talk. If an ordinary person stands around and says nothing, people think he's a dunce. But if Joe is quiet, and if he's always with strangers, they say he has 'presence' and figure he's thinking deep thoughts.

"But I'll say one thing for him: Joe doesn't kid himself. He said to me once, 'I have to laugh when a fan calls me a great man. I'm just an ordinary Joe who happens to have a talent.' Truer words have never been spoken."

Marilyn shook her head in disbelief. "People are strange. They believe what they want to believe. Here I am, a serious actress, a woman with a very high IQ, a reader of Fyodor Dostoyevsky and Aleksey Konstantinovich Tolstoy, who's looking forward to becoming a great character actress like Marie Dressler when I grow old, and who enjoys Vivaldi and Bach. Joe DiMaggio, ballplayer extraordinaire and not much else, watches cartoons on TV for entertainment. Yet he is considered a smart man and I'm regarded as a dumb blonde. Do you understand that, Doc? I don't.

"Also to the detriment of our marriage, Joe had no interest in my career. He hated the vulgarity of Hollywood and found a trip to my movie set boring, repetitive, and monotonous. According to him, baseball is much more interesting than movie-making because every ball thrown by the pitcher is unique. It never occurred to him that every movie take is unique, too. If only he had eyes to see that. No matter how creative and innovative my on-set acting was, to him it was far less exciting than watching a ball game on TV. So that's what he did—watch ball games. Night and day.

"To be honest about it, aside from admiring his tall, long-boned, graceful movements in the ball park, which looked like sheer poetry in motion, I wasn't any more interested in his games than he was in watching my films being made. Like the famous Chinese remark about horse races, everybody knows that one batter can hit farther than another, and in the long run, who cares which one can hit the farthest?

"So, aside from our lust for each other, we had little in common. According to the public and the movie magazines, our marriage was going along just fine. But in truth, we were at each other's throats all the time. Anything could set off an argument. He's obsessively neat. I'm terribly sloppy. So every sock of mine he found on the floor brought a glum and sour look to his face and/or a lecture. I bought him books; he refused to read them. When I recited poetry to him, he said he didn't get it. I wanted a social life, and he withdrew into ever-lengthening silences.

"On the rare occasions when we ate together at a restaurant, we bolted down our meals in gloomy silence. He hated the way I dressed. When I said my style of dressing was part and parcel of my job, he said, 'Quit the job!' He didn't come often to the set to watch me work because, he said, he didn't want to watch his 'half-naked wife wriggling around in the arms of another man.'

"When we weren't quarreling, we were turned off to each other. It was not a happy situation.

"Although I bought Joe a king-sized eight-foot bed for his comfort, after a while, we began to sleep in separate bedrooms so he could watch TV all night and not keep me awake. But a man and his wife should sleep together. Sleeping apart is lonely. People need human warmth even while asleep. In separate bedrooms, if you happen to think of something you want to tell your mate, you have to go traipsing down the hall or up the steps to find him. I wound up on the second floor while he slept on the first, and by the time I reached him, I may well have forgotten what I wanted to say to him in the first place.

"Half the men in the world would give their eye teeth to see Marilyn Monroe's body, and my husband preferred to look at TV! No TV sets should ever be allowed in the bedroom. Who can compete with what's on TV?

"My dream of marital bliss had turned into a nightmare. Joe was cold and indifferent, and got into moods where he wouldn't speak to me for days or even weeks at a stretch. When I tried to force him to talk to me, he would turn his back on me or bark, 'Leave me alone! Stop nagging at me all the time!' It's not an easy thing for a man and a wife to live intimately together. In fact, I think it's practically impossible. But, believe it or not, I'm still optimistic about marriage."

Although I wanted to hear the rest of the story, it was way past the end of the hour, and another patient was in my waiting room. When I indicated that to Marilyn, she said, "Already?" and stuck her tongue out at me as she left.

APRIL 23, 1959

Marilyn picked up where she had left off the day before. "Joe was an insanely jealous man who was envious even of the grocery delivery boy. He drove me out of my mind with his suspicions, most of which were unfounded. The climax came when I was making the film *The Seven Year Itch*, in which I played a shimmering, seductive enchantress who sublets the apartment above the one lived in by summer bachelor Tom Ewell.

"The Fox publicity department decided to take a promotional shot of me near the Trans-Lux theater on Lexington Avenue, which is where Joe and I went on the few occasions when we attended the movies together. It turned out to be the most famous photo of me, and possibly of anyone else, ever taken. It was a very hot summer day, and they had me standing over the subway grate to get cool. I'm sure you've seen it."

I nodded. "Who hasn't?"

"Then you know that, in the movie scene, two subways are supposed to zoom by and produce a gust of wind strong enough to blow my skirt way up over my legs and expose my white panties. No subway really went by. The air-blowing was done by special-effects people using a wind-blowing machine underground.

"Well, the scene, and the photo, drove Joe wild! Unfortunately, my panties turned out to be sheerer than I had realized. But even so, you would have thought I was standing nude on the top of the Empire State Building, thumping on my naked breasts like King Kong! The director, Billy Wilder, described the expression on Joe's face as 'the look of death.'

"Even though I wore two pairs of underwear for the sake of modesty, the material, under the powerful klieg lights, became quite see-through. Joe went berserk, and strutted away from the scene with the blackest, gloomiest look I've ever seen. I thought, *Uh-oh! I'm in trouble when I get home tonight*. Well, even I couldn't have predicted how bad the trouble would be. Joe screamed and hollered that I enjoyed standing there naked and loved showing my 'damn near bared crotch to half of New York City.'

"He accused me of being an exhibitionist and said only a whore at heart could pull off a stunt like that. When I objected that it was only a scene in a movie, for God's sake, he pushed me up against the kitchen wall and started slapping my face from side to side and punching me on my arms and back. I kept screaming, 'Stop it, Joe! You'll kill me!'

"He said, 'You deserve it.'

"I cried out, 'Take your filthy hands off me. I'm not a ball for you to bat around. I don't care how many Sicilian husbands beat their wives! I'm a grown, twenty-eight-year-old woman, and I will not allow any man to treat me that way. Tomorrow, I'll call my lawyer and ask him to file for divorce.'"

"Good for you, Marilyn!" I said. "I'm proud of you that you would not allow yourself to be abused anymore. That was real progress in my view."

She was pleased at my words and smiled. Then she continued, "It gets even better. After hearing my acerbic words, Joe was shocked into paralysis. He became desperate to change my mind, even apologizing on his knees and saying he would never, ever do such a thing again, but I proceeded with the divorce anyway.

"Abuse of a woman by a big man is not something I can find it in my heart to forgive. How could I stay married to a man when he wouldn't let me be who I have to be? He regrets his behavior to the present day, and said later, 'I don't blame you for divorcing me. In your place, I would have gotten a divorce, too.' Regrettably, it was too little too late.

"When I showed up in divorce court, mobs of reporters ganged up around me, hurling questions like knives. One asked, 'Will you and Joe be friends?'

"'Yes,' I answered, 'if I don't have to talk about baseball.'

"Although the divorce went through, Joe and I have remained the closest of friends. He became the best friend of my life, and has rescued me many times from horrors I was unable to escape myself. He even pulled me from a hurricane!"

"*A hurricane?*" I said in surprise. "Which hurricane? I never read anything about it."

"It was Hurricane Janet. Let me think for a moment and I'll tell you exactly when it was. I had left Natasha by then and begun studying with the Strasbergs here in New York, and I was working with Milton Greene—oh, so much had happened, but I'll tell you about all that later. It must have been 1955, because I was already dating Arthur— my husband, Arthur Miller—and Joe and I had been divorced for half a year at least.

"I've never told anybody about this before, and I kept it from the papers. If it had gotten around, everyone would have known what an idiot I was to fly into the Caribbean during hurricane season. Not only that, but I was foolish enough not to tell anyone but Joe where I was going. As I've told you, Joe isn't very bright, and didn't know any more than I did about hurricanes, so he didn't try to make me stay home. Or perhaps he'd learned by then that nobody makes Marilyn do anything she doesn't want to do.

"I felt exhausted and decided to fly to Puerto Rico for a few days of rest. I'd always wanted to see it. Johnny Hyde loved Puerto Rico, and I thought I'd feel close to Johnny in a place he loved. But *rest*? Ha! It was all I could do to make it out of there alive.

"Only those who know Joe DiMaggio would believe this story. I, for one, have never heard anything like it. Joe can be a wonderful guy, and sometimes, like this time, he was a real hero. I flew to Puerto Rico and had a few pleasant days resting on the beach. One day, while absorbed in reading Proust, I looked up and thought, *Gee, the waves are getting awfully high*. I moved my chair back a bit and didn't think anything more about it until the sky suddenly grew dark. *Well*, I thought, *I hate to waste all the money this trip cost, but I better get back to the hotel before it begins to storm*.

"I reluctantly gathered up my stuff and returned to my second-story room at the rickety hotel where I was staying. I had gone to Puerto Rico to be alone, and boy, was I alone! There seemed to be no one else around. It had begun to pour by then, and the plaza below began to flood. I sat there, anxiously watching as a virtual river started to rage down the street. To my horror, I saw the water rapidly rising, too close to the second floor for comfort. I began to be frightened for my life, and tried to call the front desk, but the phones were already not working.

"This is it, Marilyn, I thought. *At this rate, in perhaps another hour or two, there will be no more Marilyn Monroe. Well, you always say you want to die, so here's your chance to help things along. Jump out the window now before the room is flooded. End your rotten life forever.*

"I climbed up on the window sill and prepared to jump when, in the distance, I saw an odd-looking speck. It came closer and closer until I saw that the speck was a man swimming down the very river that was roaring down the street. I looked closely.

There was something about the man's beautiful rhythmic motion that looked familiar. *My God,* I thought, *that's Joe!* He was braving exposed wires and fallen trees, swimming through hurricane floods to rescue me! Only Joe DiMaggio would do such a crazy, stupid thing. He saved my life. Hundreds lost theirs in that very powerful hurricane.

"Our love for each other continues to this day, and has remained the most important touchstone of both our lives. Too bad our marriage didn't work as well."

APRIL 24, 1959

Marilyn came in for her session and said, "Today, I want to talk about a lovely postscript to my divorce of Joe. One of the people I turned to for solace was my friend Frank Sinatra. While my divorce was in process, I was naturally very upset. I couldn't help but wonder if I'd done the right thing in deciding to divorce him. So I went to live with Frankie for a few weeks to give me time to pull myself together.

"Frank was as miserable as I was because his marriage to Ava Gardner, the love of his life, was toppling. For a while, despite living together, our relationship remained platonic. Early one morning, when he came into the kitchen, he saw me standing in front of the open refrigerator, trying to decide if I wanted to eat or drink. 'Saw' is the right word. I was completely naked.

"'Oh, Frankie,' I said, pretending to be embarrassed, 'I didn't know you got up so early.' He made a grab for me, and that was the end of our platonic relationship. Actually, I did him a favor. Because of his heavy drinking, he had become impotent. He was getting up there in years and was too old to drink so heavily and still be able to perform in the sack. This worried him a great deal, because he'd always prided himself on his ability to satisfy women.

"We commiserated with each other about our failed love lives and then had great sex. I guess you can say we mourned together, kind of like the great Jewish custom of sitting *shiva*, but with one important difference. I'm happy to tell you that I cured him of his problem. He was extremely grateful. The only reason we didn't become serious about each other was that he was still in agony over his split with Ava. And like him, I was in too much pain about my forthcoming divorce from Joe to begin a serious relationship with another man.

"But if you must grieve, and grieve I did, Frank provided a most pleasant way to do so."

You've got to give the woman credit, I thought, shaking my head. (I did a lot of head-shaking with Marilyn Monroe.) *She knows how to use her sexuality, both professionally and personally, in the most creative ways I've ever heard of.* As she once said publicly, "Sex is a part of nature. I go along with nature." And so she did.

APRIL 25, 1959

Marilyn came in wanting to return to 1954 and the famous skirt-blowing scene.

"A whole lot of fuss was made about it. I thought: What was the big deal? Everybody knew I had two legs. But the tabloids were saying that a patch of my dark pubic hair showed through the two pairs of white panties the studio made me wear."

"Didn't you mind?"

"Not at all. Everybody has some. It's much worse not to have any. Back in the early '50s, I got a Brazilian waxing treatment, in which all your pubic hair is pulled out. *Ouch!*" she yelled, grabbing her genitals with both hands. "I looked like a little girl down there. I let the hair grow back while deciding if I wanted to keep having it removed. Joe didn't like the wax treatment. He said he wanted a grown woman, not a little girl, and that a female with no pubic hair is like a woman without a head. He was turned off by the plastic Barbie doll look. Now that I think about it, I agree with him.

"But I'll tell you what I really minded about the subway scene," she continued. "A stupid man yelled out at me, 'Hey Marilyn, I thought you were a natural blonde!' If looks could kill, there'd be one less Marilyn Monroe fan."

I couldn't help but admire her sexual freedom and total acceptance of her body, though no amount of money could have convinced me to appear in such a pose, not that anyone would have asked.

Marilyn may have become an icon precisely because of the contrast she provided to attitudes like mine. At the time, she was just what the country needed to confront our puritanical approach to sex.

In *The Seven Year Itch*, Tom Ewell's character desperately wants to possess the erotic Marilyn, but doesn't dare try, though he would likely be successful. However, the key moment comes when Ewell peeks under Marilyn's windblown skirt and, miracle of miracles, nothing awful happens. (Note to Dr. Freud: Ewell does not get castrated.)

The Ewell character was tremendously relieved, and so was the country as a whole. "The Girl," as Marilyn was called in the film credits, exemplified a new sexual philosophy—that sex was a simple, harmless pleasure and nothing to get outraged about. At least ten years ahead of her time, Marilyn Monroe became an enchanting, corrective symbol. She was one of America's first love children, helping our country move away from the repression of the Puritans and into a sexually more open society.

Marilyn wound up our session with a typical Monroe quip. "At a party given in my honor to celebrate the success of *The Seven Year Itch*, the director, Billy Wilder, came over to congratulate me and to say that he was directing *The Lindbergh Story* next. I got mad at him. He wouldn't let me play Lindbergh.

"Speaking of Billy Wilder," she said over her shoulder on the way out, "I love a comment he made to me, although you probably won't think it's so great. He said, 'Marilyn, stay away from psychoanalysis. Your charm is that you have two left feet.'" She giggled, wagged and wiggled her fingers at me, and dashed out the door.

Billy Wilder might have had something there, I thought, and laughed.

APRIL 27, 1959

"I know you've been dying to hear more about my career," Marilyn said sarcastically, a spiteful look on her face. "It would be nice if you were just as interested in me as a person, not as that movie star Marilyn Monroe. But since neither you nor anyone else is, I should be used to it by now. So let's talk about it, once and for all, and get it over with."

"Tell me whatever you like, Marilyn," I said with what I hoped was the dignity befitting a psychoanalyst.

Apparently forgetting to care whether I was interested in her or not, Marilyn proceeded to talk about the development of her career leading up to the highly successful Seven Year Itch. Although she was their biggest star and made them millions, Twentieth Century Fox refused to cast her in the serious roles she felt ready to play, and continued to pay her the niggardly salary she had signed a contract for when she was a starlet.

Marilyn understood that the studio executives, in particular Darryl Zanuck, did not believe she had the wherewithal to become a fine dramatic performer. Moreover, regardless of her wishes, they didn't *want* her to become a serious actress. She had been highly successful as a dumb blonde in comedies and musicals, and they intended to continue assigning her such roles because she brought in heaps of money.

APRIL 28, 1959

"Today I want to tell you about Milton Greene," she began. "I first met Milton in October 1953, I seem to recall, at a party thrown by Gene Kelly. I was dating Joe at the time, and coming off those first few big movies with Fox. I'd just returned to Hollywood after making *River of No Return* on location, and Milton had come to Hollywood to shoot a cover story about me for *Look* magazine.

"The first things I noticed about him were his big grin and small stature. He wasn't much bigger than me. And he looked so young and cute. 'Why,' I said, 'you're just a boy!' Not to be outdone, he answered in his croaky voice, 'And you're just a girl!' He had sweet brown eyes and looked like the black-haired Irish kid who sat next to you in English class and dipped your pigtails in ink.

"I became enthralled when he told me about his passion for photography. He said he wanted to capture the beauty in people's hearts, and to illuminate it in an elegant and natural way. It was so much my way of thinking that we immediately became intimate friends and even lovers. We didn't remain lovers for long because, frankly, he wasn't my cup of tea. In case you forgot, Doc, I prefer older men in bed, not boys. Also, his wife Amy and I soon became close friends, and believe it or not, I do have a conscience.

"Milton was like no man I've ever known. For our first shoot, we rode out to the desert looking for a rock beside a cactus as a backdrop. I started to take off my clothes, and he said, 'Don't do that!'

"I said, 'I don't mind.'

"He answered, 'But I do.'

"*A man who didn't want me to take off my clothes?* Would miracles never cease? I knew right away we'd be friends.

"I told him I was very unhappy at Fox, not only because of the poor roles I was still being cast in, but because they were paying me only fifteen hundred dollars a week, in contrast to Jane Russell, who was not bound by a long-term employment contract and was paid one hundred thousand dollars per film, or more, depending on what she negotiated. Even more important, I wanted to play serious roles and act opposite fine actors like Marlon Brando and Richard Burton, but the big wheels at Fox only laughed at me when I said so. Milton agreed that this was most unfair, and he said he was certain he could help.

"He asked to see my contract and, after his review, told me not only that it was null and void, but that I should leave Twentieth Century Fox immediately. That was exactly what I wanted to hear, so with one unceremonious phone call, I dumped my studio. They didn't like it at all, but as Milton had said, there was nothing they could do about it, since the law was on my side.

"I've heard it said that this rebellion against Twentieth Century Fox helped break the back of the old movie-making system. If so, I'm gratified by my part in it. I don't like bullies, even when they're part of an enormously successful commercial enterprise, and I'm happy to have helped defang them. And if you say I'm a castrating woman, dear shrinker, find yourself another patient!"

I smiled. Marilyn knew very well that, in her fight against exploitation, I was behind her all the way.

She continued, "For the next two years, Milton was my friend and champion, my pill supplier, and then my business partner. In fact, both Greenes remained my soul mates and closest friends for a long time.

"At Milton's first shoot, I discovered that, besides being able to cut through subterfuge and deceit, he had superb timing and a unique ability to create a rapport with a subject, so much so that I was able to open up with him more than I ever did with any photographer, before or since. If you'll forgive the cliché, I allowed him to capture the depths of my soul. I have no doubt that Milton Greene is a genius. He didn't have any doubt, either.

"We got so excited about our shared artistic values that, right then and there, we decided to form our own film production company to be called Marilyn Monroe Productions. I was to be president and Milton vice-president. Milton said he would be the only vice-president in history who didn't want the president to be assassinated. I felt great, and went around yelling, 'Hey, everybody! Guess what? I'm incorporated!'

"We planned to produce the elegant films we both wanted to make, in contrast to the junk Fox was forcing me to act in. I was sick and tired of sex roles, and I wanted to play great juicy roles, like those in Dostoyevsky's *The Brothers Karamazov*. When I happened to mention that to a journalist, he howled and said, 'Do you mean you want to play the part of the brothers?'

"I said, 'No, *dear*. I want to play Grushenka. In case you don't know, she's a girl!' Lee Strasberg said that if anybody had listened to me and cast me as Grushenka, it would've been one of the great performances of all time. He said, 'You were born to play the role.' Other people said, 'Yeah, sure, we'll believe it when we see it.' But they didn't know either Milton or me very well. Some people say they'll do something and then don't come through. When Milton and I say we'll do something, we do it!"

Marilyn was the first woman star ever to form her own production company. I shook my head for the umpteenth time and thought, *What an incredible woman Marilyn Monroe is!*

APRIL 29, 1959

"But before we started making movies together, Milton helped me renegotiate a new contract with Fox that was far superior to the old one. The studio, to their great surprise, found they were unable to replace me in the eyes of the public, and had no choice but to sign the contract, which had the most favorable terms yet given to any female Hollywood star.

"I'd be required to make only four films over the next seven years for them, and I'd be allowed to make another movie with any studio of my choosing. Plus, Marilyn Monroe Productions would be paid one hundred thousand dollars for every film we made for Fox, along with a percentage of the profits.

"Most important of all to me, a special clause in the contract gave me the right to reject any Fox film I thought unworthy of making, and to refuse to work with any director or cinematographer I disapproved of. The Greenes and I submitted a list of sixteen directors I'd be willing to work with. The studio went along, not because of their good hearts but because we had them over a barrel.

"That was in March. *The Seven Year Itch* finished shooting November 5, 1954," Marilyn said, "I had married Joe in January, and by November we were divorced. Of course, I was devastated by the divorce, and I fell into a deep depression. My dear Milton flew to Hollywood to rescue me, and brought me back to New York with him. It was at the end of 1954, the beginning of 1955, when our dreams came true and we formed Marilyn Monroe Productions, Inc. Our initial plan was to do two films, *Bus Stop* and *The Prince and the Showgirl*. We actually produced both the next year, in 1956. I consider them the finest achievements of my life."

"I decided to move to New York and learn how to really act by enrolling at the Actors Studio. I felt I could be more my real self in New York than in Hollywood. After all, if I can't be myself, what's the good of anything? In April, I subleased an apartment in the Waldorf Astoria Towers.

"I'd met Paula Strasberg in Hollywood when she was visiting her actress daughter, Susan, and I resumed our relationship as soon as I arrived in New York. To my delight, I quickly became the protégée of the Strasbergs, and an exciting relationship began among the three of us that was to change me as an actress forever.

MAY 4, 1959

In the few years that had passed since *Niagara*, Marilyn had gone from rising starlet to Hollywood goddess. For years, she'd been studying to improve her acting, and every role she played was an improvement over the previous one. She had become the top box-office attraction in America as well as all over the world. Despite the burdens of her personal and professional lives, and her status as a great star, Marilyn, in all her integrity, decided to leave Hollywood and move to New York to study acting. She was determined to become a serious dramatic actress, whatever the cost.

"I don't care about money," she said. "I just want to be a wonderful actor!"

"Why is that so important to you, Marilyn?" I said. "Many of your fans are foolish, perspiring strangers. What do *you* get out of it?"

"Well, when those foolish, perspiring strangers all sit down together in a theater, and you as an actor are in such good form that everything comes out exactly as it should, you get lifted to the heavens. It's as if you're not just *you* any more, an insignificant interloper in the world. It's kind of like all the strangers melt together into one loving piece of humanity and you finally feel at home. They become the family I never had. It's hard to explain, but once you've experienced it, life is never the same again."

I was quite moved, and we both remained silent for a while. *The move to New York would be a bold one for any actor*, I was thinking, *but particularly courageous for Marilyn, who battles terrible insecurities and all kinds of demons, external as well as internal. How many successful Hollywood actors would walk out on Twentieth Century Fox and move to New York to study with Lee Strasberg, even if he is the greatest drama teacher in the world?*

As if she felt she had opened up too much to me, Marilyn's mood shifted. She said, "A funny thing happened to me when I first arrived in New York. I'd left Hollywood suddenly without telling anyone, and nobody was at Idlewild Airport to meet me. I was lugging my beautiful white Persian cat Mitsou, who was pregnant with kittens, in a special carrier. It was quite a load to carry, seeing she was pregnant and all. Between the time the plane landed and I reached the eighth-floor apartment at Two Sutton Place that Milton Greene had found for me, three kittens were on their way.

"I immediately phoned three veterinarians, and would you believe it? When I said, 'This is Marilyn Monroe, my cat is having kittens, and I need help right away,' all three thought I was some kind of loon and hung up on me! Fortunately, Mitsou has ancestors from the jungle, where, to the best of my knowledge, they have no vets, and she is fully capable of taking care of herself. I should do as well. Incidentally, I now have four white cats."

MAY 5, 1959

"Happy May Day, Shrinker!" she said, greeting me with a smile. "Or was that last week? I'm not so good on dates." I acknowledged her greeting with a nod.

Then, with the swift changes of mood she was known for, she became very thoughtful and lay quietly on the couch for a few minutes before speaking. Soon, Marilyn returned to talking about Lee Strasberg. She said she was introduced to him by Elia Kazan and Cheryl Crawford, the founders of the Actors Studio. To everyone's surprise, Strasberg immediately recognized Marilyn's talent, and felt an excitement about it second only to his belief in Marlon Brando's genius.

Lee immediately took Marilyn under his wing. He and his wife Paula quickly became a tremendous influence on Marilyn, taking over almost every aspect of her professional and personal life. Lee gave her free private acting lessons in his apartment at Eighty-Sixth Street and Broadway and allowed her to attend sessions at the world famous Actors Studio.

Both Strasbergs encouraged Marilyn to practically move into their home. Lee Strasberg was much more to her than an acting teacher: He was her surrogate father, mentor, acting coach, friend, adviser, hero, and guidance counselor. He fully supported her ambition to become a great dramatic actress, and felt she had a rare talent that, if properly cultivated, would catapult her to greatness. He also convinced her to go into psychoanalysis.

Marilyn implicitly trusted whatever Strasberg told her, for to her he carried the aura of a psychoanalyst, a prophet, a witch doctor, and a magician. She placed her life, her career, and her future in his hands, to do with as he thought best. He was probably the greatest influence in her entire life, and next to Marilyn herself, the person most responsible for her becoming a great actress.

MAY 6, 1959

"I'm in awe of Lee Strasberg, and all he's done for me on a personal and professional level," said Marilyn. "I'm eager to hear anything he has to say, whether it's praise or criticism, if I can use it to improve myself as an actor and a person. I get both from Lee. A lot of people come into their house, but I know I'm special to him. I'm the only one he and Paula let live there.

"You know how they say that something that seems too good to be true usually is? Sometimes, I'm afraid my relationship with him is only a dream, and I'll wake up one day and find myself back with foster parents who'll throw me out any day now. He's a genius who creates truth in acting as no one else has ever done in this country."

"Tell me how he does that, Marilyn," I said, even though I knew quite a bit about the Method myself, from my late-husband and the many years I had been interested in film and theater. I wanted her to know that she truly was living in reality, and sometimes it could be pretty wonderful.

She answered eagerly. "His major technique is called emotional memory, in which you bring to mind a moment in your life when you experienced an emotion like the one the scene calls for. The memory triggers an honest emotional response, as if it were something happening at that very moment.

"You start by relaxing and then place yourself in the time you need to re-experience. You ask yourself, 'What do I see? What do I hear? What do I taste? What do I smell? What do I feel on my skin? Is it hot? Cold? On what part of my body do I feel it? What am I wearing? Is it my favorite clothing, or am I uncomfortable in it? Is anyone else there? Who are they? What do I feel about them? Do I like them? Love them? Hate them? Can I see them? Hear them? What do they look like? What do their voices sound like? And so on.

"That, my dear doctor, is the whole exercise," she said. "That's all there is to it, really. The scary secret of great acting is hereby revealed to you. You can now join the ranks of Bernhardt and Duse." She stretched out her hand. "That will be fifty dollars, please." Marilyn, it seemed, found it hard to stay serious for any great length of time.

I didn't respond.

Marilyn, not noticing, returned to her serious mood. "Like most great things, the genius of the technique is its simplicity. All you have to do is be completely there. For instance, people ask me what I do to look so sexy. I don't do anything. I just think of men, or of one man in particular who I'm yearning for. It's easy to look sexy when you're thinking about a man who's special to you. Working from the inside out is what makes for good acting."

Marilyn began to giggle.

"What's so funny, Marilyn?" I asked.

"I just remembered something that happened in class today. An actor got up and played a scene. When he finished, Strasberg asked what the guy was feeling while he was acting.

"The guy said, 'The scene made me cry.'

"'Good,' Strasberg said. 'Now make *me* cry.'"

We both laughed, and I said, "I'm sure he'll never have to say that to you, Marilyn!"

"In *Bus Stop*," she continued, "when my character Cherie got what I've always wanted, to be loved unconditionally no matter what she'd done in the past, I thought of Lee Strasberg, and how he gives me what I've always needed from a father and never gotten from any other man. He doesn't care that I say 'fuck you' to the world and even to him sometimes, that I am practically always late, that I pop pills by the dozen, and that I drink too much—or that I'm unreliable and impulsive, don't always know my lines, and sometimes lose my concentration.

"Whatever I do or don't do, Lee never yells at me. He totally accepts me, no matter what. I always feel loved by him. In doing that scene in *Bus Stop*, I remembered all that he is to me. The feelings that aroused allowed me to do the best work of my life. I've been told by many who've seen that film that it also broke their hearts."

I knew what she meant.

"If only I'd had him as my real father! How different my life would be now," she said angrily, wiping away her tears.

I found myself feeling deeply sad, too. *If only life could be lived over again, and Marilyn had the childhood she deserved! If only! If only!*

I also wiped away a few tears.

MAY 11, 1959

"Now, about *Bus Stop*," Marilyn said, as if no time had elapsed since our previous session, "I have only one complaint. Don Murray was excellent in the leading male role, even though I don't like him one bit and think he's a conceited, arrogant egotist convinced that the sun rises and sets on his talent.

"Do you know why he was so good in the role, Doctor? Because I gave him so much to work with. He didn't do a thing with the part before I made him talk right to me and look straight at me. Before that, you would've thought I wasn't in the room with him. And would you believe, he got an Oscar for his performance and I didn't even get mentioned! Boy, is that unfair! The injustice of it still stings. And Murray's never been as good in any part since."

MAY 12, 1959

"Let's get back to the Strasbergs and how important they are to me," said Marilyn. "Three days a week, after I leave here, I go to their home, where I hang out with Paula in the kitchen for a while. I tell her my troubles and she mothers me and gives me milk and cookies. I love her, but I can't help it—I love Lee more.

"Then I have my private lesson with Lee, which I live for. Those lessons are the high point of my week. There isn't a one I don't come away from refreshed, encouraged, and revitalized, feeling that Lee will help me become a great actress. I feel sorry for people who don't have a Lee Strasberg in their lives.

"After my lesson is over, I don't want to leave the charmed atmosphere, so I often stay for dinner, and they always make me feel welcome. We all sit around the kitchen table like a real family. Classical music plays in the background. There's a lovely ambience in the room—the fake Tiffany lamp sitting on the glass table lights up our faces like precious jewels. Lee often opens up and tells stories and jokes, illustrating them with clumsy gestures like a bad actor. Whether they're funny or not, we all laugh.

"One day after dinner, we were sitting around the table talking, and I keeled over from taking too many pills. Everybody got very anxious, although I wasn't, because it had happened before and I knew that eventually I would wake up. So they dragged me off to bed. I'd seen other famous actors like Franchot Tone and Montgomery Clift black out at that same table. Lee usually yelled at them, saying that what they were doing to their talent was criminal, that great actors have as much responsibility to their gifts as they do to a child.

"But for some reason I don't understand, he's different with me. He doesn't yell or even preach at me, but is tender and understanding. While I lay there in a daze that time, my eyes closed, he must've thought I was too far out of it to pick up what he was saying, but I overheard him telling Paula, 'Marilyn can't handle criticism or anger directed at her. She feels rejected. But the same qualities that make her sick will make her a great actress. With her raw sensitivity, she's able to pick up thoughts, lies, and the unconscious thoughts of other people.

But because of her past, she's not able to handle rejection . . . yet.'

Oh, that's why he is so nice to Marilyn, I thought.

"Encouraged by the word 'yet,'" continued Marilyn, "I smiled and fell happily asleep, thinking that sometimes it is worth having a terrible past, because it brings me lovely things in the present like my relationship with Lee.

"By the way, Doc," she said over her shoulder as she headed out the door, "I asked him to make love to me. He said no."

She grinned.

I grinned back.

MAY 14, 1959

"The students at the Actors Studio have been very nice to me," Marilyn said. "They seemed surprised to have a Hollywood star attend their classes, but tried to make me feel welcome. After class, we get together and go out to lunch. I was shy at first, partly because I felt older than any of them. I really wasn't that much older, but just felt like I was. When Paula also came along with me, I was able to relax and enjoy being with the group."

Then Marilyn told me that when it was her turn to do an acting exercise on sense memory, she stood before a small group of students in a panic. Strasberg asked her to recall a moment in her life in which she remembered the clothing she was wearing and what she saw, heard, and smelled. Marilyn proceeded to describe how she'd felt on being alone in a room as a child, when an unknown man had walked in.

Suddenly, Strasberg admonished her, "No! Don't tell us how you feel. Tell us what you hear and see." Marilyn concentrated for a few moments and then began to speak.

Another student, actress Maureen Stapleton, told Marilyn later, "As you described what you wore, what you heard, what you saw, and the frightening words the man said to you, you began to cry, and sobbed until the end of the scene, when you seemed almost annihilated." I thought, *This is the real Marilyn Monroe, a vulnerable, shy woman, but a woman who'll be a great actress one day.*

"Later, I did something very brave," Marilyn said, in one of the rare times I heard her brag.

"What was that?" I asked.

"Well, a student at the Studio did a scene. Afterward, actor Eli Wallach was critical. 'I don't think the scene was very clear,' he said. For the very first time in class, I raised my hand and said, 'I don't know about that, Lee. It seems to me that life isn't very clear.'

"Good for you, Marilyn," I said. "That took a bit of courage."

She smiled from ear to ear.

Shortly after, Marilyn called to tell me that she had overcome terrible bouts of terror to appear at the Actors Studio in Eugene O'Neill's *Anna Christie*. It was the most serious acting she had ever attempted, and required great courage. After all, she was the most famous actress in the world, and performing badly would have made her the butt of jokes and forever consigned her back to the ranks of dumb blondes.

There was standing room only at the Studio, as every possible member attended her performance, even actors who hadn't been to the Studio in years. Many hoped to see the great screen goddess fall flat on her face. She fooled them. From all reports, she shyly told me, her performance was superb—a *tour de force*, in fact—so that even the highly critical Strasberg was thrilled.

I later heard from another patient who was a member of the Actors Studio, and who didn't know Marilyn was my patient, that the scene was magnificent, and after it was finished, the whole Studio broke into applause for the first time in its history.

MAY 18, 1959

Marilyn entered my office on this day looking very excited and began speaking before she even reached the couch. "I had a wonderful dream about the Strasbergs," she said. "I call it 'The Strasberg Dream.' I was a little girl, and they both picked me up until I reached a little over their heads. That made me bigger than I would have been." She began to cry, and said, "That tells the whole story, doesn't it? Since I've been studying with Lee, I can act parts like Anna Christie, which I never could've done before. I'm a far better actress now than I ever would have been otherwise."

"Yes, Marilyn," I said. "Your dream speaks the truth. You are indeed a better actress than you would have been."

She smiled happily through her tears.

And I? I felt as happy as if I had played Anna Christie myself.

MAY 20, 1959

"I can't sleep, Doctor! And you're no help."

"What do you usually do when you can't sleep?" I asked.

"I take pills—lots of them. But they don't work anymore, or at least not most of the time. Do you know who I always depend on the most? Believe it or not, it isn't friends or strangers, but the telephone. The telephone is my best friend. When I'm unable to sleep, I really enjoy calling my friends. I pick up the phone and call the ones who don't mind, or at least say they don't mind, talking to me at 3 a.m. Some of them can't sleep, either, but sometimes they just don't pick up the phone.

"The Strasbergs told me I can come to their home any hour of the day or night, so last night I decided to test that out. I went there depressed, unwashed, naked under my soiled bathrobe, with my hair greasy and uncombed. I thought, *My fans should see me now!* How long do you think I would remain Hollywood's number one sexpot if they saw me like that, shrinker?

"Speaking of my fans," she digressed momentarily, "I hope they'll like my new serious self as much as I do. So far, the only 'lines' they've wanted from me aren't written in English—they're my curves. A woman is often measured by the things she cannot control. She's measured by the way her body curves or doesn't curve, by where she's flat or straight or round. She's measured by thirty-six, twenty-four, or thirty-six inches and ages and other numbers—by all the outside things that don't ever add up to who she is on the inside. I want to be measured by who I am on the inside.

"Paula welcomed me in her huge black Mother Hubbard night-gown," Marilyn continued, "as graciously as if it had been lunchtime.

She gave me some hot tea with milk, but what I craved was champagne. She poured me a little, but when I reached for the bottle, she grabbed it away and pulled me into her big, gelatinous bosom. I nestled into it for a few delicious moments. It was soft as a pillow, but ingrate that I am, Lee's embrace was the one I craved.

"When I tearfully cried out, 'Lee, Lee, I need to see Lee!' she shook him awake, saying, 'Lee! Marilyn's here. She badly needs to see you.' Without missing a beat, he stood before me in his old bathrobe, threads hanging from the bottom, wearing his wrinkled blue-and-white seersucker pajamas.

"I was glad to see he didn't look much better than I did. His hair, at least what was left of it, was quite rumpled. He lifted me up and carried me into the bedroom and we spoke about how awful I was feeling. Usually, that's enough to make me fall asleep, but last night, even that didn't work. So he cradled me in his arms and said, 'Darling, you just need to be held. Nobody ever held you as a child.'Then he sang softly:

"'Lullaby, and good night, with roses bedight, Lay thee down now and rest, may thy slumber be blessed!'"He gently caressed my fine hair. Nobody would've thought this tender, loving man was also the stern, highly critical dictator who terrorized so many famous members of the Actors Studio. My eyes drooped as I cuddled against him, and I soon fell asleep. When I woke up in the morning, I was still in his arms."

Marilyn turned around to look at me and smiled triumphantly. "Now that's what I call therapy, Doctor!"

I was too moved to argue.

MAY 25, 1959

The Strasbergs' lack of rigidity made Marilyn want the same kind of treatment from me. Her regular analytic appointment was at four o'clock. One day, she showed up at three. In a rare coincidence, my three o'clock patient had cancelled, so I was able to see Marilyn then. The next day, she didn't come at her regular hour, but showed up at five instead. I was with another patient. Marilyn left a note which said, "Kilroy was here. Where were you?"

MAY 28, 1959

At her next session, I said, "What's with this coming at odd hours, Marilyn? Analysis is not a cafeteria where you come whenever you feel like it, even if I were available around the clock, which I am not."

She was very upset. "I can't see a mother-person by appointment." She began to weep. "I had so much hoped you'd be here at five yesterday. I wanted you to be on the same wavelength as me and know when I needed you. I gave up on my mother long ago. She didn't know I existed, let alone have any awareness of when I needed her. I have no hope she'll ever change. I wanted to try with someone who'd understand and be there. My mother and I have only a painful relationship. I wanted to try with someone new. But you failed me, just like her."

"I'm so sorry you feel I failed you, Marilyn. In a better world, your mother would have been there for you when you needed her. I wish I could make up for her shortcomings, but I can't."

JUNE 1, 1959

After giving me this picture of her current relationship with the Strasbergs, Marilyn moved on to her husband, Arthur Miller. She had begun dating him soon after her move to New York.

In fact, she had first met Miller before marrying Joe DiMaggio. It was at a party, probably during the spring of 1951. She said to a friend, "See Arthur Miller over there? I'm going to marry him someday."

The friend said, "Come off it, Marilyn! How can you marry Arthur Miller? He has a wife."

Marilyn merely smiled.

"I was awed to be meeting a Pulitzer Prize winner," Marilyn recalled. "You know me: I always feel inadequate because of my lack of education. I blushed and stuttered and stammered until he must have thought, *She's really the dumbest blonde I've ever met!*

"We met again later that year, when he watched me do a scene set in a nightclub. I had to walk across the floor in a black-filigreed lace dress. When he came back to see me after the scene had been shot, a stagehand whistled at the way I walked. In front of this brilliant man, I was embarrassed. Miller tried to make me feel better, and said he knew the way I sway my hips when walking was natural to me.

"He said he'd once followed me on the beach and seen that my footprints were in a straight line, the heel coming down right before the last toe print, and throwing my pelvis into motion. I didn't know that, and thought, *Hmmmmm. He followed me on the beach! He must really be interested in me. Maybe he doesn't think I'm such a dumb blonde after all.*

"About that same time, we met again at a party thrown for him. A number of beautiful young women had been invited. I was happy to see that he ignored every one of them but me. Me, he asked to dance, and I melted into his arms as if I'd been born there. We danced on and on, and I never wanted to stop. It was like hugging a tree, like a cool drink when you've got a fever.

JUNE 5, 1959

"At that party I referred to last time, Arthur and I talked into the early hours of the morning," she said. "According to him, he was impressed by my sensitivity and sense of reality, but it was more likely that Arthur, who was then about thirty-five, felt flattered to seemingly be desired by a glamorous, sexy, and famous woman.

"Without even saying anything, it was he who had inspired me to sign up for a UCLA extension course in literature and art. I'd always worked on a program of self-improvement, but now I wanted to feel more his intellectual equal if I could.

"We didn't see one other, or start dating, for another four years because both of us were married, especially him, and we were on different coasts. But I thought about him all the time, and had fantasies that we would meet again. For a while, he replaced Clark Gable in my dreams, and became the pillow I hugged at night. In my mind, I even acted for Arthur when I was making a film. I used to imagine him watching me work and wanted to be marvelous in his eyes because he said I ought to act on the stage.

"When I got to New York and found enough nerve, I contacted Arthur, who couldn't resist my invitation. It was May 1955." A married man, Miller lived in Connecticut with his wife and their two children, Jane and Bob. A simple thing like his marital state didn't stop Marilyn from going after the man she wanted.

"He said he had been thinking of me a lot, and trying not to call me. We met regularly that whole summer and autumn, despite the fact that Arthur was still married and felt guilty—as he did about almost everything else. Miracle of miracles, we were able to keep our various rendezvous secret, by meeting in far-out places like greasy diners that nobody had ever heard of. Who cares about food when you're in love? Love is the closest we humans get to Heaven. Without love, life has no meaning.

"One day, we joyfully threw our desserts out the window, yelling, 'Who needs chocolate when they have love?' I hope some dogs enjoyed our discards. Arthur and I were happy just to be together. We also walked and rode our bikes around the city a lot. Nobody expected Marilyn Monroe to be riding a bicycle, so our meetings remained hidden from everyone. In a magazine interview in July that year, I let slip that I was thinking of buying a house in Brooklyn. When the interviewer asked why, I said I'd always loved Brooklyn—me, who, before I met Arthur Miller, thought Brooklyn was a small river in England!

"The journalist noticed my beloved English bicycle in the kitchen, and I explained that I rode it in Central Park and on Ocean Parkway in Brooklyn. What I didn't tell him was that the person cycling with me was Arthur Miller."

Marilyn interrupted herself to add, "I must tell you more about the Greenes—you know, Milton Greene, whom I told you about. They were so wonderful to me at this time! I lived with them in their Weston, Connecticut farmhouse before I married Arthur in 1956. Milton couldn't have been a better friend. He believed I deserved a star's lifestyle, and that it was unbecoming for someone of my fame to be mired in shabbiness. To make that a reality, he mortgaged his home and borrowed money to the limit of his credit.

"The cost of 'maintaining' me was $50,000 a year, which included $100 a week for the care of my mother, $125 a week for psychoanalysis, $500 a week for beauty treatments, $50 a week for perfume, and money for my secretary and press agent. He also bought me a new black Thunderbird sports car and a wardrobe costing $3,000.

"He even quit his $50,000-a-year job at *Look* magazine to devote himself to my career and our production company. He gambled everything on his conviction that Hollywood could not afford to pass up the gold mine that I was. He proved right, of course. But where do you find a friend like that, who's willing to gamble his whole life on his belief in someone else? Everybody should have such a friend, but nobody I know besides me is so lucky.

"I tried to pay the Greenes back as best I could by babysitting their year-old son Josh whenever possible, and help feed and bathe him. I even babysat him on New Year's Eve, so the Greenes could go out on a date together. Josh and I had a wonderful time playing together. It was better than any New Year's Eve date I ever had.

"I would slide down the banister with him sitting on my lap, and bounce balls off the wall for his amusement, and together we would leap up and down together on the guest bed. Baby Josh would jump over the footboard and fall into my outstretched arms to get tickled to death. Then we would laugh and laugh until both of us were exhausted. I used to pretend he was my baby, and loved to cuddle him, rock him, tickle him, and—don't tell Milton—let him fall asleep in my bed in my arms. We had the most delightful times together, and I suspect that neither one of us will ever forget them.

"Along with Josh Logan, Milton helped to develop the *Bus Stop* movie project. He was assigned by the studio to handle my make-up and lighting, and was largely responsible for the movie's critical success. A genius photographer, he lent to the character of Cherie a pale white-and-black aspect, so it was easy to believe she was a creature of the night who rarely saw the sun.

"Milton also arranged to obtain *The Prince and the Showgirl* as a vehicle starring me and Laurence Olivier. And all this time, he was taking fabulous photos of me, including some of the most famous of all time. Little Norma Jeane was doing OK. During our nearly three years together, I did fifty-two photographic sessions with him, with the superb results I'm sure you've seen.

"Milton is a man with more impressive talents than anyone else I know. At the youthful age of twenty-three, he was called 'color photography's wonder boy,' and was instrumental in bringing fashion photography into the realm of fine art. He first became famous for his high-fashion photography, but is best known for his fine photographic portraits of artists, musicians, and film, television, and theatrical celebrities, of which I'm happy to state I'm considered number one.

"He was also a fine director, using the same abilities as in his photographic art to capture the qualities that personify real people. He's the author of many publications, and has had innumerable exhibitions of his work. It seems there's nothing he can't do.

"Have you ever heard of a person with so many talents? All I can do," she said mournfully, "is act, sing, and dance."

JUNE 8, 1959

Marilyn continued the story of her relationship with Arthur Miller. "We dated secretly, hidden from the eyes of paparazzi and friends alike. I listened wide-eyed to his every word, thinking I could learn enough from the world's greatest playwright to make up for my educational shortcomings. Arthur, naturally, was flattered to be desired by a younger, famous movie star. He talked and I listened, at least in the early stages of our relationship. He lectured me about the theater, books, music, and Communism. He talked a lot about Communism. Mesmerized by him, I carefully wrote down his words and memorized every tidbit.

"We tried to keep our dating out of the newspapers. One way we did so was by having the actor Eli Wallach escort me to where Arthur and I were planning to meet. Rumors got around that Eli and I were an item. Eli's wife, the actress Anne Jackson, heard them and got very upset, until we explained that Eli was just a beard for Arthur. Then she laughed and we four began to double-date.

"But gossip has a way of winning out despite all precautions. On June 10, 1956, Walter Winchell wrote in his column, 'Playwright Arthur Miller, who reportedly is the next husband of Marilyn Monroe, will finalize his divorce tomorrow. His next stop is certainly trouble. A sub-poena issued by the House Un-American Committee will check into Miller's entire circle of friends, which also happens to be Miss Monroe's inner circle. All members are former Communist sympathizers.'

"That bastard! How dare he publicize a pack of lies! Me, a Communist sympathizer? I know as much about politics as a monkey in the zoo. I only know what's in my heart, and if there's any Communism there, it's news to me. Besides, Arthur has wonderful friends who're the backbone of the American theater.

"I have only one criticism about what he said to the Congressional committee. When they asked him why he wanted to travel to England, he answered, 'A production of my play, *A View from the Bridge*, is in the planning stages in London. I'll be there with the woman who will then be my wife.' The committee hadn't known about our impending marriage. Neither had I. It would have been nice if he had asked me first, instead of my finding it out along with millions of strangers. But that's Arthur for you—as honest as the day is long."

Despite her idealization of Miller, Marilyn hesitated to marry him because she wasn't sure they were right for each other. He dazzled her with his brilliance, but she didn't believe she was intelligent enough to hold his interest. She retained this fear in our session together, three years later, after the early difficulties in their marriage.

"What will happen when he finds me out?" she lamented.

Right around the time of the subpoena, Miller told a *Time* reporter that Marilyn was the most womanly woman he could imagine. He said that people who are with her want to die. "Men become more like who they really are when they're around her. A phony becomes phonier, a shy man shyer, a kind man kinder, a confused man more confused. She sets up a challenge in everybody she's with. She is like a litmus paper, a lodestone that draws out of every man his essential qualities, so that he's more himself than he's ever been. She's literally incapable of saying anything that isn't the truth. In her acting, she looks for the basic truth in a situation, which gets her to its very core."

Isn't this pretty much what Jung meant when he wrote: "There are certain types of women who seem to be made by nature to attract anima projections; indeed one could almost speak of a definite 'anima' type. The so-called 'sphinxlike character' is an indispensable part of their equipment, also an equivocalness, an intriguing elusiveness—not an indefinite blur that offers nothing, but an indefiniteness that seems full of promises, like the speaking silence of a Mona Lisa. A woman of this kind is both old and young, mother and daughter, of more than doubtful chastity, childlike, and yet endowed with a naive cunning that is extremely disarming to men"?

"I didn't feel like a lodestone," said Marilyn, "but I loved that Arthur thought I was one, and that he considered me a completely honest person."

JUNE 12, 1959

Apparently, Miller's feelings about Marilyn assuaged her doubts, at least for the moment, for during a very rushed private service, they were married in New York in a civil service in 1956. Marilyn was so besotted with Arthur that she converted to Judaism, although according to all available records, she practiced her new religion only for two weeks.

"Whether I was a practicing Jew or not didn't matter to Egypt," Marilyn said with a grin. "Would you believe that all my movies were banned the day after my marriage by the Egyptian government, along with all the other Islamic countries? 'Marilyn Monroe is outlawed in Egypt,' they shouted to the Egyptian masses, who'd always been among my biggest fans. She's married a Jew and is now a Jew herself!' Fuck them! My films are a gift to my public, and I don't want any bigots taking pleasure in looking at me!

"Thirty friends and relatives were present at the ceremony," she continued. "My absent-minded genius of a husband forgot to buy a wedding ring, so we had to borrow his mother's. He bought me one the next week, which he had inscribed, 'A to M, June 1956. Now is forever.' Nice, huh?

"When a journalist asked me about my feelings for my new husband, I said, 'I'm deeply, passionately in love with this man. Arthur has helped me to change—for the better, I hope. He's interested in knowing all about people and everything about life, and I learn from him. Since I've known Arthur, my life has grown a lot bigger. Movies are my livelihood, but he's my everything. As Ruth said to Naomi, "Whither thou goest I will go." Where Arthur goes, I go, too. There's no question who the boss is.'

"Did I actually say such a thing? I can't imagine.

"On July 13, 1956, two weeks after we were married, we left for a working honeymoon in London, where we rented Parkside House, a large, beautiful British mansion. I was to star with the great British actor, Sir Laurence Olivier, in the film *The Prince and the Showgirl*. We traveled with twenty-seven suitcases, incurring excess baggage charges of fifteen hundred dollars. How many of those bags would you guess were mine? Twenty-six," Marilyn quipped.

JUNE 16, 1959

Olivier had originally played the role in Terrence Rattigan's *The Sleeping Prince*, the stage play on which the movie was based. His wife, Vivien Leigh, had co-starred with him.

Marilyn went to England full of misgivings. "I started making the movie with two strikes against me," she said. "First of all, I was starring with the greatest actor alive. Who do you think the audiences would prefer—a man knighted by the queen for his brilliance on the stage, or a woman famous for being a dumb blonde? Don't answer that, Doc!

"Most people are too stupid to make up their own minds about what good acting is and isn't and, like a bunch of sheep, will immediately jump to the conclusion that the critics know best. But how could I compare to Vivien Leigh, an actress who just happened to win an Oscar for playing Scarlett O'Hara in *Gone with the Wind*?

"Sir Laurence must have compared the two of us all the time, to my detriment, I'm sure. I was so scared at the thought of little Norma Jeane from the orphanage pretending to be equal to a knighted actor and an Oscar winner that I spent the first day of shooting shivering under my fur blanket, and arrived on the set late."

Intimidated as Marilyn was by co-starring with screen royalty, she never lost her sense of humor. The American columnist Earl Wilson spoke of the formality of the British press, in contrast to press conferences held in the United States. He said that in England, Marilyn was seated apart from journalists and politely applauded. At one meeting in New York, Olivier was startled by the boisterousness of the press. He asked Marilyn, "Are they always like this?," to which she wryly replied, "Well, this is a little quieter than usual."

Marilyn continued her story of *The Prince and the Showgirl.* "Olivier started the film with much more enthusiasm than I, sporting a roguish glint in his eye and lust in his heart. Unfortunately, his ardor was short-lived. In his memoirs, he wrote that he began the movie expecting to have an affair with me. After all, how many actresses would turn down the opportunity to have sex with the great Sir Laurence?

"To his surprise, but not mine, we ended up hating each other. My habitual lateness to the set drove him wild, and as master of an acting technique less spontaneous than that taught by the Strasbergs, he detested my use of the Method. In particular, he loathed my coach, Paula Strasberg, who'd accompanied me to England to tutor me. Olivier tried to have her removed from the set, but when I refused to proceed without her, he had no choice but to grant her access. It didn't help to lessen his hatred of both Paula and me."

JUNE 19, 1959

Who was it who said that troubles always come in threes? This certainly was true for Marilyn Monroe. Around the same time as her acting problems with Olivier, Marilyn began experiencing trouble in her young marriage.

Marilyn read me what Mabel Whittington, the Millers' maid at their rented London house, told a newspaper: "They seemed happy in the beginning, but as the months wore on, I could hear him nagging at her mercilessly, usually about how he thought she should be preparing for the day's work. He picked on her a lot. I think Miller wanted to stay on the good side of Olivier, and worked hard at avoiding Olivier's criticism at all costs. He wasn't even a loyal friend who stuck up for his wife, let alone a good husband. I felt sorry for her.

"At first, she seemed interested in his opinion, but there came a point when she'd had enough, particularly when he criticized her acting. She walked around the house trying to memorize her lines. She had a lot of trouble remembering them, and repeated them aloud over and over.

"He was annoyed and kept correcting her. She barked at him, 'When you begin making pictures, Arthur, we'll discuss this! Until then, I'll do the acting and you stick to the writing, such as it is these days.'"

"This account was largely correct," Marilyn said.

I thought, *Hurray for you, Marilyn Monroe! We'll make a feminist out of you yet!*

I believed that, in her thinking, Marilyn already was a world-class feminist well before her time. But she was a victim of female bigotry that could have been prevented had feminism been more established during her lifetime.

I put aside my thoughts on feminism and saw that Marilyn had begun to wring her hands. "Two weeks into rehearsal," she moaned, "my world fell apart. I idly walked past the dining room table at Parkside and noticed a notebook that Arthur had 'accidentally' left open on. I glanced at his entry for that morning—about the trouble I was causing Olivier at rehearsals, and how disappointed and ashamed he was of me. I read it over and over again because I hoped I'd read it wrong.

"That sometimes happens, you know. But unfortunately, my eyes had not deceived me. After I read it the final time, all the blood drained out of my face and I grasped the tablecloth to keep from falling to the ground. It didn't help that I fell anyway, pulling along with me a huge vase of red roses.

"I lay there, soaking wet and covered with roses I'd paid for myself, and sobbed. Nobody came to pick me up. I was convinced that Arthur had purposely left the notebook in full, open view because he wanted me to know how he felt. How could I possibly fail to notice it when I walked through the dining room twenty times a day?

"I was completely demolished by his betrayal, and consulted the wisest man I knew, Lee Strasberg, about the criticism. But even the brilliant Strasberg couldn't convince me that Arthur had written it in the heat of the moment, and that it did not represent how he really felt.

"When I called him, Lee said, 'Marilyn, darling, if Paula left me every time I said a nasty word about her, our marriage would have gone kaput twenty years ago!'

"I wasn't convinced, and I believe that what Arthur called 'hastily written words' were the beginning of the downfall of our marriage. I could live with the fact that he never sent me flowers—I could buy all the flowers I wanted myself—or that he never gave me gifts, even though I always bought *him* beautiful and expensive things. Scratch that! I felt like the little schoolgirl who didn't get any valentines. But what I truly couldn't tolerate was that he was rude and contemptuous of my problems and considered me an inferior. *Inferior!* Can you imagine? I was more famous than he was, and paid all our bills.

"His treatment of me dragged me back to the orphanage days, when no one was lower on the totem pole than I. From the moment I read his 'hastily written words,' we began to fight all the time, and I did little to hide my blazing temper. Arthur is a meek man who refuses to defend himself. His reaction to my rages was to pull away even further and go deeper into himself. That just made me more and more furious.

"I followed him around the house, screaming at him, until he barricaded himself behind his office door and wouldn't unlock it, no matter how loudly I banged. I began drinking champagne throughout the day and lacing it heavily with vodka. Even worse, I took an ever increasing number of pills, until I got so groggy I couldn't remember how many I'd taken and kept downing more and more. I was half-conscious much of the time, trying to numb my emotional pain."

JUNE 22, 1959

Marilyn's state of mind naturally affected her work on *The Prince and the Showgirl.*

She said, "I arrived at work later and later, and sometimes was so dazed with pills and alcohol that I was unable to work. On many days, I didn't come in at all. When I did manage to get there, I often forgot my lines and they had to reshoot the same scene over and over again. Both cast and crew were so angry with me that many of them stopped talking to me.

"John Huston, the director, was very concerned, and had a talk with Arthur. Huston said, 'Arthur, you'd better get your girl off the drugs, or she'll pretty soon be dead!' As if Arthur had any more influence on me! Arthur told Huston that he'd often tried to get me off drugs, but that I wouldn't listen to him. 'Those are her demons,' he said. 'I don't understand her. I do everything I can to please her, but she never is satisfied.' He couldn't have been more right. All I wanted was for him to love me, and he didn't, or he never could've written such devastating words.

"I had never felt lonelier. When I looked in the mirror, I saw a wrinkled brow on a face filled with sadness, tension, and disappointment. My blue eyes had lost their sparkle and were circled with red from weeping. My cheeks were as gaunt as the dead. My mouth was the ugliest feature of all. My once 'sexy' lips were cracked like a broken vase. My hair fell into snake-like strands that did justice to Medusa. I thought, *Whoever said I'm the most beautiful woman in the world should take a look at me now.*

"The studio became so alarmed at my behavior and appearance that they even sent me for a few sessions with Anna Freud, daughter of the great Sigmund."

I would have given an arm or a leg to know what transpired during her sessions with Anna Freud. I leaned forward, wishing to question Marilyn about every word the great woman had spoken.

Dream on, Darcey! Apparently even Miss Freud was of no help to the rapidly deteriorating Marilyn, who never mentioned her again. Curious as I was, I could not in good faith pump her for information. She had been exploited by far too many people, and I did not want my name added to the list. Unfortunately, the words of the great Anna Freud to superstar Marilyn Monroe are lost to posterity forever.

Damn!

JUNE 25, 1959

These are the infamous words Arthur Miller wrote in that infamous journal: "I have second thoughts about being married to her. She's totally different from what I expected, a child and not a woman. She isn't as intelligent or knowledgeable as I'd believed and, instead, I find her pitiful. I'm also worried that my career is endangered by associating with her. I'm terribly disappointed."

Arthur had heard that Laurence Olivier considered Marilyn a "spoiled brat." To his journal entry, Miller added that he didn't know how to respond to Olivier's accusations, because he basically agreed with him. To make matters worse, Olivier had called Marilyn a bitch. Arthur went along with him there, too. He knew that Marilyn didn't like Olivier, but felt she wasn't trying hard enough to get along with him.

"Why should I have to try to get along with Olivier?" she asked me. "Why didn't he try to get along with me, Doctor? He went out of his way to show his distaste for me and my acting, which made me dislike him even more. You know me: I won't pretend to feelings I don't have."

Miller's words had brought out Marilyn's worst fear: that she would be uncovered as a fraud, someone who wasn't as smart, as talented, or as nice as she had made Arthur think when they were dating. When she spoke to Lee Strasberg about her discovery, his response somewhat reassured her. Perhaps, he said, on a deep level, Arthur didn't at all mean what he'd said, but was merely having negative thoughts.

"Haven't you ever had such thoughts, Marilyn?" Lee asked her. Marilyn couldn't in all honesty say she hadn't, and tried to follow Strasberg's advice to attempt to make a success of her marriage. But Arthur's words had left a mark, and she never felt the same about him again.

She said, "I made up my mind that Arthur never again would get all of me. He would only get what I wanted to show him. That was my revenge."

I thought: *The part you would never show him again was your vulnerability, Marilyn. It hurts too much when you are betrayed.*

JULY 1, 1959

"Back to *The Prince and the Showgirl*," she said, starting the next session with a bang. "The only good thing about making the film was that, surprise of surprises, despite all the *sturm und drang* of making it, it turned out to be quite good, and I got rave reviews. I'll never understand how I could feel so lousy and come across so well on the screen. I guess I must have talent after all. Even the illustrious Olivier confessed to the press that he thought I was wonderful in the movie and, would you believe it, said I was even better in it than he was? There's something decent about the man after all!

"It was very dreary in London and seemed to rain the whole time. Or was it me?

"As if that wasn't enough of a problem, Arthur abandoned me when I needed him the most. After two miserable weeks of filming, he flew back to New York to see his children. I was very upset about it, and truth be told, jealous that he loved them more than he loved me.

"To get even with everybody, I called a stop to the filming, insisting I was suffering from colitis. Most people knew I resented being deserted, especially when I was feeling most vulnerable. I had another reason, however, for stopping the filming that nobody knew about. I thought I was pregnant. Tragically, I had a miscarriage almost immediately.

"In Arthur's absence, I made Colin Clark, the assistant to the assistant director, my comforter and adviser. What else could I do when my husband abandoned me? Colin was staying in my room one night when I awoke in pain. 'Help, Colin! I'm having a miscarriage. It's Arthur's baby,' I said, in tears. 'It was a gift for him. He didn't know about it. It was supposed to be a surprise. I wanted to prove to him that I can be a real wife and mother. I didn't dare mention it to anyone, in case it wasn't true.'

"Colin sympathized with me in the nicest possible way, but I remained overwhelmed with grief."

JULY 7, 1959

After the miscarriage, Arthur came back to London to rejoin Marilyn. She said, "We wrapped up the film's shooting in November, and were set to leave London to go back home, but not until after a public farewell in which the Oliviers hypocritically tried to squelch rumors that they had bad feelings about the movie.

"It was a carefully staged performance, utterly lacking in sincerity, which nauseates me to remember. You know how much I hate falsehood, Doc. Aside from the Peter Brook production of Arthur's play, *A View from the Bridge*, the trip had truly been a disaster for my husband as well as for me. As Arthur remarked, 'England humbled both of us.'

"Shakespeare wrote, 'When sorrows come, they come not as single spies, but in battalions.' He must have been talking about the Arthur Millers. After barely recovering from our British traumas and my miscarriage, the House Un-American Activities Committee announced its decision, more than a year after first subpoenaing Arthur—you remember, that took place before our London trip. My conscientious playwright was found guilty of contempt for refusing to reveal the names of a literary group suspected of being Communist sympathizers."

If Marilyn couldn't give Arthur the baby she wanted, she was still a loyal wife in a way that was a credit to her integrity, using her influence and risking her career to accompany Miller to the hearings, despite her studio's warnings that she would be finished if she supported him publicly. Like her studio, Marilyn's friends and lawyers unanimously cautioned her that if she persisted in standing behind Arthur, she might never work again.

Marilyn was never one to follow advice blindly, especially when it was something she didn't want to do. Disregarding everyone's counsel, she went with him to Washington to testify about his character at the contempt hearings. In my opinion and that of many of my friends, Marilyn's support of Miller during his confrontation with HUAC was her finest hour and a choice example of her courage and integrity.

"And listen to this, Doctor! When he was in Washington, Arthur received an offer from Francis Walter, chairman of HUAC, to cancel his hearing entirely if I would pose for a photograph with him. Can you believe it? How corrupt can our government be? Don't answer that, or I'll be here all day. Arthur said, 'That's how dangerous he really thought I was.' Arthur, of course, said no. If he hadn't, he and I would have been through. My opinion of the committee was unambiguous: They were all sons of bitches. Arthur had to tell them to go fuck themselves, but as a Pulitzer Prize-winner, he spoke in more civilized language than I could."

The HUAC investigation put extreme and consuming pressure on both Marilyn and Arthur Miller during the first year of their already challenging marriage. And what marriage wouldn't be threatened under so crushing a burden? Marilyn's loyalty during this crisis was heartwarming to Miller, and they never were as close or as happy again. He always believed that her courageous intervention helped to overturn his conviction.

JULY 9, 1959

"I forgot to tell you," Marilyn said hesitantly, "what happened to disrupt my wonderful relationship with Milton Greene during this time. It was partly Arthur's fault. He disliked Milton from the first time he met him. I think he was jealous because he knew how important Milton was in my life and career, and Arthur wanted to take over, which he did as soon as we got rid of Milton.

"My relationship with Milton collapsed while we were in England shooting *The Prince and the Showgirl*, when he announced publicly that he wanted to set up a British branch of Marilyn Monroe Productions, with Jack Cardiff, the master British cinematographer, as its first director. Arthur was furious that Milton had gone over our heads to make such arrangements, even announcing them to the media, and convinced me Milton was out of line.

"Milton also wanted to take over publicity about me, including photographs—even to be in charge of organizing my scrapbook. I can see now that he wanted to take the company and me over, lock, stock, and barrel. I didn't set up my company to pay out 49.6 percent of its earnings to Milton Greene! I also didn't like the fact that Milton was friendly with Laurence Olivier, whom I had no doubt was my enemy. Nobody close to Olivier was a friend of mine, including Arthur Miller!

"Before Milton left England, my buyout of his interest in our production company was a done deal, or so I thought. I'd offered him fifty thousand dollars for his share of Marilyn Monroe Productions but, to my surprise, he turned it down, saying he believed in me with all his heart and would never sell his stock in the corporation. Apparently, he later changed his mind, and in 1957 sold me his stock for eighty-five thousand dollars. The partnership was *finis*, and, unfortunately, so was our friendship.

"Why do all my relationships end so badly, Doc? Is it something I'm doing? On second thought, better not answer that! I don't think I can take the answer. I'm sorry to say that I tend to dump people when I'm finished with them.

"Shedding people when they're no longer useful to me is the only way I know. Otherwise, I'd hang on to them forever, and I'd never get anywhere. I want to be a great actress, and will do anything in my power to achieve that goal.

"Sometimes, I miss Milton, and I'm sorry our friendship had to end that way, but if I were to grieve for everybody I've lost along the way, starting with my unknown father and crazy mother, I'd be submerged in tears forever, and no one would ever hear of Marilyn Monroe. You understand why I have to operate this way, Doc?"

She burst into tears.

JULY 13, 1959

In our next session, Marilyn returned to the story of her relationship with Arthur Miller.

With gratitude to his wife for standing by him, and their anxiety considerably abated, Miller took Marilyn on a second honeymoon to Ocho Rios in Jamaica with his cousin Morton Miller and his wife.

"Why he had to drag them along, I'll never know," Marilyn grumbled.

"Still, I was able to lead a relaxed life away from the problems of my career, and I relished the simplicity of the open-ended days when we could do exactly what we felt like doing when we felt like doing it. Isn't that what I really need, Doctor—a simpler life?"

I didn't tell Marilyn, but that was exactly the conclusion I had come to when she told me about her sister's more ordinary life. Perhaps we mortals who lack the gift of the gods are much better off than people like Marilyn, whose heads become bloodied and bowed under the weight of their genius.

"We walked on the beach and watched the fishermen catch fish," she continued, "although the sight of the fish gasping for air distressed me considerably. I fiercely believe in protecting helpless animals—I know what it feels like to be helpless—and get absolutely outraged when somebody kills a fish. Although I eat fish—you've got to eat something—I can't bear to see them murdered. I'm just as concerned about the fate of all animals. On returning to the city from Idlewild Airport, we came across the bloodied body of a dog which had been hit by a car. I shut my eyes, buried my face in my hands, and shrieked."

Marilyn and Arthur further recuperated from their stress by spending the summer of 1957 at their farmhouse in Amagansett on Long Island. Marilyn walked around the wood-floored house in shorts and a polka-dot shirt, when she wore anything at all. They played badminton (Marilyn won) and swam together, driving along the beaches and back roads in a Jeep. Arthur went fishing in a baseball cap and bathing suit, while Marilyn, in a white bikini, ran in the surf. They often leaned on each another as they walked through the shallow waters. They seemed like an ideal couple.

Marilyn said, "In the fresh ocean air, with my loving husband by my side, my spirits revived, and I began to look young and healthy once more. I felt brimming with life. In fact, I was. I was pregnant again, and this time prayed to make a real live baby. It was to be a gift to Arthur, who at age forty-two was no spring chicken. I loved being pregnant. It was so normal. I even liked feeling nauseated—that's the way pregnant women are supposed to feel. I felt complete for the first time. I don't believe any woman is whole unless she has a child.

"Arthur was no longer under the immediate threat of imprisonment by HUAC. Hollywood was a distant place—somewhere I used to live and never wanted to see again. I was completely rejuvenated at the idea of giving birth to a child.

"I had fantasies night and day about having a beautiful little baby girl, and about what a terrific mother I would be. I would name my child Ana, after my wonderful Auntie Ana, of course. I would take her with me on my location shoots, and sing to her in the dressing room between takes. I was already boning up on 'Rock-a-bye Baby,' and other lullabies. I knew three by then. I would never let baby Ana be alone, and I would hire a tutor to make sure she was properly educated. I would hug and kiss her all the time, not like my cold, indifferent mother.

"In fact, I would let her sleep with me until she got married—I wouldn't care what the experts or my husband had to say about it—and cuddle her all night long. And I would never, ever punish her. I would simply say sternly, 'Ana, Mommy doesn't like it when you do such and such.' And she would love me so much she would immediately behave. I would pile her room with all the beautiful new toys any little girl could possibly want. She wouldn't have to wrap a handkerchief around a clothespin and pretend it was a doll, as I did.

"I would order every great book ever written, including all of Shakespeare, and read to her every single day starting the minute she was born. She would grow up listening to beautiful music around the clock so she wouldn't have to feel inferior in the company of intellectuals. When she went to college, her instructors would be so flabbergasted at her wealth of knowledge, they would say, 'What a wonderful mother you must have, to have educated you so well!'

"I'd put Ana in her carriage and proudly walk her around the block whenever I could, hoping to show her off to all the neighbors who thought I was stuck-up. And I'd beam whenever they couldn't resist peeking into the carriage and saying, 'How beautiful! She looks just like her mother!' Ana would have the perfect childhood, and at last I would have the mother-daughter relationship I'd always dreamed of.

"At the time, I was considerably overweight, but I considered myself voluptuous and didn't care! I enjoyed luxuriating in the sun all day and daydreaming if I wanted to. I loved listening to the pounding of the surf as we walked beside it, hand in hand. Sometimes Arthur and I sang my movie songs together, looking into each other's eyes and smiling.

"One day, when we wore matching orange-cable sweaters I'd bought in a boutique in town, I imagined everyone we passed could see that we were lovers, although some stupid old frump asked if we were father and daughter. I remember stopping and throwing my arms around Arthur and kissing him hard on the mouth, saying, 'Thank you, thank you, Daddy, for bringing me here. Thank you for giving me the happiest day of my life!'

"For a while, I adored playing the role of housewife and trying to learn how to cook. Like everything else in my life, I was an original at it. You've always said I'm a creative person, Doctor, so of course you understand I'd have to be creative in my cooking, too.

"I decided one time to surprise Arthur by baking him a chocolate cake. At the last minute, I had the bright idea of making it a chocolate orange cake, so I ground up some orange peels and mixed it into the icing. Later, I watched Arthur eating, or perhaps I should say trying to eat, the cake. He had a funny expression on his face as he kept twisting and pulling at his mouth, unable to separate his upper teeth from his lower teeth. The icing, it seems, had congealed, gluing his teeth together. I said, 'Arthur, I will never, ever bake you a cake again!' And I never did.

"Another time Arthur found me hanging homemade pasta over the backs of chairs and drying it with a hair dryer. For some reason, it didn't taste like the spaghetti in Frankie Sinatra's Villa Capri restaurant.

"Whadya think, Shrinker? Should I change careers and become a chef?"

JULY 17, 1959

"Unfortunately, when something seems too good to be true, it usually is," Marilyn said. "Our summer idyll turned out to be too good to last. It suddenly ended on the first of August.

The night before, I had a dream that predicted a tragedy.

"In the dream, I was visiting my gynecologist, who said, 'I'm sorry to have to tell you, Marilyn, but your baby's heartbeat is weak. I have to do an ultrasound to see what the problem is.' When she did, the doctor gasped and said, 'Oh, no! Your baby is dead. You've pushed too hard, and your baby has died.' I slowly watched the placenta detach itself from a beautiful little baby girl and float around in my womb. I began to scream hysterically, 'I've killed my baby! I've killed my baby!'

"I woke up in terror but reassured myself it was only a dream. But, unfortunately, it wasn't. Somewhere in my unconscious, I must have sensed the terrible truth. While weeding in the garden, I doubled over in pain and Arthur had to rush me to the hospital. The pregnancy was diagnosed as ectopic and had to be terminated to save my life. I'm not sure it was worth it. It was not the first time I'd lost a baby, and it would not be the last. But somehow this time was different. Baby Ana was so real to me, I couldn't have grieved more if she'd actually been born.

"My gynecologist said my uterus was a mess, and at least ten years older than the rest of me. He thought that numerous septic abortions had contributed to my scar tissue and infertility. I'd also suffered from numerous, untreated pelvic infections, he said. It was then that I truly gave up hope of ever being a mother. When the doctor came into my hospital room to tell me the bad news, I said, 'Thank you, Doctor. I already know.'

"When I told Arthur about the miscarriage, he said something that took him a little further down in my estimation. He said he was glad I had had the miscarriage. He was afraid that, with my endometrosis and history of miscarriages, we might well have had a Down Syndrome child. And if the child—let's assume it was a girl—had gone to term, he said he would probably have wanted to institutionalize the infant immediately after birth, and never see her again.

"I was horrified and said, 'Oh, Arthur, how can you think that way? You'd desert a human being? Your own child? If the baby were mine, I'd never allow you to do that. If I were the child's mother, I would love and cherish her, and give her a good life at whatever level was possible. I wish I had her now! I wish the baby I just miscarried had been that Down Syndrome child! She would've been a living baby, and that's all that matters. I'd have loved her with all my heart, no matter what she was.'

"Arthur said, 'I know it sounds cruel, but all of our lives—mine, yours, and the baby's— would've been ruined had we kept the child, versus the life of one retarded baby who wouldn't know the difference.'

"I burst out crying. 'No, Arthur, no! You're wrong. She was a human being. She would have known how heartless you were being! Nobody deserves that kind of treatment. That's more callous than putting me in an orphanage as a child. At least my mother and aunt came to see me when they could."

I tried to understand Arthur's thinking, but was unable to find any rationale that excused his nastiness. I ran to our bedroom, locked the door, and kept it locked no matter how loudly he pounded. Then I cried myself to sleep. I tried to put my new knowledge on the back burner, but in my heart of hearts, it was just one more thing I'd never forgive Arthur for.

"Whether it was the miscarriage itself, my lost hopes, or a continuing depression, I retreated more and more into drugs, and the tension between Arthur and me deepened. There was a solidity to my despair he was unable to penetrate, and I kept taunting him with his inability to rescue me.

"Around that time, I had another dream. I call it 'My Sealed-Off-Self Dream.' In it, I'm carrying a cigar box filled with solid concrete, and the concrete seals the box shut. I'm carrying it to the Salvation Army and looking for another empty cigar box in exchange, but there aren't any available. My box is very heavy, and getting heavier all the time."

"What do you think your dream means, Marilyn?" I asked.

"I think it means that I'm locked in grief and there's no salvation for me."

Her interpretation of the dream was correct, but I was too terrified to tell her that.

"In your dream," I said, "you are seeking salvation. Let's hope we will find it together."

One evening, Arthur found Marilyn collapsed on her bed from an overdose of sleeping pills and called emergency services, who fortunately were able to pump out her stomach. She survived—barely.

On another occasion, Norman and Hedda Rosten, their Long Island friends and neighbors, received a 3 a.m. call from Marilyn's maid. When they arrived, they learned that the maid had called emergency services, who again found themselves pumping out her stomach after an overdose. Marilyn seemed determined to do away with herself.

When she regained consciousness, all she could say was, "Still alive? Such bad luck!"

JULY 22, 1959

On August 4, 1958, around six months before she began analysis with me, Marilyn had recovered enough from her 1957 miscarriage to begin filming a movie called *Some Like It Hot*. It was a bit of a regression for her, because she would've preferred to act in a high-quality drama rather than a comedy. But she needed to make another movie, and the script, to her, didn't seem bad, so she decided to accept the role. It was one of the best decisions she ever made.

Joe and Jerry, played respectively by Tony Curtis and Jack Lemmon, are two struggling musicians on the run from the mob after witnessing the St. Valentine's Day Massacre in Chicago. They try to find a way out of the city before the mob kills them. The plot is hilarious, but Marilyn didn't think the beginning was at all funny.

The two men are depicted as unemployed, hungry, and without winter coats in freezing Chicago weather. "If the writers were cold and hungry, we'd see how much laughing they would do!" she declared. That was the empathic Marilyn for you. But as she got deeper into telling me the plot, she began to laugh along with me.

"The only job that will pay their way out of town is an all-girl band. At the booking office, where the men are trying to be hired, Joe asks, 'What kind of a band is this?' Sig Poliakoff, the booking agent, answers, 'You gotta be under twenty-five.' Jerry says, 'We could pass for that.' Sig says, 'You also gotta be blonde.' Jerry answers hopefully, 'We could dye our hair.' Sig Poliakoff says, 'Oh yeah, well, you gotta be girls.' Jerry says, 'We could—' 'No,' Joe interrupts, 'we couldn't!' But it turns out that they can. Using the names Josephine and Daphne, the two musicians dress up as women and manage to board the train to Florida with the all-girl band. "Their disguises were dreadful, and anyone would know immediately that they were men, but the studio proceeded anyhow," Marilyn said.

I had seen the movie when it came out in March, four months earlier. I absolutely agreed with Marilyn's assessment and thought Curtis and Lemmon made the clumsiest, most unappealing women I had ever seen. Nevertheless, they were very funny in the film.

"After a hilarious train ride," Marilyn said, "they arrive in Miami. Joe falls in love with Sugar Kane, originally Sugar Kowalczyk, the ukulele player—me, of course—but she believes he's a woman. He says adoringly, 'Look at her, will you? Watch how she moves. Just like Jell-O on springs. I think she has a kind of motor built into her. Believe me, she's a whole different sex!'

"It delighted me how much Tony seemed to mean it as much as his character, Joe. That still comforts me, even with everything that happened later.

"But why, oh why, do they keep casting me as a dumb blonde?! When Joe offers Sugar diamonds, she says, 'Diamonds? They must be worth their weight in gold!' How stupid can you get? I was born under the sign of Gemini. That stands for intellect!

"Anyway, Joe invites Sugar Kane out to a yacht owned by Osgood Fielding III, a rich millionaire. Jerry, as Daphne, keeps Osgood dancing so that Joe can pretend he owns the yacht. Osgood Fielding keeps harassing Daphne throughout the film, nagging her—really him—to visit his yacht.

"But as the playwright said, all's well that ends well. Everything gets straightened out, and all the would-be lovers get together. The film ends with the best movie line of any I've ever heard. The Lemmon character reveals to Osgood that he's really a man, yet Osgood proposes marriage to him anyway, saying, 'Well, nobody's perfect!'

"We had a lot of fun making the film. Lemmon and Curtis had a great time being coached by a German drag queen, and rehearsals were filled with jokes and laughter. We often went to the Formosa restaurant together for lunch. 'Josephine' and I took frequent trips to the ladies' room to see if he was getting away with his disguise. We rocked with laughter when nobody gave him a second look.

"The whole cast took a lighthearted approach to making the

movie, which added to the pleasure of working in it. It was one of the few movies where I felt a real part of the cast—until Tony ruined it for me.

"Many of the cast and crew were very upset by my habitual lateness. So what else is new? You'd think they'd have accepted my idiosyncrasies by now and be grateful I make their films so successful. But they were all saying how difficult I was to get along with. Nobody mentioned that the men directing me have had as many problems as I have. Billy Wilder is a monster and a sadist. John Huston is a drinker and gambler, and you never can tell when he'll be under the influence. Howard Hawks is a big bully who reminds me of Wayne Bolender with his belt out.

"But I was most upset by what Curtis said about me at the end of the film. A reporter asked Tony what it was like kissing me. 'It's like kissing Hitler!' he responded. I cried when I read his remark and refused to talk to him after that. He later denied that he'd ever made the comment, but in my mind the damage had been done.

"Despite all the problems, the film turned out to be the greatest financial success of any movie I ever made. People lined up for blocks to see it. And, according to the reviewers, I was wonderful in the movie, so my performance greatly added to my reputation.

"So there, Tony Curtis! Call me Hitler, why don't you? You'd be lucky to be half the actor I am."

OCTOBER 2, 1959

For some reason, Marilyn now wanted to return to the months after her debacle in London with *The Prince and the Showgirl*, before the Ochos Rios vacation and Marilyn's subsequent miscarriage, when Arthur Miller's fate was still in question.

"Arthur and I patched things up, or so it appeared," Marilyn said. "We were riding back to New York one day from his farmhouse in Roxbury, Connecticut when, from the driver's seat, he suddenly burst out laughing. I was surprised, because he'd been pretty glum lately.

"I said, 'What's the joke, Art?'

"He answered, 'I can't tell you. It isn't very nice.'

"'Oh, come on, Arthur!' I said. 'You and your conscience! This is not the House Un-American Activities Committee. For goodness sake, I'm your wife! Don't be such a prude.'

"He said, 'OK, but don't say I didn't warn you.' I waited as he struggled with his conscience. This time, unlike most times, his conscience lost.

"'Did you see that big brown building we just passed?' he said shyly.

"I shook my head. He said, 'It's the ugliest piece of architecture, if you can call it that, ever designed. A cow could have done better. I've never seen anything like it. It looks like a giant turd . . . Who do you think owns the building?'

"I said, 'It must be Yale University.'

"We both burst out laughing."

I struggled to keep from laughing, too. When I got myself under control, I said, "Marilyn, dear, we know that you often run away from troubling subjects by making a joke. You are very witty, but are you trying to push away something unpleasant that happened on that car ride? I cannot imagine that you and your husband sat enclosed in a car for—what was it? Two hours?—and had nothing more important to exchange than a dirty joke."

"For a change, Dr. Freud," she answered, "you're right."

I did not take the bait.

"As a matter of fact," she confessed, "we had a terrible argument that lasted most of the trip."

"Tell me about it."

"He was all huddled up, sulking as far away from me as he could get and looking out the window. I knew he needed to be quiet a lot, so I bit my tongue to keep from intruding. Finally, I couldn't stand it any longer and said, 'What are you thinking about, Arthur?'

"He looked irritated and answered, 'Nothing much,' and sank even deeper into the door. His silence said to me, 'Don't bother me, you moron. I'm thinking about something a dumb blonde like you couldn't possibly understand.'

"Tears ran down my cheeks. I said, 'Arthur, talk to me. Please. I'm lonely.'

"He answered, 'For God's sake, Marilyn, can't you amuse yourself without me for one moment? Think about your next film. Open a book. Look at the scenery. I'm supposed to be a playwright, and a playwright has to have solitary moments so he can think.'

"'But that's all you ever have, Arthur—solitary moments,' I said. 'You never talk to me anymore except to say, "Please pass the salt." Why do you want a wife if you need your privacy so badly?'

"'Good question,' he said. 'I've been asking myself the same thing lately. I need a wife who understands what a playwright requires, not a little child who needs her hand held all the time.'

"I said, 'You dare say that to *me*, the breadwinner in this so-called marriage? I need to have my hand held all the time? Why didn't you say that when I turned over one hundred thousand dollars to you to build your little office where you could be alone all the time. You didn't even ask me for the money, but just said in that pathetic little voice of yours, 'I wish I had enough money to build a nice little office under the pine trees. Then I'd be able to write.''

"'Even after you pocketed my money and built the loveliest office in Connecticut, you're still not writing. How come, Mr. Pulitzer Prize Winner? Every time I come in there, you're smoking that stinking pipe of yours and looking out the window. No wonder you're not earning any money!'

"He said, 'If you'd leave me alone and not make me worry about you all the time, maybe I could write. All I have time for is protecting poor Marilyn from the paparazzi, making sure she doesn't take too many pills, counseling her about every little detail of her life, down to whether she should eat now or later. I take her here, pick her up there, see that she isn't taken advantage of by the producers. It's Marilyn, Marilyn, Marilyn, until I forget what it feels like to be Arthur Miller. I've become Mr. Marilyn Monroe! No wonder I can't write.'"

Marilyn interrupted herself to say to me, "Sometimes when you're angry, you say terrible things. I'd give anything if I could take back what I said next. I know Arthur, and he'll never forgive me for it."

"What could you possibly have said that is so unpardonable?"

"I shouted at him, 'I have nothing to do with it! I'm just a convenient peg for you to hang your lack of productivity onto. You've lost it,

Arthur Miller. Admit it. *Death of a Salesman* was a fluke. In fact, there was nothing original about it. You just copied down the lines your family said. You'll never write another good play, because you've used up all they had to say. Why don't you accept the truth and become a salesman like your father? At least *he* paid the rent.'"

I was shocked, so I asked Marilyn, "What did he say?"

She sobbed. "He said, 'Maybe you're right,' and curled up even further into the car door. When I looked over at him, tears were running down his cheeks.

"I felt awful that I had hurt him and I said, 'Oh, Arthur, I'm so sorry! Please forgive me. You know I didn't mean it. You know I think you're the greatest playwright in the world. I was just trying to rile you up so you'd talk to me. Even fighting with you is better than living with your terrible silences.'

"He didn't answer me, and didn't say a single word for the rest of the trip. In fact, he hasn't spoken to me since, not even to say, 'Please pass the salt.' I'm scared, Doctor. Do you think he's going to leave me? That I couldn't bear."

Actually, I, too, was afraid the marriage was doomed. I knew that Marilyn was too fragile to hear the truth, but lying to her was not an option. Coward that I was, I said, "All married couples have arguments, Marilyn. Let's hope this one blows over, too."

NOVEMBER 30, 1959

"I dreamt I fell into a deep dark well, into the very depths of depression," is how Marilyn began our next session. "I extended my arms to you, pleading for a lifeline to draw me back up. You approached the well and knelt down. I couldn't see you but felt your presence. I grabbed hold of you and wouldn't let go. You stood up abruptly and announced that you had to leave, but that my mother would be waiting for me *downstairs.*"

How terrible it was—and how worrying—to hear that after all of our time together, Marilyn still felt that I was like her mother, who stood by and watched her drown.

DECEMBER 1, 1959

One ghastly session relentlessly followed another. As often as not these days, Marilyn turned her back on me and torpidly went through the motions. I felt her excruciating pain and tried to comfort her.

"Stop!" she shouted. "Stop! You'll kill me with your kindness! I want to die . . . to die . . . to die! Every morning I wake up and cry that I'm still alive."

I remembered Sheila Scott, a suicidal patient I had treated as a young analyst. The referring physician had sent Sheila to me with the note, "Her life is not worth anything to her or anyone else. Therapy is the only choice at all for any kind of future for her. If it succeeds, there's everything to gain. If it fails, it is no great loss to Sheila."

The astute physician was preparing me so that I would not feel guilty if Sheila killed herself. But against all odds, Sheila had gotten well. If I could help the miserable creature that Sheila was when I first set eyes on her, then I could help Marilyn, who had so much more than Sheila to live for.

DECEMBER 7, 1959

And still her melancholy continued. "I'm miserable, Doctor. Nothing in my life makes me happy. I'm a nothing—an absolute nothing. And you know what? You may be a doctor and all, but you're a nothing, too. A nothing, a nothing, a nothing! Just like me." Her eyes filled with tears.

"You're right, Marilyn. I am," I said. "In the big scheme of things, we matter no more than the smallest flea."

She looked at me in surprise.

"Why's that fact so hard for me to accept?" she asked.

"When you are taught the lesson too early," I said, "as when your mother only sporadically recognizes your existence, it is too terrible to bear. Perhaps when we are mature enough, we can accept the truth in small patches."

"Well," she said, "I'm obsessed with it. I want to show people what nothings they really are—each and every one of them, whether they're Pulitzer Prize winners, movie stars, directors, or big-name producers. In the millenniums of time, nobody matters one iota, and not a one of them would honestly deny that.

"No amount of family or education or success can ever change that. The more inconsequential anyone feels, the more they have to do to disprove it. I think that's the one thing in all the world that's hardest for me to endure. From nothing we come, and to nothing we return."

My eyes filled with tears.

Marilyn was right. The truth, like death itself, was too terrible to bear.

DECEMBER 12, 1959

In the days until our next appointment, I could do nothing but worry terribly about what Marilyn might do to herself.

What I had learned from our sessions was this: If Marilyn did kill herself, it would be because she did not want to live. There was no way of knowing which was stronger in her, the Life Instinct or the Death Instinct. There was no way to predict which force would triumph over the other.

But as long as she continued seeing me, at least a small part of her wanted to live, and I would do everything I could to keep it that way.

DECEMBER 22, 1959

Marilyn was quiet for the longest time. I said nothing.

Finally, I said, "Isn't there anything you want to say to me today, Marilyn?"

"You're always bugging me," she angrily retorted, and got up to walk out of the session.

When she reached the door, she turned her head and said, "Go have *your* head examined, Doctor! Maybe it'll do *you* some good!"

DECEMBER 23, 1959

She came into the office looking quite hostile, her brows drawn together and a sullen expression on her face.

"What's with you today, Marilyn?" I said. "You seem mad as hops. Is there something I said or did that made you so angry with me?"

She didn't answer for a few minutes, and then she said hesitantly, "It probably has something to do with a dream I had about you."

"Oh? And what was that?"

Her stutter grew more noticeable, an indication of true emotion. "Has—has anyone ever told you that you look s-sinister? There is s-something about you—I don't know what—that looks—particularly dark and evil."

"Many people feel that way at certain stages of their analysis," I answered.

"Maybe so, but I have to find out if it's real."

"I quite agree with you. What in particular gives me this sinister look?"

"You remind me of an orphanage head nurse whom I hated. In my dream, you looked just like her. This nurse once tried to do a rectal examination on me. She pulled down my pants and came at my ass with a thermometer. Her face was bright red and distorted, with a twisted expression I'd never seen before. She terrified me. I wondered why she needed to stick it up my ass when the doctor took my temperature through my mouth. I screamed 'No! No! Go away!' and kicked her so hard she said in disgust, 'All right. Just skip the whole thing. Don't get your bowels in an uproar!'

"In my dream, you also came at me, like she did, to take my temperature, and I thought, *Brother, if she tries to take my temperature that same way, it's all over for her!*"

"Do you think I want to do a rectal examination on you?"

"I wouldn't be a bit surprised!" she answered.

DECEMBER 24, 1959

"I had two fantasies about you recently," Marilyn said at the next session. "In both of them, I was furious with you. In the first one, I was so enraged, I ripped up your whole office. I tore down the drapes, slashed open the pillows, and broke your fancy Chinese statues into a thousand little pieces. In the second fantasy, I went outside and killed everybody I saw, getting back at the members of my so-called family and everyone else who's ever abused me."

"I prefer the first fantasy, Marilyn," I said. "It is good that you can be angry with me and tell me about it without acting on it. And Marilyn, I know how depressed you are, but I do want to wish you a Merry Christmas, and extend to you my sincerest hopes that the next year will bring a much better time in your life."

"Hah!" she said. "I didn't even know it was Christmas," and walked out without saying another word.

JANUARY 4, 1960

The night before, I awoke with a start. I had dreamt that Marilyn was screaming, "Help me! Help me! Help me! I don't want to kill myself!"

When she came in for her appointment the next day, I said, "Marilyn, what were you doing last night around midnight?"

"Why do you ask?"

I decided to tell her about my dream.

"That's funny," she answered. "I was asleep too and also had a dream in which I screamed and screamed. But in my dream, nothing came out of my mouth. It was like I was locked in a pressure chamber and nobody could hear me, no matter how loud I screamed. It was horrible."

"That was what it was like when you were an infant, Marilyn. You screamed and screamed and nobody came. But you don't have to scream anymore. I hear you now."

JANUARY 6, 1960

Things began to get a little better after Marilyn learned that it was all right to have negative feelings about me and to express them. It helped, for example, that she understood I had no interest in doing a rectal examination on her, unlike the nurse in the orphanage. Gradually, Marilyn came to realize that I really cared about her, and she began to speak more and more of her warm feelings toward me.

I was delighted, and kept my fingers crossed that her progress would last, and that even if she regressed at times, which was to be expected, she would have a safe, emotional place to return to. A few months passed in which she continued to come in for her sessions and to attend the Actors Studio, where, by her account, she continued to improve a great deal and earned the near-unanimous respect of her acting student colleagues.

As for me, I was able to relax in her presence without worrying so much that she would kill herself, and could enjoy the wit, humor, and insight of this fascinating and oh-so-vulnerable woman.

FEBRUARY 24, 1960

It was now more than a year since Marilyn had begun coming to me for analysis. One day, she came into a session looking downcast. "I hate to tell you this, Doc, but we have a problem," she began.

"Yes? And what is that?"

"I plan to finally divorce Arthur, and I think I'll be happier with a change of scenery. The West Coast will remind me less of my failure with Arthur. Plus, all the film companies are located in Hollywood, where I have to be to stay in the middle of everything. I think I have to relocate to Los Angeles permanently, so I won't be able to come to see you anymore."

Then, beginning to cry, she said, "I don't want to go!"

"What? I cannot believe you are serious," I said sternly. "Of course you must go to Los Angeles. I trust you are just testing me to see if I will let you."

She was silent.

"Sit up, Marilyn! Yes, get up off the couch and sit facing me. We have to talk!"

She sat up like a small child being chastised by her mother and opened those gorgeous blue eyes of hers as wide as they would go.

"You are feeling better now, Marilyn. You have been working well here, and developing your art, and you seem to be enjoying your life more. If you are in Hollywood, you will have a better chance of landing those juicy dramatic roles you so want—the roles you have worked for and striven for, sometimes to and past the point of collapse, for years. Now you are about to decide against that? Why would you do such a thing? I will not allow it."

"You're my confidant, my friend, my surrogate mother, my alter ego," Marilyn said haltingly. "You're all ears when I'm here. You never act like you're waiting for me to finish so you can talk. I can't really confide in anyone else. I'm too shy. And other people aren't really interested in me, but only in how soon they can run their hands over me or get my autograph. I don't know if I can get along without you."

"That is not true, Marilyn. It just feels that way. A little girl cannot leave her mother, but you are not a little girl anymore and I am not your mother. I am only your analyst. You can find a new one to replace me in Los Angeles who will listen to you just as well."

"No, I can't!" she cried out. "You understand me like no one ever has. For the first time in my life, I've found someone I trust who cares for who I really am instead of what they can get out of me. And you want me to leave that for the sake of some dumb set of opportunities I'll probably mess up anyway? No, ma'am, I know when I'm well off. I'm staying right here."

"Well, Marilyn," I said, getting to my feet, "I am honored that you think so highly of me. But your analysis is not truly working if it keeps you a little child." I added more kindly but no less firmly, "You will take me with you to California. As my teacher, Dr. Theodore Reik, once said, 'People who love each other don't have to stay together to feel together.'"

I strode to my desk, picked up my address book, and opened it. I then wrote a name and phone number on a piece of paper and handed it to Marilyn.

"Dr. Ralph Greenson," she grimaced.

"Phone him tonight, Marilyn, and make an appointment for next week. Tell him that I am referring you and that it is urgent. I will contact him, too, and advise him that you will call. I am very sorry that we will not have more time to terminate properly, but we have several more sessions to talk about things and prepare you for leaving as well as we can."

"See, I always suspected you didn't really like me," she said in tears, "or you wouldn't let me leave you."

I took her in my arms and we cried together.

She went to California, of course.

But I suggested, in one of our final face-to-face sessions, that, as a form of personal therapy, she write me regularly from Los Angeles, even if she had nothing to say, and I promised to write back if she asked me to.

She agreed. I also promised to let Dr. Greenson know that she would be doing this and make sure he had no objection.

Meantime, I hoped the referral to Dr. Greenson, who was a great analyst, would work out for her.

PART 2
Letters from Marilyn

JULY 2, 1960

Dear Doctor:

Starting in April of this year, I began to make a movie called *Let's Make Love*, and during it, I had an affair with my co-star Yves Montand. You won't believe it! Or maybe you will, knowing me and my history of failures in love.

Arthur and I were in L.A. in bungalow number twenty-one of the swanky Beverly Hills Hotel. As luck would have it, we were directly across from the bungalow housing Montand and his famous actress wife, Simone Signoret. When I heard that, the thought crossed my mind, *I hope Arthur and Simone go away, so Yves and I can make love.*

You know how the sages say, 'Be careful what you wish for, or your wish may come true'? Well, in this case, those words couldn't have been more fitting. My wish came true, and oh, how I wish it hadn't!

"I tell you this without guilt, Doctor, because my marriage with Arthur is just about *finis*, so I was not terribly worried about being unfaithful to him. As far as Yves's marriage is concerned, I don't consider it my problem if a man strays. I don't believe any third person can ruin a good marriage, and if it's not good, then what's the difference?

I was determined to make this movie a big success. In fact, I didn't believe it could fail. The script was written by the wonderful Norman Krasna, the director was the great George Cukor, and Yves had recently been quite successful in the French movie version of Arthur's *The Crucible*.

But despite the great lineup, I wasn't happy with the script, and was sorry I'd signed the contract to play the role. I was delighted when a writers' strike broke out and no one was available for revisions. I hoped the dearth of available writers would mean they'd have to cancel the film. But unfortunately, Jerry Wald, the producer, asked Arthur if he would revise the screenplay.

To my dismay, Arthur agreed. I'd thought him a great liberal, who always took the side of the underdog, and there he was crossing the union picket line. I couldn't believe it at first, and then lost what little respect I had left for him.

What I'd always loved most about Arthur was his integrity, and here he was betraying his and my ideals. Instead of feeling love for him, I felt shame, and I couldn't look him in the eye anymore without wincing.

In a way, I understand why Arthur took the job. He hadn't been making any money and I was actually supporting him. In fact, I'd taken on this movie purely to bring in some cash. Of course, he was embarrassed by this.

I suspect he took on the rewriting job to bring in a paycheck and, even more, to put me in my place. After all, he was in charge of writing the words I had to speak before the cameras. It was his nasty way of being top dog and getting even with me, and it made me dislike him even more.

In the film, I play the part of musical comedy actress Amanda Dell, who's acting in an off-Broadway review that satirizes Jean Marc Clement, a billionaire industrialist played by Yves. Clement attends a performance, where he instantly falls in love with me. But he's afraid I'll love him for his money and not for himself, so he develops a plan to woo me without revealing his true identity.

We acted out several hot love scenes, which greatly aroused me and fed my passion for Yves. I don't know how other actresses can play hot love scenes and not get sexually aroused. But then they don't play the truth in a scene, and that must be evident to the audience. It's part of my gift that I really get turned on in a love scene, or else I refuse to play it.

Of course, Clement winds up winning the heart of Amanda. It's unfortunate that real life does not always follow *reel* life.

Because of my disillusionment with my husband, I guess I was more open to being comforted by another man. It so happened that Arthur had to go to Nevada with John Huston to scout out locations for *The Misfits* (more about that later). At the same time, Simone returned to France to make a film. Yves and I became close friends—*very* close.

One day, I was too exhausted to attend a rehearsal. Yves was concerned about me and came to my bungalow to see if he could help. Well, you know how things are, Doctor. One thing led to another. He took me in his arms to comfort me and then leaned over and kissed me passionately. He said he couldn't help himself. And then we made love. It was great—just what I needed to help me recover from Arthur's indifference and one-upmanship.

Yves was so gentle and warm and considerate a lover that I fell head over heels in love with him. His penis was superior to any I'd ever seen, and you know I've seen plenty! I guess people know what they're talking about when they say the French make great lovers. In my opinion, a woman hasn't been loved until she's been loved by a Frenchman.

I've also heard it said that the more equal two people feel in their love for each other, the happier the union will be. Well, it felt to me that Yves loved me as much as I did him, and I had no doubt we'd both divorce our spouses as soon as we could and marry each other.

We made hot and passionate love for two months, from April to June, and a better two months I've never spent. But as usual, my experience in paradise was short-lived. Did you ever think you were in Heaven, Doctor, only to have the bubble suddenly collapse around you? Well, that's what happened to me.

When the film wrapped up, I was astounded and horrified to learn that Yves had no intention of marrying me, and instead would immediately return to his wife. The Montands began to work hard at putting their marriage back together again, and I found he had no room in his life for me.

It was as difficult for them as for me because when Marilyn Monroe takes a lover, the media has a holiday and plasters details of the romance all over the front pages, so the whole world knew that Yves and I had been lovers. But Simone Signoret is a wonderful woman, and I admire her despite the fact that she caused my heart to break. She told the newspapers that, of course, Yves had an affair with Marilyn Monroe. What man could resist doing so? But Yves was never as serious about Marilyn, she said, as I apparently was about him. "I'm sorry Marilyn was hurt, but our marriage is a living thing that can conquer the hurdle of an extramarital affair," she said.

Even more humiliating was when Yves affirmed his wife's assessment. He told the papers that "Marilyn is a simple girl without guile. I'm sorry if I made her feel our affair was permanent. I thought a great screen actress would be more sophisticated, but I was wrong. Marilyn isn't sophisticated at all, and in her heart is a child who believes in fairy tales. She doesn't know that what she had was a simple schoolgirl crush on me, and in no way is a threat to my long-standing, deeply loving marriage."

Can you believe it, Doc? *A simple schoolgirl crush*? He had the nerve to say that to the whole world, as if I hadn't turned my heart and soul over to him! Doctor Dale, I've been rejected many times, starting with my father. But I don't know that any rejection hurt me as deeply as this one. Or maybe it was as much the public humiliation as the private rejection.

The pain was so piercing I thought I'd surely die. In fact, I hoped I *would* die. I went to bed and stayed there, sobbing for over two weeks. I thought, "I'm going to bed and will never get up again," and then fell in and out of a stupor for at least another week. When I woke up, I found myself clasping the telephone cord in my hand, as if to retain at least the possibility of contacting Yves. I stopped trying to reach him only when he refused to take my calls. Even I caught on then that he and I were through.

I thought, What should I do? What can I possibly do to make myself feel better? I feel so alone in the world. I am alone in the world. My friends are sick and tired of hearing about my painful love affairs. Anyway, they're all suffering from unrequited love themselves. If it's possible, Frankie Sinatra is even more heartbroken about Ava Gardner than I am about Yves. *Arthur*? Forget it! And because my sister Berniece has a happy marriage, she couldn't possibly understand my pain.

—Marilyn

I wrote her back as follows:

Oh Marilyn. I *am* so sorry! So very sorry. It was contemptible of Yves to use you and then dump you. He is not the person you fantasied he was and isn't worth grieving over. You are mourning a lost fantasy and not a real person.

I know it is hard for you to agree with me now, but believe me, the old adage that time heals all wounds is very true. Trust me, I know that you will get over this, as you have gotten over other romantic setbacks in the past. You will someday find real love.

To my surprise, she wrote back:

Dear Shrinker:

I feel as if you've kissed the wound in my heart, and it's beginning to close up.

You say, "Time heals all wounds." I'd rather hope that "time wounds all

heels," and that Yves gets what he deserves!
—Marilyn

Good for you, Marilyn. If you can make a joke about it, the healing process truly has begun.

JULY 20, 1960

(With apologies to Christina Georgina Rossetti)

Oh, promise me, Jack, someday you and I
That again together we will try
Upon a bed our love to renew,
And forget the troughs where our problems grew,
And remember the moments of our earliest springs,
Which whisper to us both, and then we'll sing
Of our blessed union yet to be.
Oh, promise me, Jack! Oh, promise me!

Dear Shrink:

On the night of July 13, 1960, I was lying on my massage table getting massaged by my friend and masseuse, Ralph Roberts, when we heard the history-making broadcast from Los Angeles's Memorial Coliseum, in which Governor Adlai Stevenson said, "Ladies and gentlemen, I have the honor of announcing that the Democratic nominee for President of the United States will be Senator John Fitzgerald Kennedy."

I have to tell you, Doctor, I have a bit of a thing for Jack Kennedy. I know his sister Pat—Patricia Kennedy Lawford—pretty well, from the very first day I was back in LA. I met her at a party. She's just about my age—thirty-five—and just in case you don't know, she's the sixth of Joe and Rose Kennedy's nine children.

Pat's husband is Peter Lawford, the actor, and he's the one who introduced us. Well, I just about leapt out of my chair at the sight of Pat—she's the living image of my dear departed Auntie Grace! She has Grace's energy, she talks like her, she thinks like her, she even laughs like her. When

I first heard her laugh, I thought, *Watch it, Marilyn! You're just like your mother—you're hearing voices.*

Like Grace, Pat never sits still for a moment, and has the same riotous sense of humor. They could easily have passed for sisters. Knowing her is almost as good as having my beloved auntie back and alive. In fact, we feel like we're related. Pat even said later I was like a sister to her.

Pat and I took to each other right away, and I thought she'd become my new best friend, to replace you, who are my *old* best friend. We tête-à-têted all evening at that first party, and were so engrossed in each other that I actually ignored all the men in the room.

But I'm not going to ignore them now! Let's get back to Jack.

Two nights later, I was once again having a massage when Jack gave his acceptance speech, in which he said, "I accept it with a full and grateful heart, without reservation, and with only one obligation—the obligation to devote every effort of body, mind, and spirit to lead our party back to victory and our nation back to greatness . . . The rights of man—the civil and economic rights essential to the human dignity of all men—are indeed our goal and our first principles."

Then I leapt up and off the table and shouted, "Hurray, Ralph! Jack Kennedy's going to be our next president! And someday I may get to be First Lady!"

Ralph said, "Lie down and let me finish, Marilyn. He'll still be running a half hour from now."

Love,
Marilyn

OCTOBER 24, 1960

Dear Dr. Darcey:

I'm nearly finished shooting my next film, The Misfits. It has not been a pleasant experience, what with a three-way strain between Arthur and me, director John Huston and me, and Huston and Paula Strasberg. Lately, the problems have been worsening so drastically, they're becoming intolerable. We may all collapse under the tension.

I've been worried that the film would be ruined because of all our squabbling, but it's turning out really well, at least based on the dailies I've seen. Critics may even say I've done some of my best acting in it. Will miracles never cease?

Meantime, though, Arthur, who wrote the script, told the newspapers that the experience has been both sad and exhilarating for him. "What is sad," he said, "is that I'd written the screenplay to make Marilyn happy, but instead it resulted in her complete collapse. At the same time," he added, 'I'll always be glad I wrote it for her, because her dream was to be a serious actress."

And yes, Virginia, there is a Santa Claus!

—Marilyn

NOVEMBER 2, 1960

Dear Dr. Darcey:

About that complete collapse that was mentioned in my last letter: When Henry Weinstein, the *Misfits* producer, called me, he said I responded in a thick-tongued, rambling voice that frightened him to death. He called a doctor, and they once again had my stomach pumped out.

It was getting to be a habit, and it didn't even feel disgusting anymore—just an unpleasant routine. Unfortunately, I again recovered. And once more, I was irritated to be alive. Afterward, it took a long time before I experienced a single moment when I felt glad to still be on this earth.

One day, I badly needed to talk to Arthur about *The Misfits*. I hated my character and thought she read like a caricature. Although Roslyn was supposed to be based on me, and Arthur had the nerve to steal much of the dialogue from our actual conversations—doesn't the man have any imagination?—he made Roslyn entirely too passive a woman. He also had her speaking platitudes, which I try not to do.

I had to play the most difficult role of my career, a distorted mockery of myself, and I wonder if that gives me grounds to sue him for invasion of privacy or some such thing. Can you sue a husband you hope to get a divorce from? I'll have to consult my lawyer on that one.

Anyway, Arthur made Roslyn a recently divorced clinging-vine type who depends on the men in her life for her very existence. And she's supposedly based on me, who never was supported by a man in my life! Nowhere did he ever mention that I, the woman, had supported him, the "hero," for at least a coupla years.

The lines in the script he'd transcribed directly from our conversations embarrassed me terribly. Maybe I *will* sue him!

Even worse, he kept changing them after I'd learned them, and right before they were to be filmed, too. He seemed out to show the world all my character flaws. If a Pulitzer Prize were to be awarded for keeping a person off-balance, Arthur Miller would have been at the top of the nominees list.

Maybe that wouldn't be such a bad thing. At the rate he's writing, or not writing, that's the only Pulitzer Prize he could ever win again.

In the script, Roslyn Taber—me—has established residence in Reno in order to seek a divorce. Guess who that's patterned after?

At a bar, she meets two friends, Guido and Gay, and falls in love with Gay—played by Clark Gable. Roslyn and Gay move together into a house Guido is building. Like Gay, Guido falls in love with Roslyn. It seems that every man she meets falls in love with her. It should only happen to me!

The resourceful Guido thinks up a plan to capture wild mustangs, called misfits because they're too small to ride on the Nevada salt flats, slaughter them, and sell the meat for dog food. My dear friend Monty Clift plays Pierce, a beaten-down, out-of-luck rodeo rider. Monty's a pleasure to be with, both as a friend and a member of the cast. He's the most professional actor alive, despite his addictions and neuroses. I'll have to ask him how he does it.

Anyway, the four of us set out for the salt flats to look for the horses, though Roslyn is unaware of the scheme. When she finds out, she's horrified, just as I am when I see animals abused.

Roslyn screams—I got laryngitis from all the screaming I did in all the takes—and pleads with Gay not to go ahead. At first, he resists her entreaties, and then is so struck by her goodness of heart that he cuts the ropes and lets the animals go free. Again, would that real life was more like reel life.

Well, back to that son of a bitch I married. Much as I wanted to talk with him, this man who claimed he still loved me locked himself in his office and would have none of me. I have a pretty bad temper when I get riled up, and believe me, I was riled up! I tore through the living room and began to bang on his door.

He refused to come out. I started screaming, "*The Misfits* is not *your* movie, Arthur! It's *our* movie. You said you were writing it for me. Well, you sure fooled me! All you wanted was to use me to regain your prestige. You changed the script right under my nose. Roslyn's not like me at all. I hate her! All you care about are the male characters!"

There was no answer. I kicked over some tables, started banging on the keys to my white piano, and in the kitchen grabbed a champagne bottle, slamming it against the mirror behind my bed until it was covered in shards of glass. (Later, when I lay down on the bed, I got cut in the most inconvenient of places. I'm still picking the slivers out of my ass.)

In any event, I kept thumping my body against Arthur's door until I was black and blue all over. When he still didn't answer, I crumpled in a heap on the floor, sobbing, and fell asleep right there. When I woke up, he was gone. He must have stepped right over me. He has not slept in that apartment since.

What led up to all this tumult? The day before, Arthur came into my bedroom just as a doctor was looking for a vein in which to inject the sedative Amytal. I screamed, 'Get out of my bedroom, Arthur Miller! Get out of my life! I don't need a betrayer in either one!' He cringed and backed away, saying he'd continue working on the The Misfits script. He went on making small alterations, which angered me no end, because, as I said, he kept rewriting scenes overnight after I'd already learned the new lines he'd written the day before.

Worst of all, he continually revised the movie's ending. He couldn't bring himself to allow the film to close with the human misfits going their separate ways. Unfortunately, what worked in his head did not work in real life, and we've agreed to a divorce.

I've been playing a role called Marilyn Monroe all my life. Half the time, I'm just doing an imitation of myself. Well, I'm sick and tired of pretending to be somebody other than who I am. I just want to be me, even if it's little Norma Jeane, the orphan girl. At least she knew who she was.

That's one of the reasons I fell in love with Arthur. I thought that being with a great playwright would help me find myself. It didn't. With him, I have had to play Marilyn Monroe more than ever, because I feared that he wouldn't love me otherwise. I can't take it anymore, and I'd like nothing better than to kill off that great movie star who I really don't know Marilyn Monroe.

All a girl really wants, Doc, is for one guy to be different from all the other men in the world. Unfortunately, what Arthur taught me is that whichever man a woman picks will eventually turn out to be just like all the rest. They're all cut from the same cookie cutter, and see only my surface instead of what's inside.

I can't imagine how things could get any worse. My marriage to Arthur is a failure. I have nobody of my own. I don't see how I can go on.

—Marilyn

In a brief return note, I reassured Marilyn that she often thought and spoke this way, and that just when I thought all was hopeless for her, she always managed to rally and come back to her best self.

Oh, how I hoped that was true this time around! But deep inside my gut, I was not so sure.

NOVEMBER 5, 1960

Dear Dr. Dale:

I need to tell you more about *The Misfits*. Despite my problems with Arthur, both as a husband and scriptwriter, I was initially elated because I believed the movie had great possibilities. For one thing, the director was to be John Huston, who'd directed me in *The Asphalt Jungle*, and I couldn't wait to work with him again.

Unlike my other directors, Huston had no qualms about directing me. He told me, "Marilyn, you may be trouble, but God, you're worth it!"

The rest of the cast—Clark Gable, Montgomery Clift, Eli Wallach, and Thelma Ritter—were the best thing about the movie. Clark was warm and affectionate, and the loving look in his eyes was, for me, a childhood fantasy come true. He really loved me—I have no doubt of that. For that reason alone, I'm glad I was in the movie.

Despite all my problems, sometimes I'm the luckiest woman in the world. Who else do you know whose deepest childhood wish comes true? Clark Gable loves me! The first time we danced together, I couldn't believe it and turned the color of my red chiffon dress. I kept thinking I was dreaming and would wake up the same lonely Norma Jeane, the orphan girl, hugging an empty pillow!

Everybody wonders if I slept with him. I'll keep them guessing, but I'll tell *you*, Doctor. I didn't. It would have felt like incest! Also his wife Kay was pregnant with Clark's first child, and I wouldn't do that to a baby before he's even born. Not that I wouldn't have liked to! Clark's hand accidentally touched my breast one time, and I got goose bumps all over.

Eli Wallach also was absolutely wonderful in the film. He's a great actor, and I hadn't known before that he was so good. He should be considered a great star. It's a pity he's never gotten the acclaim he deserves. He was a good friend to me and helped make the heat of the desert bearable.

My darling Montgomery Clift was his usual wonderful self. I love Monty dearly, and it was great to have him around, although his illness frightens me. Of all the people I know, he's the only one worse off than me.

And Thelma Ritter provided the perfect light touch.

Yes, sometimes it's good to be Marilyn Monroe, even if I was married to Arthur Miller.

That was the big irony. We shot the film mostly in Reno, which had handled five thousand divorces the year before. Living those months in Reno reminded me of my ill-fated marriage to Joe, which had ended there.

For Arthur, whom I loathe, shooting there brought back miserable memories of his first failed marriage. And he seemed to take that out on me. Our relationship was so awful that I don't know how we ever got through the movie. Arthur and I spoke less and less to one another, until eventually we weren't speaking at all.

I think I said this earlier, but Huston took Arthur aside at one point and begged him to get me off drugs. If he failed, Huston said, Arthur would feel guilty the rest of his life. To be honest, Huston had no idea how exhausted Arthur was from his fruitless efforts to help me. We got along worse and worse, until on one occasion I actually drove off and left Arthur behind, rather than allow him in my car.

Fortunately or unfortunately, he was rescued by Huston, who said afterward, "If I hadn't happened to see him, he'd have been stranded out there for a long time."

I was so mad at Arthur I couldn't help it!

I had a dream that showed just how furious I was with him. In the dream, the city was under attack by enemy planes and our home was being destroyed. Bombs were going off all over the place, and the houses that remained were crawling with huge, disgusting water bugs. I woke up in horror and tried to reassure myself that it was only a dream. But you've taught me too much for me to believe that, Doc, and we both know that the destruction in the dream is what's really going on between Arthur and me.

Divorcing him will be such a relief. I just have to get away from him! I just *have* to leave him. We have grown light years apart. I can't stand his gloomy face any more or the way he's ignored me.

It's better that we're apart now. There was no way to go on living with the rage we felt for each other. We argued all the time over the most trivial details, like the time he slipped on a sock I'd dropped on the floor. He made me feel miserable for days about it. Big deal! I dropped a sock! I couldn't help it that he hurt his back. He shouldn't have been so clumsy.

The constant fighting was unendurable. He made me a nervous wreck. I felt rejected and lonely. I went into seclusion to try to recover, but felt as alone in the world as I did in the orphanage. It began to feel like my marriage to Joe. I was lonelier in Arthur's presence than when I was by myself.

Arthur pretends to be a caring person, but in his heart of hearts, he's an S.O.B.! He said he was in despair about our separation. If that's despair, I'd hate to see happiness. He was always writing about how much he loved me. Some love!

We weren't even officially separated and he was already hanging around the set, mooning over that skinny broad with the butchy hair-cut, the photographer Inge Morath. Everybody on the set knew Arthur was two-timing me. It was very embarrassing! There was even talk that he was going to marry Inge. How *could* he, after being married to *the* Marilyn Monroe?

Here I was, supposedly the greatest sexpot in the world, and this plain little Nazi steals him away right under my nose! As Bette Davis said in *Of Human Bondage*, "Good riddance to bad rubbish"—and that, incidentally, is one of my favorite movies. I'd love to play her part if they ever redo it, but nobody would ever cast me in it.

Well, I thought, "You know my song, "After You Get What You Want, You Don't Want It?" Well, I got what I wanted—the great Arthur Miller—and, believe me, I didn't want him anymore.

Even Joe did better than Arthur. Joe always loved me, even after our divorce. He still loves me, and as far as I know, never has replaced me. That's love for you. Maybe I should go back to him. He had a few little shortcomings, but he has it all over Arthur when it comes to being there for me.

I better add one thing so you know I'm telling you the full truth, Doc: I've been unfair to Inge. I met her while she was taking photographs of the actors, and she really is nice, and not at all a Nazi. I'll have to try to remember—it's Arthur I'm mad at, not her.

—Marilyn

NOVEMBER 17, 1960

Dear Shrinker:

I was awakened at 4 p.m. by the most terrible news I've ever received in a lifetime of bad news. My darling surrogate father, Clark Gable, died of a massive heart attack at the relatively young age of fifty-nine. Clark, my wonderful Clark Gable, gone from my life forever! No hope now of ever finding my psychological father.

I can't bear the thought. Just when I've finally found him after a lifetime of looking, he's permanently gone from me. Besides being overwhelmed with grief, I am riddled with guilt. I am terrified that by keeping him waiting such long stretches in the hot Nevada sun, I contributed to his death, not to mention the stress my behavior caused him on the set. In fact, Kay, Gable's wife, told the newspapers that she believed the strain of working with me had contributed to Clark's death.

—Marilyn

Knowing the overwhelming guilt Marilyn was feeling, and the impact that could have on her psyche, I wrote her back:

My dear Marilyn,
I am so sorry.
I know how much you loved Clark Gable.
I wish I could do more, but know that my heart is with you, and I am grieving for you as well as for him and his family.
—Dr. Dale

How useless my words were, and how I wished there was more I could do or say to comfort her.

NOVEMBER 20, 1960

Dear Shrinker:
After leaving Arthur and learning of Clark Gable's death, I've gone into a bottomless depression. I can't even feed myself. I just lie in bed all day.

There's no end to the pain. Everything is gray and bleak and far away. I really can't describe what I feel because I can't let myself feel it. If I ever really felt it, I'd surely die.

You once asked me how you could help me. I'll tell you how: Tell Dr. Greenson to help me die.
—Marilyn

I went into a panic yet again. I had really tried everything I knew and did not know what else to do.

I felt powerless to rescue her from her utter despair and desolation. Just reading about her suffering was intolerable.

I could only try to let her know I understood the enormity of her pain, which I again did in a short note.

NOVEMBER 22, 1960

Dear Shrinker:

I was still so distraught about Clark's death that I decided to jump out the window of my thirteenth floor apartment. I knew I'd have to commit to my decision before climbing out on the ledge, or somebody would surely recognize me, call the police, and stop me in the act.

I was terrified that I'd be in terrible pain when I hit the ground, until I remembered reading somewhere that people who jump out of windows lose consciousness before they hit bottom.

I walked to the window and started to climb out when I noticed a woman walking on the sidewalk. I knew her! In fact, she lived next-door to me. How could I jump out the window and risk killing a neighbor?

So I gave up the idea of jumping and thought I'd look for a better way to kill myself.

—Marilyn

NOVEMBER 23, 1960

Dear Shrinker:

I'm thinking of quitting analysis. When I'm this way, everything goes black and negative. All I can do is lie under the covers, day after day after day. All I want to do is die ... die ... die."

—Marilyn

With foreboding letters like these, I felt I had no choice but to alert Dr. Greenson, who was well aware of Marilyn's situation, and to write her back.

NOVEMBER 27, 1960

Dear Marilyn:

I know you won't like the idea, but you ought to be in a hospital. You need more help than I can give you. There is no shame in admitting you are in serious trouble and need more help. I can have you admitted to Mount Sinai here tomorrow. I can come see you in the hospital and continue our sessions. Or you can have Dr. Greenson do the same in Los Angeles.

What do you think?

—Dr. Dale

NOVEMBER 30, 1960

Dear Shrinker:

What do *I* think? You should know what I think! No! No! That's what I think! I'll not go into a hospital! If I went to a hospital, they'd surely say my situation was hopeless. No analyst in the world would disagree, except you.

So how can you even ask me such a thing? I told you, this is the end of the line. Either I kill myself with the help of someone who cares for me, or I won't do it at all.

—Marilyn

In spite of Marilyn's protestations, she entered the Payne Whitney Psychiatric Clinic in February 1961, and transferred soon after to Columbia Presbyterian Medical Center.

Her letters resumed March of the following year.

MARCH 22, 1961

Dear Shrinker:

I was invited by Kay Gable to the christening of Clark's son, John Clark Gable, and I was delighted to attend. I even looked forward to seeing a miniature Clark Gable face. But as soon as I arrived, I peeked under the huge white christening cap. What a disappointment!

To my dismay, the baby didn't look like Clark at all, but resembled a wizened old man. I thought, *Oh well, he's Clark's son and will probably get better looking as he gets older. He couldn't get any homelier.*

Then I held him close to my breast and kept sniffing him, hoping at least he'd smell like his father. He didn't. He just smelled like any other baby.

Nevertheless, I held him so long that people became uncomfortable, thinking, "What kind of nut is this?" I didn't care, because I was lost in the fantasy that John Clark was a baby Clark and I had together. I told everyone there that John Clark was now my true love and the big man in my life, even if he was a bit young for me.

—Marilyn

The following letter did not come until a year later, once Marilyn had had some time to recover:

MARCH 1, 1962

Mirror mirror on the wall
Who's the wisest shrink of all?
Guess who?

Hi Shrinker!

I'd like to share some of my latest musings with you, if you're still interested in a movie star who hasn't starred in anything for a while. I want to talk to you anyway, and would like to believe you feel the same way about me, although it wouldn't be the first time in my life that someone who professed interest in me has dumped me. I usually make sure to dump them first.

I know I've mentioned to you that I'm crazy about Jack Kennedy. ("I'm just mad about Jacko, and he's just crazy about me!") He's now the main man in my life and in my dreams.

Which is what this letter is about. I'm a person whose dreams have all come true. I wanted to be a great movie star, and I am. I wanted to be a great actor, and I hear tell that, in that department, I'm quite the genius. I wanted to sleep with Marlon Brando, and I did. All my life, I wanted Clark Gable to love me, and miracle of miracles, he did! I dared to dream that I, little Norma Jeane from the orphanage, would win her independence from the movie moguls, and I have. In fact, I'm the first woman ever to have defeated a major Hollywood studio. I dreamt I would be the president of my own production company, and I'm the head and sole shareholder of Marilyn Monroe Productions! Not a bad record for a little girl from an orphanage.

Doctor, is someone a megalomaniac who thinks all her dreams will come true and they do? I doubt it. People who think fairy tales never come true have never met Marilyn Monroe. I've fought like a banshee (whatever a banshee is) to make my dreams a reality.

I just looked up "banshee" in the dictionary and found that in Celtic folklore, it's a supernatural being that's supposed to warn a family of the approaching death of one of its members, by wailing or singing in a mournful voice.

Oh my God, I hope I'm not a banshee! I hate to think I've foreseen the death of a Kennedy. Ignore the word, please! Forget that I ever called myself a banshee, and maybe the thought will disappear into the universe.

Anyway, back to the purpose of this letter. My latest dream is that I'll become the wife of the President of the United States, and thereby become the First Lady of the United States. Perhaps I can make this dream come true, too.

Am I crazy, Doctor? Dr. Greenson thinks so. Knowing my past history, I hope you'll agree with me, not him.

Love,

MMM (Marilyn "the Megalomaniac" Monroe)

MARCH 3, 1962

(To be sung to the tune of "You Are My Sunshine")
You're still my shrinker,
My bestest shrinker,
You make me happy
When life is gray.
You'll never know, dear,
How much I miss you.
Please rejoin me, oh shrinker, today.

Dear Shrinker:

I hope you're well and don't miss me too much. It's four o'clock in the afternoon, at what used to be our regular shrinking hour, so I thought it a perfect time to drop you a line. All is well so far, but I don't want to waste your time on boring details.

Over the past coupla years, I've loved being around the Kennedy family, with their loads of children, and those packs of dogs running free and yapping at whichever Kennedys are playing touch football. I was deeply thrilled when Pat said to me shortly after we became friends, "Marilyn, you're a Kennedy now."

I even have a family role: Pat's allergic to animals and keeps as far away from them as possible, but I just love their menagerie and make sure the dogs are always bathed and groomed whenever I'm around.

"I don't know why you don't like dogs, Pat." I said to her once. "They're like little people."

"Yeah?" she answered. "Fortunately, Marilyn, little people don't go around shitting on my white carpets!"

I have to give you another example of Pat's sense of humor. This incident makes me laugh every time I think of it. We were in Las Vegas together, and Pat had brought along her then two-and-a-half-year-old daughter, Victoria. Although children ordinarily aren't allowed in the casino, Pat, by using Kennedy influence (and cash), was permitted to bring Victoria in with us. Pat plopped the child on top of a blackjack table and said, "Here's the story, Marilyn. I'm going to play one game of blackjack. If I lose, I'm going to leave my kid right here with you. If I win, she'll be my prize."

She then proceeded to play her hand, with me standing right beside her. Well, she lost, and stood up and started to walk away. I got very alarmed, and yelled after her, "Pat . . . P-P-Pat . . . Come back! Come back here at once! You can't do that to me! I don't know how to take care of a little girl."

She returned, of course, and scooped up her daughter. By that time, I realized she'd been joking and was laughing so hard I was in hysterics. She loves to tease me, because she knows she'll always get a rise out of me.

Pat told me in confidence (and I trust you not to tell a soul) all about her marriage to Peter. It seems that Joe Kennedy despised Peter, and was openly against the marriage from the beginning. He said, "If there's one thing I hate worse than an actor, it's a British actor!' He actually had Peter investigated by FBI Director J. Edgar Hoover, and was told that Peter was neither a homosexual nor a Communist. That he was Protestant didn't help matters any in Joe's Catholic eyes, though. And much as he tried, Peter still couldn't get his future father-in-law to become a fan.

In a last, desperate attempt to wean Pat away from Peter before the planned marriage, Joe shipped her off on a trip around the world. It didn't work. Pat was a woman in love, and Joe's maneuver flopped badly. No sooner had Pat's plane set its wheels down in Tokyo than she turned around and flew back home to Peter.

It took a lot of courage for her to stand up to the old man. Not many people could have done it. I don't know if I could've.

But Pat quickly regretted not listening to her father, for the union was plagued almost from day one by Peter's drinking, and an almost lascivious attachment to Frank Sinatra's Rat Pack.

In addition, Peter's infidelities began right after the wedding and even continued during Pat's pregnancies. But Pat was accustomed to the practice because of her father's outrageous philandering right under the nose of his wife Rose.

Nevertheless, she insisted on separate bedrooms. She said, "I refuse to sleep next to a man who's having sex with another woman," and made the sign of the cross each time before having sex with Peter. She's probably the strongest, most courageous woman I know. I wish I had her balls!

I felt sorry for her until I thought to myself, "Who are you to feel sorry for her? Your last two marriages left plenty to be desired." Some people are talented at making good marriages. Unfortunately, Pat and I are not among them, at least so far.

"I wondered why such a famous woman could possibly need me in her life. (As you well know, self-confidence is not my biggest asset, despite my many hours on your couch.) I decided that Pat must be comfortable with movie stars (remember, her father had had a long affair with Gloria Swanson).

As a top movie actress, I suppose I add Hollywood glamour to Pat's high-society lifestyle. She loves show business, and was a TV producer for a while. She also adores the movie world so much that she's known as "the

Hollywood Kennedy," and is well liked by many famous movie stars. It's no accident that she married one, though she feels her ultimate duty is to the family business—politics.

The fact that Pat is friendly with me, an important movie star, must give her something intriguing to discuss with her highly successful siblings, especially Jack, the President of the United States, for whom, as I may have said, I've long had a thing.

Apparently, he's long felt the same way about me. He had major surgery on his back in 1954, when he was only thirty-seven. On his hospital wall, while recovering, he placed a poster of me in blue shorts standing with my legs spread apart. Wouldn't you know it, though? The poster was posted upside-down so that my feet stuck up in the air.

But it wasn't until fairly recently that Jack asked Peter to arrange a meeting between us. Peter complied, introducing us at a dinner party in the president's honor.

We mostly meet now at Peter's and Pat's place on the beach at Santa Monica. We also get rooms at the Holiday House Motel in Malibu, and once an old hotel on Sunset Boulevard. We went for drinks at the Malibu Cottage, which had the raunchiest bar you ever saw. (Well, maybe not you, my pure-of-heart shrink. The raunchiest bar *I* ever saw!) It had only eight barstools and the floor was covered with sawdust. But who cares what's on the floor when you have a date as classy as Jack Kennedy! Drinking all night long between trips to the bedroom, we fit right in.

I've been in love with Jack from the beginning, but I often wonder if our affair is as important to him as it was to me. I know he loves to have sex with me, and reassure myself that his coolness is just his aloof, upper-class way of behaving, but something inside of me never really feels secure in his love. I was relieved when I overheard Peter telling a guest of his, "The President is very enamored of Marilyn. He thinks she's enchanting, even though she's not really at ease with him. She's so impressed with Jack's charisma and charm that she's starry-eyed about him, like a high school girl in love with the Big Man on Campus."

Peter got that right. That's exactly how I feel about Jack.

At that first dinner party when he met, something awfully nice happened. Jack said to me, "Would you mind saying hello to somebody for me?" Then he phoned his father and said, "Guess who I'm sitting next to? Marilyn

Monroe! I'll have her say hello to you?" Then he put me on the phone.

Papa K had had a stroke a few months earlier, but it was exciting to speak with the old gent, who was such a part of the history of Hollywood, to say nothing of the USA. I was delighted to tell him how much we all loved Jack and to thank him for his part in getting him elected. Later, Jack said his father seemed as thrilled as I was about the conversation.

On one of our clandestine dates, I arrived at Jack's hotel only an hour late. I'd made a special effort to be on time, in honor of the president. My escort was Milt Ebbins, Peter Lawford's business partner. I stopped in the doorway of a room packed with famous faces, stood up to my full five feet six inches, smoothed the wrinkles out of my form-fitting dress, which was so tight I could hardly breathe, and said in what I thought was my deepest Marilyn Monroe voice, "I'm ready." Unfortunately, what came out sounded more like the croak of a frog. To the best of my knowledge, no one but me seemed to notice, unless they were just being polite.

When I walked in, the people in the room split in half, like when the Red Sea parted to let Moses through. Only I was Moses. About twenty-five celebrities were there, and you'd think none of them had ever seen a movie star before. Everything came to a halt, as if they were stumped while playing "Charades." Everybody stopped talking and even drinking, and a hush came over the room. I'd never seen anything like it. At first, I wondered if one of my boobs had popped out of my dress, but then I realized that news travels fast in that circle and they probably just wanted to see who JFK's latest sexual conquest was.

Well, they got an eyeful. Jack gave me a big smile, took my arm, and ushered me off to the main table, but first he turned and winked at Peter Lawford, no doubt to thank him for being his pimp.

To be continued ASAP.

Love,

Marilyn

P.S. I'm so glad you like my "poetry" and think it's a good way for me to express myself. You may be sorry you encouraged me, however, because now I'll continue sending you my poems.

MARCH 20, 1962

(With apologies to Emily Dickinson)

Hope is the thing with feathers
That perches in the heart,
And sings a tune without the words,
When Jack and I are apart.
I've heard it in the coldest land,
And deep inside my head,
And when I do not hear from him
I wish that I were dead.

Dear Shrinker:

Jack called me personally the other day. I didn't even mind waking up to take the call.

He said, "Good morning, Marilyn. Did I wake you?"

"Of course not, Mr. President," I lied. "I've been up for hours."

"So you know who this is?"

"Of course, Mr President. Is there anyone on earth who wouldn't recognize that Hahvard accent?"

"Marilyn," he said, getting right down to business, "I'm going to be in Palm Springs this weekend. Will you join me there? My private plane, *The Caroline*, will fly you in. Jackie," he added casually, as if in an afterthought, "will not be with me."

It was all I could do not to say, "She better not be!"

"Thank you, Mr. President," I said primly, disguising the flood of pleasure overwhelming my heart.

So that's what I'll be doing this weekend!

Love,

Marilyn

MARCH 25, 1962

Oh, JFK, king of men,
I can't wait to see you again.
I give you great head
And am yours to the letter
So why do you still like Jackie better?

Dear Shrinker:

In Palm Springs, dinner was set for eight o'clock, but now that I knew Jack was interested in me, the pressure was off and I could take my time. At nine o'clock, I was still sitting in front of my dressing table mirror, putting the finishing touches on my make-up. It felt good to know that I could keep the President of the United States waiting and there was nothing he could do about it. I suppose you shrinks would say I'm getting even for all the years I waited for my father. Maybe. Or maybe I just like feeling powerful. When I finally arrived an hour later, the President was standing by the door, and I could tell by the way his face lit up that he was captivated by me.

"Finally! You're here," he said with a big smile, showing those perfect white teeth. Then I heard him whisper to Peter Lawford, "What an ass! *What an ass!*" He turned to me and said, 'There are some people here who are dying to meet you.' *Some people?* I was descended upon by a mob. I guess they just wanted to breathe in the fragrance of Jack's new girl. Peter Lawford played the beard again and escorted me to another party, at which Jack and I spent some time gamboling in the guest house. I poured him a glass of champagne, of which he sipped very little. He was too busy staring lustfully at me over the top of the flute. I put on a record and danced to it. He grabbed me and guided my dance steps toward the bedroom.

I know I made him very happy that night, but I can't say he did the same for me. He didn't romance me with sweet words and sentimental speeches. And I've had teenagers make better love to me. But as Angie Dickinson once quipped about his sexual proclivities, "It was the best twenty seconds I ever spent."

"Nevertheless, after we were finished, I said, 'You know what, Jack? I think I'd make a wonderful First Lady."

"'I'm afraid you're not really First Lady material, Marilyn,' he answered without missing a beat.

That really knocked me for a loop. I said I had a headache, excused myself from his company, and ran right to my room. I tried to reassure myself that he was just joking, but it didn't help, and I sobbed myself to sleep. There are other difficulties being involved with JFK—security difficulties that I've never had to deal with before. Whenever and wherever we make love, Jack always has to leave a light on. If the light woes out, Secret Service men are to break down the door and burst in.

Once, when we were at Peter's place in Santa Monica, we took a shower together. As we came out of the bathroom in the buff, who should walk by but a Secret Service man! Not a great feeling!

Some people felt that Jack has a major character flaw—his womanizing—which leaves him open to blackmail and assassination. I don't know about that, but I'd think a president of the United States who wanted to run for reelection would be worried about being seen stepping out with the country's hottest movie star. But not JFK. He seems to think he walks on water, as far as women are concerned. He apparently said once, "Dad told all the boys to get laid as much as possible. I always follow my father's advice."

He bragged to me that he never held back where a beautiful woman was concerned. Don't I know it! Even including his earliest days in the Navy, when he was nicknamed "Shafty," he never ceased his womanizing. I knew of this before we got involved, so I guess I have no right to complain now, but I wonder: Millions of men want to sleep with me. How come I'm not enough for JFK?

I once told my friend and masseur Ralph Roberts, whom I confide in about most everything, that I was going to see Jack soon, and asked Ralph about the soleus muscle, which the President had told me was bothering him. I'd just been reading *The Thinking Body*, a book by Mabel Elsworth Todd. I told Ralph I'd been discussing the muscle system with Jack while massaging his back. I then called him and had Ralph speak with him about his muscles. He thanked me and said he found Ralph's advice helpful. But what I really think is that it was my other efforts that made his back feel better.

At heart, I'm still a little orphan girl who, incredible as it sounds, enjoys the sexual favors of the leader of the free world. After all, I'm a fatherless girl, and the president is the father of the country. I'm so proud that I'm sleeping with the most important man in the world, who I'm sure will turn out to be a great president on the level of Abraham Lincoln. Some people might say I'm just being patriotic.

Love,

Marilyn

MARCH 26, 1962

Dear Shrinker:

Here's something funny about me that you may well understand. Even when making love to President Kennedy, I mostly address him as Mr. President. Although I'm ecstatic about having him there, it's almost as if I am making love to an institution, not a man. I might as well be making love to the White House.

Does that make sense to you? Did I marry the American institution of baseball with Joe DiMaggio? Was it the institution of the theater I married in the great playwright Arthur Miller? Is that why my love affairs never work out for long? I'm not happy if I feel a lover wants me because I stand for Hollywood and not for myself. I drop him. Could my men feel the same way?

I think I've always been deeply terrified to be someone's wife, for life has taught me that one cannot ever truly love another person. My sex life, in and out of marriage, has often been lousy. One reason, I suspect: It's difficult to have an orgasm when making love to an institution. I'm not a promiscuous woman, and never cheat on a man unless I'm ready to let go of him. In the beginning, the man is not an institution, so the sex is better.

Here's another funny thought I have about Jack, which I hope I'm wrong about. Even though he seemingly loves to sleep with me, I have a nagging feeling that deep down inside of him, I don't really matter. I suspect he reveres no woman, not even his wife. He loves only John Fitzgerald Kennedy.

He makes me think of Alexander the Great, who I read about in school.

Alexander needed to conquer the world, including all the women in it. (I used to daydream that I lived in those days and, because I was so beautiful, he couldn't resist me, becoming the first woman he was ever able to love.)

In the dark of my sleepless nights, I worry that, to Jack, I'm just one more conquest, a trophy sexpot who becomes another notch on his belt, and not a real love.

It's said that it takes one to know one. Could the same be true of me—that, like Jack, I only want to make a great conquest and don't really love anyone? If so, we're well-matched.

—Marilyn

MARCH 27, 1962

(With apologies to Percy Bysshe Shelley)

My name is Marilyn, Queen of the Screen.
Look on my works, ye Mighty, and despair!
Nothing will remain. Round the decay
Of the colossal wreck that is me,
The lone and level sands stretch far away,
While the queen of sex fades into the dust.

Dear Shrinker:

It may be my imagination, but it seems to me that the President's affection for me is cooling down. It may just be that as President, he's terribly busy, and has more important things to deal with than little Norma Jeane, but in my gut, I don't think that's the reason. I have a sixth sense for how people feel about me, and I can detect the slightest change in voice or glance. No wonder! As a child, I learned to be on constant alert for when I was about to be kicked out of another foster home.

I really am worried that my relationship with JFK is on the way out. This spring, it's become obvious that his interest in me is little more than an affectionate, even careless, self-indulgence. He still calls me for an occasional roll in the hay, but he seems more lackadaisical about it, and one time even forgot we'd made an appointment to get together. I sat and waited for him for hours, and felt like the little orphan girl who waited and waited for a mother who never showed up. Like then, I cried myself to sleep.

Something dreadful happened today. The President had set up a special private line for me at the White House so I could call him any time I wanted. I phoned him often, and he always answered, if only to say he couldn't talk (as when he was with Jackie) and would call me back later. He always did, as soon as he could. It was great. We could always talk, even when we couldn't see each other.

Well, I called today as usual. An operator answered and said the line had been disconnected. I hoped it was a joke, and that he'd call me right back and say, "Ha! Gotcha!" Or maybe it was a mistake, and the phone company had inadvertently disconnected the line.

It was no mistake! I got more and more desperate and kept calling the White House switchboard every few minutes. Finally, an operator got on and said, "That line has been disconnected," and started to hang up.

I said, "Wait a minute! Just a moment! This is Marilyn Monroe speaking and I need to get in touch with the President right away. If you don't connect me, I'll see that the President has you fired." The operator answered snottily, "I know who this is, Ms. Monroe, but I'm afraid the President is not taking any calls right now," and she hung up before I could inquire further.

I'm terrified at what this all means, and can only hope that Jack will get in touch with me soon and explain everything. After all, there may be a perfectly understandable reason why the line has been disconnected.

Do you think he's abandoned me? Is it because I'm not educated enough for him, that I'm not in the same class as his refrigerator-of-a-wife Jackie? I'll bet she'd love to know some of the things he's told me. Did he want me only as a plaything? Did he get what he wanted, like in the song, and now he doesn't want me anymore?

Well, I'll find out soon enough. I just got a call from Bobby's secretary that Bobby's coming to visit me tomorrow. When I asked her why, she said she couldn't give me any information. I'll have to find some way to get through the next twenty-four hours. Maybe I'll take so many pills they'll knock me out until then.

Love,

Marilyn

P.S. I'm enclosing a check for one thousand dollars to compensate you for your time and effort reading my long letters, assuming, of course, that you do read them.

MARCH 28, 1962

Row row row your boat
Fiercely down the stream
Smash the oar upon Jack's head
For life is one long scream.

Dear Shrinker:

Well, Bobby was here, and the situation is even worse than I thought. It seems Jack sent Bobby as an emissary to deliver the message that it is all over between us. Apparently, Jackie was getting worried about the seriousness of our relationship, as were others, especially the political types. A Catholic man divorced right before he ran for a second presidential term never would be reelected, and it would mean not just the end of his political career, but perhaps that of the entire Kennedy dynasty as well.

Bobby got quite nasty, as only he can. He said I am a pest who demands constant attention, and had better get out of Jack's life P.D.Q.! Me a pest? *Me*? Marilyn Monroe, superstar, supposedly the most glamorous woman in the world?

Dr. Dale, I'm heartbroken. What a cruel way to end a loving relationship! Our President may try standing up to Castro but, when it comes to me, he's a coward! The least he could have done was come and tell me the bad news himself, or to call me. And knowing how important his career is to him, I'd have tried to understand.

I know you'll say I'm responding as if I've lost my father again. Be that as it may, I don't know if I can live through such a loss another time.

I feel so terribly worthless, like a piece of meat too old even to be thrown to the dogs. I feel like the waif I always was, the still ugly Norma Jeane, whom people are only nice to for what they can get out of her. Nobody loves me. Nobody ever has. Life isn't worth living anymore.

Which reminds me of a terrible dream I had last night. I was sitting at my little white desk, which I love, and opened the drawer where I keep my writing paper. It was filled with cockroaches—so many that they swarmed all over me and then down to the floor. You know how much I hate cockroaches. I screamed in horror.

Well, Doctor, I know what this horrible dream means. I'm in an overwhelming rage at Jack Kennedy. In the beginning of the dream, the drawer is closed, which means I didn't know how furious I was.

The sheer amount of rage I feel is overwhelming, and I'm afraid I won't be able to contain it, so I go out of my mind and do something irreparable.

Do you agree with my interpretation? Actually, you don't have to weigh in, Doc. I know I'm right.

I can promise you this: In some way, as soon as I can manage it, I *will* get my revenge! No man, not even the President of the United States, can treat Marilyn Monroe so badly and get away with it!

—Marilyn

APRIL 25, 1962

Be it ever so humble
There's no place like home,
Unless, like Marilyn,
You live in it alone.

Dear Shrinker/ Friend:

Thank you so much for your sweet note and for returning my check. It's not so much the money. I'm moved that you actually want to read my letters—that you find them of interest.

Love,
Marilyn

APRIL 29, 1962

To buy or not to buy,
That is the question.

Dear Shrinker:

Well, I have some great news! Dr. Greenson suggested that I buy a house of my own, which he believes will bring me a sense of security and help me get over what he calls my obsession with JFK. I thought, Why not? Nothing else has helped. I've never owned a house by myself before. In fact, I'm thirty-five and have never really had a home at all.

I'm tired of living in apartments. Over the last sixteen years, I've rented more than thirty-five (!) different homes, apartments, and hotel rooms. Isn't it about time I get a place of my own? Maybe having a house to care for and furnish to suit only my preferences will make me stop worrying about Jack so much and think more about me.

I asked Eunice Murray, whom, on Dr. Greenson's recommendation, I hired as my housekeeper, to help me find a house in the Brentwood area of Los Angeles. The single-story, Spanish renaissance-style house we found is simple but lovely, with white stucco walls surrounded by vines, flowers, and thick green foliage. The air is thick with the sweet smell of blossoming flowers.

How different from the dusty air of New York! The house has gorgeous wood-beamed ceilings that I adore, a large central living room with a fireplace, and several small bedrooms. It's located at the closed end of a cul-de-sac, and will give me privacy from curious fans. (Much as I love them, I don't want them peering through my windows.)

Can a person fall in love with a house, Doc? If so, I'm in love (even though I had to borrow the money for the down payment from Joe DiMaggio). It's near Dr. Greenson's office and home, which makes me feel more secure. I can run to his house, or he to mine, in a few minutes, should it ever be necessary. The house is actually a smaller version of his—Mexican decor and all. I fell in love with it the moment I saw it, and had hardly crossed the threshold when I said to the agent, "I'll take it!"

Despite my love for the house, I burst into tears when I signed the contract. After all, I thought, I'll have to live in it alone. There's no joy in buying a house by yourself, for yourself. Unfortunately, loneliness is an internal thing, and follows you wherever you live. At worst, however, having a house of my own will keep me busy for a while as I furnish it.

I also discovered that I love gardening, which I never really had the opportunity to do much of before. I love kneeling down and inhaling the aroma of fresh earth and getting my hands as dirty as I please, with no one to be angry about it, as Ida Bolender was when I was a child. (Will I ever grow up, Doc?) And it is a joy to watch each new bulb slowly blossom into a flower. If I can't have babies, as least I can grow flowers!

A funny thing happened when the owner's housekeeper first allowed me access to the property. Her eyes widened when she saw me. She said, "Are you *really* Marilyn Monroe? I don't believe it!"

"I don't believe it either," I answered. "Everybody tells me that's who I am, but you can't prove it by me. "

To be continued tomorrow.

Love,

Marilyn

APRIL 30, 1962

A house, a house
My kingdom for a house!

Dear Shrinker:

I was a bit shocked when I looked at the tile above my new house's front door. The engraving reads, in Latin, "Cursum Perficio," or, "I am finishing my journey." I gulped and thought, "I hope not! Maybe it just means that I'll live out my life in this beautiful home."

But if it is the end of the line for Norma Jeane and Marilyn Monroe, who cares? Who really gives a damn if I finish my journey or not? Certainly not I.

So far, the year 1962 hasn't been all bad for me, though some days I've been so depressed I couldn't get out of bed. On those days, I felt as down as I was during my the end of my in-office analysis with you. I would think, "Why should I get up?" I could think of no reason to get out of bed.

In spite of this, the year has had two high points: the purchase of my beautiful home, and winning a Golden Globe Award as the "world's film favorite." (Norma Jeane, the orphan girl, now the favorite film star of the whole world? Incredible!)

My use of drugs improved for a short while, but life was so barren I soon began to slide back into old habits, meaning I gulped down pills by the fistful. When friends asked if I wasn't worried that I would OD, I answered, "I hope I do. Hell hath no fury like an unloved woman." It would be a pleasure to leave this cauldron of misery behind me forever.

Love,

Marilyn

P.S. Speaking of pills, last night I had a terrible nightmare. A large, heavy man (much bigger than me) was wielding a knife in my bathroom, which is where I keep most of my pills. The man was slicing off his flesh and screaming. An older man (Dr. Greenson?) was looking in but doing nothing. I think the dream speaks for itself. I'm actively destroying myself, and no one is helping, including me.

Analyst's Note: I hoped I was wrong, but when I read this dream, I began to lose all hope that Marilyn would win out over all the evil, internal forces, symbolized by the large heavy man in her dream, that were pulling her to the grave.

MAY 17, 1962

Shrink shrank shrunk
I am not a drunk
No matter what you thunk.
I take a sip now and then
And maybe another one again
But I am not a drunk
Or am I?
What do you think, Shrink?

Hi Shrinker!

Here's a funny story about my poetic 'Am I a drunk' question. My friend Jimmy Haspiel says that in the eight years he's known me, he's never seen me drunk—in fact, he said he's never even seen me tipsy. One day, though, he showed me a photo of me in which I obviously had been drinking too much. He said, "Marilyn, this photo was taken in an elevator in Marlene Dietrich's house. You were very high."

I asked, "What floor was I on?"

Love,

Marilyn

MAY 18, 1962

(With apologies to William Blake)

I was angry with my beau
I told him not, my wrath did grow.
And I watered it in fears,
Night and morning with my tears.
And it grew both day and night,
Until it was a ghastly sight.
Come morning I was glad to see
My foe lay dead beneath a tree.

Dear Shrinker:

Peter Lawford has asked me to come to Madison Square Garden to sing "Happy Birthday" to the President at his birthday celebration. According to Peter, Jack laughed heartily when somebody ran the idea by him, and he apparently thinks it's great. I said I'd love to do it, although the studio is having a hissy fit and has threatened to fire me from that stinko movie, *Something's Got to Give*, if I don't show up for work on Monday. (It's already seven and a half days behind schedule.)

I have to tell you a little about the film, so you'll understand why I'm not terribly happy being in it. It's yet another variation on *My Favorite Wife*, a comedy Cary Grant and Irene Dunne did way back in 1940.

Yikes! Can't any studio come up with something original these days? The only thing I like about the movie is that it's a film interpretation (the sixth!) of a poem by Alfred Lord Tennyson called "Enoch Arden" that I read and loved in my UCLA literature class. Besides the professor, I'm the only person I know of who's ever heard of it. (That includes the screenwriters.)

In *Something's Got to Give* (what's got to give is the whole movie!), Enoch Arden's name has been miraculously changed to Ellen (me), who is declared legally dead after being lost at sea. Her husband Nick (Dean Martin) has just remarried. He and his wife Bianca (Cyd Charisse) are on their honeymoon when Ellen is rescued from the island she's been stuck on for five years. In the script, I was supposed to ask my rescuers, 'Who's the president now?' When they answered, "Kennedy," I asked, "Which one?' That made me laugh.

Ellen returns home, where the family dog remembers her, but her children don't. They take a liking to her, however, and invite her to stay, proving, I guess, that blood runs thicker than water (although you'd never guess it from my relationship with my parents). Ellen takes to using a foreign accent and pretends to be a woman named Ingrid Tic. Nick, married to two women at the same time, tries to keep the truth from his new wife and to quash her amorous advances. That's supposed to be funny. Maybe I have a peculiar sense of humor, but I see nothing funny about a woman's amorous advances being rejected. To me, it's heartbreaking.

If you can overlook the sentimentality, the film's ending is quite touching (somehow I didn't mind it as much when Tennyson wrote it). Ellen sees her husband and children happily engaged with each other. Good-hearted woman that she is, she walks away from the marriage and the home, leaving her husband, wife number two, and family to their newfound happiness, which, believe me, I would not do for all the emeralds in India.

Bobby Kennedy personally called Milton Gould, a member of the Fox Board of Directors, to ask them to reconsider their threat to replace me in the movie if I took part in the Madison Square Garden festivities. "I'm sorry, General," Gould answered, "but we just can't do it. The lady has caused us all sorts of trouble and gotten us way behind schedule."

To that, I'd have said, "Fuck you, Fox-Twentieth Century," but Bobby did it for me, even though I strongly object to the anti-Semitic epithet he used. He called Gould a "Jewish bastard," and slammed down the phone.

According to a spy on the set, the producer, Henry Weinstein, joked that I was enough to make everyone in the movie turn Republican. I'm not laughing.

I don't care if they fire me. It will be no great loss to me. I've made up my mind that, come hell or high water, I am going to sing "Happy Birthday" to the President. Am I being patriotic, as everyone thinks? Hell no! My wish to take revenge on the Kennedy brothers for their mistreatment of me takes precedence over everything else in my life. Even more than usual, I stay up nights thinking of ways to do it.

As President Kennedy's birthday approaches, no one connected with the film believes that I'll be able to keep my commitment to the White House—I'm not in the best of shape, physically or emotionally. But they don't know me very well. I'd return from the grave to carry out my plans.

For the occasion, I've ordered a transparent silk soufflé *pièce de résistance* from the famous couturier Jean Louis. It's a flesh-colored, apparently-nude dress except for a few intricately woven, hand-stitched rhinestones and mirrors sewn on in strategic locations. I told Jean Louis to design a dazzling, one-of-a-kind, historical dress that only Marilyn Monroe could (and would) wear. The dress will cost me $1,404.65, with $321.89 for the rhinestones and mirrors and an extra $55.40 for the beading. My white stiletto shoes come in at a cheap $35.68.

I may not have the biggest of bank accounts, but paying for the outfit is worth every penny. Revenge is that sweet.

I'll come on stage in Madison Square Garden wearing my ermine stole, and drop it to the floor when I take the microphone. I expect that people will gasp, and have to do a double-take to make sure I'm not actually naked. The dress will be unlined and so tight that no curve of my body will be able to hide, including the outlining of my pubic area. Of course I will wear no underwear, other than that stitched into the gown by the designer.

I'll sing in the breathiest, sexiest voice I know how, and I don't have to tell you how sexy the sexiest woman in the world can sound. When

I sing, I'll run my hands over my body, including my breasts, looking straight at the President as I do so. There will be no doubt in anyone's mind that I'm making love to him in front of millions of people.

Then everybody in the world will know that the President of the United States and Marilyn Monroe are, or should I say were, lovers. I refuse to be kept in a closet, to be pulled out whenever it suits those S.O.B.s. I've learned from you that I must not let men abuse me. This will teach them that they cannot exploit Marilyn Monroe and get away with it.

By the way, I think I shocked Jean Louis, despite all his experience clothing famous women. When he came to my house to take my measurements for the dress, I climbed up on a footstool and dropped my robe, standing there completely naked. When I saw the horror on his face, I said, "Why do you look so flabbergasted? I want you to see what I look like. You'll be much more accurate if you measure me without clothes on." Shy as he is, he had to admit I was right, although he flinched when he wrapped the tape measure around my buttocks. I didn't.

I knocked myself out for three straight weeks practicing "Happy Birthday." During lunch breaks at Fox, I was coached by Lionel Newman, the music director. I shouted out the lyrics while bathing in the tub, and recorded my singing on a tape recorder. All for a silly little jingle that everybody knows!

What do you think of my idea?

On second thought, I couldn't bear it if you tried to talk me out of doing it, as Paula Strasberg has been trying to do. Susan told me that her mother said, "I hear that 'Happy Birthday' keeps getting sexier and sexier. If she doesn't stop soon, it'll turn out to be a complete caricature." I don't know about its being a caricature, but "sexier and sexier" is exactly what I have in mind.

Don't miss the President's birthday celebration at Madison Square Garden. One way or another, it'll go down in history.

Love,

Marilyn

MAY 19, 1962

I'm just a little lonely girl
As sad as I can be.
Won't some kind sir
Please come along
And make a pass at me?

Hi Shrinker!

Today I'd like to talk about loneliness, because—you guessed it—without the Kennedys, I'm feeling a bit lonely. I know I've told you a lot of this stuff before, but I'd like to put it all together so maybe I can understand why I'm always so lonely. Then maybe I can get some relief.

I woke up this morning feeling a cold hard lump of loneliness in the pit of my stomach. It grew and grew until that's what I became—a bundle of loneliness screaming, "Love me! Hold me! If you loved me, I'd never feel alone."

Who was supposed to do the loving, you might ask? Jack? Bobby? Beats me. I'd settle right now for either one. As the saying goes, "Beggars can't be choosers."

Well, that's not quite true. You and I know that everything goes back to my mother. I never felt she even liked me, let alone loved me. In fact, she never seemed at all interested in me. I am forever haunted by her absence, like someone else's shadow attaching itself to me where I expect to see my own. Where my mother's love would fit so naturally, I find loss and hurt instead.

I'm loneliest when I wake up in the morning. I think, "Why should I get out of bed? The whole day lies ahead, and there's nobody in my life who loves me." Sometimes, I lay in bed until five o'clock in the afternoon.

The days my maid Lena Pepitone comes in are a little better. At least I have someone to talk to. She brings me coffee in bed. I sneak in a little vodka and maybe a few wake-up pills. Then she makes me get up and take a bath, which, depending on the day, I may not have done for over a week. When I lie there surrounded by warm soapy water, I feel a bit better. I'm not happy, but I'm comfortable. I think, "Why don't I just sink below the suds and stay there forever?"

Oh, I know what you're thinking, Doc—that I just want to crawl back into my mother's womb. Well, do you blame me? That was the only time I ever had a real mother. On good days, when Lena drags me out of the tub and pushes me back into my life, such as it is, I am sometimes able to go about my business. Sometimes I even show up at work.

But the next morning, the whole thing starts all over again, and I don't want to get out of bed. I pull the covers over my head and yell, "Go away, Lena! Go away and let me sleep!" Sometimes she does.

I was always lonely—that's why I so loved the movies. Thank goodness for them! I could sit there all day and completely forget myself. When I got home, I closed the bedroom door and acted out what I saw on the screen, especially those romantic scenes where the actors were hugging and kissing the lady star. For a twelve year old, it was serious pantomime. I had a crush on every movie star, especially the men. But as you know, my real heartthrob was Clark Gable.

Can you believe that I thought getting married would cure me of my loneliness? Don't make me laugh! If my own father ran away before even meeting me, what can I expect from men who're strangers? I'm always alone, no matter who's in my life. I remained just as lonely throughout my three marriages, all of which, of course, ended in divorce.

I had nothing in common with my first husband, Jim Dougherty, in our arranged marriage. My second husband, Joe DiMaggio, was a sullen, silent sourpuss, at least when he was around me, and he spent most of his time watching sports on television. After a while, we didn't even sleep in the same room. It makes me feel lonelier even to think of it.

My third marriage to Arthur Miller? That was no better. Arthur closed himself up in his office and spent his time thinking and smoking his pipe. I don't know what he thought about, because he certainly didn't come up with any more Pulitzer prizes, but he was no help to me. If I'm going to be alone, it might as well be by myself.

What about women friends? What are they? I don't have any. I couldn't even find one to be my maid of honor at my wedding to Arthur. It doesn't help that women are often jealous of me and ignore me. I've been to parties where no woman spoke to me for the whole evening. The men, fearful that their wives or girlfriends would feel jealous, give me a wide berth. The ladies gang up in a corner to discuss my lasciviousness. I walk around rooms pretending to be interested in the paintings or books. I doubt I fool anyone.

There's something terrible about me that seeps through the glamorous gowns and jewelry the studio lends me to wear to parties. I'm sure I frighten the other guests. Somewhere deep inside, they're aware that I'm the kind of girl people find dead in a hall bedroom with an empty bottle of sleeping pills in her hand. They steer clear of me, except for the men who want to sleep with me. And even they push me away after they've gotten what they want.

In my career, I've found little relief from loneliness. Yes, a career is wonderful, but you can't cuddle up with it at night.

Of course, loneliness has its advantages at times, and has contributed to my becoming a star. Talent is developed in privacy. An actor needs aloneness, which is something I don't think most people understand. It's like having certain kinds of secrets for yourself that you'll let the whole world in on only for a moment, when you're acting.

Religion wasn't much help to me, either. God, the only one who supposedly loved me and watched over me, was someone I couldn't see or hear or touch. I used to draw pictures of God when I was little. In my pictures, He looked a little like Clark Gable.

To me, Sunday is always the loneliest day of the week. All the men I know are spending the day with their wives and families, and all the stores in Los Angeles are closed, so you can't wander around in them looking at the pretty clothes and pretending to buy something.

I spend some Sundays at Union Station. You learn a lot by watching people there. You learn that beauty is not everything, that pretty wives adore homely men, that good-looking men adore homely wives, and that people in shabby clothes, carrying raggedy bundles, and with three or four small kids clinging to them, have faces that can light up like Christmas trees when they see each other. I observe really homely men and women, fat ones and old ones, kissing each other as tenderly as if they were lovers in a movie. Most people envy me my stardom and fame. Little do they know I'm as jealous of them as they are of me.

I once wrote in my diary, "Help help / Help / I feel life coming closer / when all I want / is to die." I know exactly how I felt the moment I wrote that. I feel the same way now. It's as if I'm abandoned on a tiny desert island no bigger than your kitchen. I have no doubt the tide is going to rise, the ocean will soon cover this little island, and I will drown.

Well, dear shrinker, I'm sorry to burden you with my tales of woe, but you know that my moods often change quickly, and perhaps tomorrow I'll feel better. I may even jump out of bed tomorrow morning and shock the cast and crew by getting to work on time and perfectly doing my lines on the first take .

Thanks for reading. Can you believe it? I feel some relief just knowing that you are reading and caring.

Love,

Marilyn

MAY 20, 1962

Now I lay me down to sleep,
I pray thee, Lord, my soul to keep.
Please let me die before I wake,
As life is much too hard to take.

Dear Shrinker:

Yesterday at 11:30 p.m. I sashayed out in my skin-tight gown and my four-inch heels before twelve thousand Democrats in Madison Square Garden and was introduced by Peter Lawford as the "late" Marilyn Monroe. (Although everybody laughed, I personally didn't think it was so funny. I'd have liked a little respect shown the Queen of the Screen.)

My throat closed up and suddenly I didn't think I could do it. Then I said to myself, "By God in his Heaven, Marilyn, you'll sing it if it's the last thing you ever do!" And to my surprise, a sultry, super-sexually charged rendition of "Happy Birthday," sung as no one ever had done it before, poured out of my throat, just as I'd rehearsed it, only sexier.

The audience was screaming and yelling so loud I don't know if anyone could hear the words I'd practiced for so long. It was like nothing so much as a mass seduction. Jack was seated about twelve feet away from me. I looked at his face, and he flushed a deep red, but there was nothing even the President of the United States could do about me. He could only pretend to be happy about the whole thing, and say, "I can now retire from politics, after having 'Happy Birthday' sung to me in such a sweet and wholesome way."

I'll say one thing about Jack Kennedy: He sure knows how to keep his cool. I was in the driver's seat for the first time, and he couldn't have liked it very much. I had my revenge and it was sweet, indeed.

The sweetness didn't last long, though. After the concert, attended a small party at the Upper East Side townhouse of Arthur Krim, the president of United Artists. Jack, Bobby, and I were all there. My "date" was Isadore Miller, Arthur's father. I took him up to the President and said, "Mr. President, I'd like you to meet my former father-in-law, Isadore Miller."

Jack said "hmmmph" and turned his back on us. It was the coldest reaction I've ever received. You'd think we were strangers meeting for the first time. I wanted to shout, "What's with you, Jack? Don't you remember the wonderful times we shared in bed?"

I called back to him. "Just a moment, Mr. President," I said. "I have a small birthday gift for you," and handed him a package. A "small gift"? It was an eighteen-caret gold Rolex "President" watch, engraved on the back with the words, "To Jack, with love as always from Marilyn, May 19, 1962." The watch cost me five thousand dollars—more than a month's pay. I'd bought it for him before he dumped me, but I decided to give it to him anyway.

I guess I still had a tiny shred of hope that such a beautiful and expensive gift would bring him back to me. But he handed it to an attendant, muttering something like, "Do something with this." Five thousand bucks and I don't even get a simple thank-you! What a rude man our president is!

More important than the watch, I had written him a poem and tucked it inside the box. It said:

Let lovers breathe their sighs
And roses bloom and music sound.
Let passion burn on lips and eyes
And pleasures merry world go round
Let golden sunshine flood the sky
And let me love
Or let me die!

It was my desperate message to Jack, telling him that, without his love, I didn't want to live. And I meant it. But Jack seemingly couldn't care less. In fact, I wonder if he even read it.

I dropped Isadore Miller off at his home, and went back to my apartment, where my masseur, Ralph Roberts, was waiting to give me a massage I hoped would put me to sleep. It didn't. I was too upset for even his golden hands to do the trick.

Going through my mind were the lines from Macbeth, "Macbeth hath banished sleep. Macbeth shall sleep no more." Only in my head it went, "Kennedy hath banished sleep. Marilyn shall sleep no more." After Ralph left, I sobbed until daybreak, and then slept a fitful hour or two before my maid Lena came in with my boiled egg and toast.

My father had rejected me before I was born. You and I know that Jack's rejection is a terrible repetition of my original loss. The truth is that I don't want to live without Jack, just as I never wanted to live without my father. Life's not worthwhile if your father doesn't want you alive. So maybe I won't be. That's the only way I know to make both Jack and my father happy.

To love without hope is the saddest thing in the world.

Love,

Marilyn

MAY 21, 1962

(With apologies to my friend, Robert Frost)

Two roads diverge in a misty wood,
I knew I could not travel both,
So long I stood
And debated the choice as much as I could

Two roads diverge in a wood,
One leads to death and one to life,
I chose the one that beckons me,
And cures me of all pain and strife.

Dear Shrinker:

As you can see from my poem, I woke up wondering if I should take an overdose of pills, or wait a little longer. Then I thought of an anecdote I read a long time ago about someone I've always admired and adored—Abraham Lincoln. He, like me, was a depressed person much of his life. At one point, he believed there was no good reason for him to go on living, so he determined to kill himself. We don't know why, but he didn't, and then six months later, he was elected president of the United States.

Is there is a moral in there for me somewhere? Is that the reason I've always been enamored of Abraham Lincoln and sometimes keep his photograph at my bedside, to have his story as an example to follow in my times of desperation? Can my life take a similar turn for the better? Is it still possible that Jack will realize how badly he's treated me, and resume our love affair?

I've never been able to endure any form of criticism or rejection and, as a result, have attempted suicide a number of times. I've always returned to consciousness sorry that I was still alive, and if (or should I say when) I try again, I'll make sure I do it right.

I know I'm insecure and needy. With three failed marriages behind me, I find Jack's rejection absolutely unbearable. I know I should find a man who will compensate for the fact that I never had a father. Is there hope that, at my advanced age of thirty-five, one will still turn up? I don't think so.

Be that as it may, I'll temporarily put aside the pills. Tomorrow is still another day.

Love,
Marilyn

MAY 27, 1962

(With apologies to Edwin Arlington Robinson)

Whenever Marilyn went downtown,
Hordes of people gathered 'round.
She was a sight from toe to crown,

Glamorous, sexy, in a gorgeous gown.
She was always beautifully arrayed,
And always human when she talked,
And fluttered pulses when she said,
"Good-morning," and glittered when she walked.
And she was rich—richer than a king,
And admirably schooled in every grace:
In fact, they thought she was everything
To make them wish to be in her place.
So on they worked, and hoped for the light,
And went without meat, and cursed the bread,
And Marilyn Monroe, one calm summer night,
Went home and put a bullet through her head.

Dear Shrinker:

Don't worry. The poem's just my humorous rewrite of "Richard Cory."

We're continuing production on *Something's Got to Give*, and things aren't getting any better. The chief production executive at Fox—the man supervising the movie—is Peter Levathes, a onetime advertising executive who should've stayed with his former profession as far as I'm concerned. He's known for his hostility toward actors and, upon my return to work, made no secret of the fact that I was at the top of his "do not respect" list. Just what I need—someone else to hate me!

Love,

Marilyn

Analyst's Note: On receiving this letter, and especially the poem, I immediately sent the following telegram to Marilyn:

Please pick up your phone STOP Call me immediately STOP —*Dr. Darcey Dale* STOP

She did call me, and we had a short conversation, the essence of which was her comment, "Can't you take a joke, lady?"

I answered, "It was not very funny, Marilyn."

"Sorry about that," she said, and started to hang up.

I said, "Hold on there a moment, Marilyn. Please, no more jokes."
"OK," she answered. "I promise," and took her leave.
So why am I not reassured?

MAY 28, 1962

Jack is nimble,
Jack comes quick.
Jack, you make me
Good and sick!

Dear Shrink:

I need to backtrack a bit to bring you up to speed. April 23, about four weeks before Madison Square Garden, was the first scheduled day of production for *Something's Got to Give*. But wouldn't you know it? I woke up feeling terribly sick. I phoned producer Henry Weinstein to inform him I had a severe sinus infection and wouldn't be able to come to work that day.

Apparently, I'd caught the infection on a recent rainy trip to New York City to visit Lee Strasberg to go over my role. It seems some germs decided to make my nose their home. I wasn't too happy with my boarders. They didn't even pay me rent.

Fox sent staff doctor Lee Siegel to my home to examine me. He recommended that I stay in bed for a month, and that the studio postpone the start of shooting. But director George Cukor refused to follow the doctor's recommendation. Instead, he reorganized the schedule to shoot scenes without me.

At 7:30 that very morning, he telephoned Cyd Charisse to immediately come to the Fox sound stage, where they shot a scene, out of order, with the two children building a tree house. I can imagine Cyd cursing me up and down the lot. Sorry, Cyd! Your pushed-up appearance really wasn't my fault. In the unlikely event you're reading this, I really was too sick to work.

Over the next month, filming continued without me most of the time, because by then I'd developed a fever, headaches, chronic sinusitis, and bronchitis, and was able to show up on the set only occasionally.

Unfortunately, production fell ten days behind schedule, for which I was extravagantly blamed, of course. As if I chose to be sick!

By this time, the production was well over budget, and the script still wasn't completely finished. They rewrote it nightly, leaving me increasingly frustrated at having to wipe the old lines from my mind and memorizing the new ones, and even entirely new scenes, every day. Despite my physical misery, I spent much of my time on the set in my dressing room with my drama coach, Paula Strasberg, working on my part.

More later.

Love,

Marilyn

MAY 30, 1962

My body is me,
Just look and see
That I am my body
And my body is me.

Dear Shrinker:

Upon my return from New York, I decided to give the film a publicity boost by doing something no major Hollywood actress had ever done before, and something that, incidentally, I had a lot of fun doing. There's a scene in *Something's Got to Give* where my character, Ellen, is swimming at night. While still in the family pool, she calls up to her husband Nick's bedroom window and invites him to join her in the pool. Unaware that Ellen is nude, Nick asks her to get out of the water, and is staggered when she emerges without a stitch of clothing.

A body stocking had been made for me, but you know me. I wouldn't be caught dead in one. I simply took it off and swam around naked. The set was closed to all but necessary crew—

with one major exception. I'd asked some magazine photographers to come in, and after the film day was over, they photographed me swimming nude in the pool, climbing out, and drying off.

I love how I look in that scene. If you'll excuse my lack of humility, I was particularly pleased with the lovely curve of my back, which I'd never noticed before. I fell in love with my body all over again.

But guess what delighted me most about the photos? The knowledge that their publication would be sure to knock Liz Taylor off the front pages. Cheer up, Liz! It's just as well that the photos are of me and not you. Can you imagine fat Liz Taylor in the nude, Doc?

Everyone's been making such a fuss over how this'll be the first Hollywood motion picture of the sound era in which a mainstream star is depicted in the nude. I say, "Big deal!"

Love,
Marilyn

JUNE 23, 1962

Happy birthday to me,
Happy birthday to me.
I'm 36 years old now
And sad as can be.

Dear Shrinker:

Well, I've been fired. I said I didn't care, and I don't.

On June 1, my thirty-sixth birthday, Dean Martin, Wally Cox, and I shot a scene in the courtyard set. My stand-in, Evelyn Moriarty, brought out a sheet cake, purchased from the Los Angeles Farmer's Market for all of seven dollars. A studio illustrator drew a cartoon of a nude me holding a towel which read, "Happy Birthday (Suit)." This was used as a birthday card, and was signed by all members of the cast and crew.

Some birthday party! The whole thing lasted a half hour, and everybody was too exhausted to enjoy it.

I must add that the cast had attempted to celebrate my big day when I first arrived on the set, but that S.O.B. Cukor insisted they wait until 6 p.m., the end of the working day, because, he said, he wanted to get a "full day's work out of that broad." I was furious. How mean can you get?

What makes it even worse is that Fox had thrown a huge birthday shindig for Elizabeth Taylor, who's holding up the works on *Cleopatra* worse than I am with *Something's Got to Give*, and she doesn't get half the fan letters I do. I don't think her figure compares with mine, either, even if she is seven years younger.

Why do you think they treat her so much better than they do me? I'm a bigger money-maker for them, and certainly a better actress.

Well, my birthday was not all bad. The Greensons gave me a champagne flute etched inside with my name. Now I'll know who I am when I'm drinking.

I'm also glad about one other thing. If you've got to be thirty-six, it's great to be a thirty-six where teenagers still whistle at you. I'm in better shape now than I've ever been, and miracle of miracles, my breasts are as firm as ever. I sometimes look at them in the mirror from the front and the side, and still can't believe what I see. I wonder how and why I've been so blessed. Every other woman I know who's my age has breasts hanging down to her navel.

The photographer Bert Stern wrote one of the nicest things about me imaginable. He said I was the wind, the light, the goddess, and the moon. The dream, the space, the danger, and the mystery. Could anything be lovelier? Of course, I don't feel like the wind and the light, let alone a goddess. But I'm happy he thinks I am. As I said, not bad for a girl of thirty-six!

I left the so-called party with Wally Cox, dressed in the borrowed fur-trimmed suit I'd worn to work that day, to attend a muscular dystrophy fundraiser at Dodger Stadium that evening with Joe DiMaggio. Joe loves me very much, but he can be mighty stingy. He failed to buy me a single lousy birthday present.

All in all, I hope my thirty-seventh birthday, if I have one, is better.

I called Henry Weinstein the Monday after to tell him I wouldn't be in that day. The cold night air of the Dodgers game had caused my sinusitis to flare up again, and my temperature was over one hundred degrees. My illness didn't go over well with Cukor, who I'm told lashed out at a meeting of the Fox board of directors, insisting that I be replaced on the film.

To my surprise, I was fired from the project on June 8. It was Elizabeth Taylor's fault. Her epic film *Cleopatra* was far over budget. Fox officials had planned for a Christmas holiday release of *Something's Got to*

Give to generate revenue and make up for *Cleopatra's* increasing cost. I want to know one thing: Why didn't they fire her instead of me?

Peter Levathes told the newspapers, "We have let the inmates run the asylum and they've just about destroyed it." With my history, you can imagine how I felt about being compared to an inmate in an asylum. Worse yet, he said the studio would proceed to sue me for a million dollars for breach of contract.

To generate some public sympathy following my firing, I quickly gave interviews and authorized photo essays to *Life*, *Cosmopolitan*, and *Vogue* magazines. Life featured me on yesterday's cover, wrapped in the blue terrycloth robe I'd worn in the pool scene of *Something's Got to Give*, with the headline, "The Skinny Dip You'll Never See." I'm not so sure. After all, I *am* Marilyn Monroe, the greatest sexpot in movie history.

My interview with Richard Meryman, to be published in Life on August 3, is my favorite ever because of its depth, and the way it includes my reflections on the positive and negative aspects of fame.

"Fame carries with it its own special burden," I told Meryman. "I don't mind at all carrying around the heavy weight of being sexual and glamorous. After all, we are born sexual creatures. I feel sorry for the many people in the world who crush and despise this natural gift. In my opinion, real art and everything worthwhile comes from it. Fame itself, despite its glamour, is very fleeting, and isn't what really matters. I now live in my work and in my relationships with the few people I really can count on. Fame will pass on, and good-bye, Fame, I've had you. I've always known you're fickle. You're something I've experienced and sometimes enjoyed, but that's not where I live."

Where *do* I live? I wish I knew.

I trust Meryman and gave him permission to say practically anything he wanted about me. The only restrictions I imposed were that he not show pictures of my house. I don't want the whole world to see how and where I live. After all, a person has to keep something private. I also asked him to be careful not to write anything that would hurt Arthur's kids—my one-time stepchildren. He was careful to comply.

Fox originally announced that I was to be replaced by actress Lee Remick, who had similar measurements to mine (without my glamour or sexiness, I'm happy to add) and thus fit into my costumes. What a lousy dollars-and-cents reason to cast someone in a role—that they fit into already existing clothing! How about casting somebody for her ability to act, Fox?

If I didn't already despise them, this bit of pound-foolish casting would make me do so. But fortunately for me, Dean Martin had final approval of his leading lady and refused to continue without me. He's told Fox he has nothing against Lee Remick, but he'd signed to appear with me, and that's the only way he'll do the picture. Now that's what I call a real friend, and I'll be forever grateful.

Love,
Marilyn

JULY 18, 1962

(With apologies to Rudyard Kipling)

On the road to Mandalay,
Where the old Flotilla lay,
I would like to go tomorrow
For a very lengthy stay.
Away from shrinks and lovers,
From movies, come what may,
That is where I wish I was,
On the road to Mandalay!

Dear Shrinker,

Things are looking up a bit. (They couldn't have gotten much worse!) Bobby called me, said he was sorry he'd had to bring me such a painful message several months earlier, that he'd enjoyed meeting me despite the terrible circumstances, and that when he was out in LA again, he'd love to personally console me.

My first reaction was to jump up and say, "Yes! Yes! Anytime. If I can't be a queen in the Kennedy dynasty, I'll settle for being a princess. And who knows? Maybe Bobby will be elected president after Jack leaves office, and I'll get to be first lady after all! Stranger things have happened, especially to Marilyn Monroe."

Then I thought: "Is Jack simply passing me on to Bobby? What's he thinking—that I'm just "One silver dollar / changing hands / changing hands ...?"

Anyway, I said to Bobby, "Of course, Mr. Attorney General. I'll be delighted to see you. When would you like to come?"

Without missing a beat, he answered, "How about tomorrow?"

It should be interesting.

Love,

Marilyn

JULY 20, 1962

(Adapted from an old English folk song)

Bobby Kennedy's gone to sea,
But as he said on bended knee,
He'll come back and marry me,
My loving Bobby Kennedy!
Bobby Kennedy is sweet and fair,
I just love to ruffle his hair,
He's my love for eternity,
My sweetheart, Bobby Kennedy!

Dear Shrinker:

Well, Bobby came, and somehow he didn't look as puny as I once thought he was. In fact, I wondered why I'd once thought so. He looked like Jack, he sounded like Jack, and his skin felt like Jack's.

How do I know what his skin felt like? It didn't take me long to find out. If I can't have Jack, Bobby certainly is a great substitute. With him, I can stay close to Jack and the first family, who've already adopted me.

From the way he behaves, I think Bobby has fallen madly in love with me. He's much warmer than Jack, who really is a cold fish. Being with Bobby is like basking in the sunshine after a winter of ice and snow.

I have to tell you that, in at least one other important way, Bobby's a distinct improvement over his big brother. He's a much more considerate lover. He takes his time and makes sure I'm satisfied before he is. No wonder he and Ethel have eleven children!

A day or two after his consolation visit, I was taking a bath when the doorbell rang. Since nobody else was in the house at the time, I flew out of the tub and rushed naked to the door. After all, I didn't want to miss anybody. It was Bobby standing there with a grin on his face. He had come to surprise me.

I leapt into his arms dripping wet. We kissed passionately and then went down on the floor right then and there. He didn't mind one bit that his suit got soaking wet. (I wonder how he explained his damp, wrinkled clothing to Ethel. I hope she gave him a hard time.)

Love,

Marilyn

JULY 22, 1962

(Adapted from an old English nursery rhyme)

Norma Jeane sat on a wall
Marilyn Monroe had a great fall
All the wise sages including the shrinks
Cannot put Marilyn together, methinks.

Dear Shrinker:

No fun and games today because last night I had another terrible nightmare. No wonder I don't look forward to falling asleep!

I dreamt I was undergoing an operation. The surgeon, the finest in the land, was Lee Strasberg. I didn't mind being cut open by Lee because you, Dr. Darcey, were the doctor giving me anesthesia, and you agreed with Surgeon Lee on what had to be done to bring me back to life and to cure me of the horrible disease I was suffering from.

The most terrifying part of the dream is what Lee found when he opened me up: absolutely nothing! You and he were shocked to discover this. Both of you had expected much more to be there—more even than you ever dreamt possible. Instead, the two of you discovered I was completely devoid of all human feelings—joy, love, hate, even terror.

The only thing you found within me was finely-cut sawdust, like that of a Raggedy Ann doll someone gave me once when I was in the orphanage. The sawdust spilt all over the floor. You picked up some and, with a puzzled look on your face, tasted it, looking as if you suddenly understood that I was a new type of case never before discussed in psychiatric annals, such that you had to give up your belief that you could permanently cure me. Lee's face fell, too, because he realized that all his hopes and dreams that I'd become a great actress would come to naught. Well, Shrinker, what do you think of your star patient now? No wonder I'm not improving. There's nothing to improve upon. Why don't I just kill myself and get it over with?

—Marilyn

JULY 26, 1963

Things can be bad
and sometimes are great,
But whenever I've needed you,
You've shown up to date.
Yes, times can be good,
And also be blue,
But from deep in my heart, Shrink,
I say "Thank you!"

Dear Shrinker:

Thanks so much for your phone call and your wonderful interpretation of my nightmare. It made me feel much better.

Of course you're right. As you said, my marriage to Arthur disintegrated, and if I'd allowed myself to, I'd have fallen apart with grief. Then my heart was broken over Jack's rejection. You're right; it's all too overwhelming for me to cope with right now.

If I let myself fully feel all this, I'll surely die. My own solution: don't feel anything, then I won't have to hurt so much.

As you said, I'm not really empty at all, but just the reverse. I'm pushing away a torrent of painful feelings to protect myself from completely falling apart and maybe even dying. You're right that it isn't a bad temporary solution.

I only hope that, in the near future, I'll grow strong enough to tolerate my grief and become a living, feeling human being again, and make you, Lee, and Paula proud of me.

Maybe things are looking up. Because Dean Martin had Fox by the short hairs, they were forced to relent and rehire me, even agreeing to pay me more than my previous salary of one hundred thousand dollars. I had to consent, however, to make two more films for them. The deal will be made official on August 1.

Much as I loathe Fox, I accepted on condition that the S.O.B. Cukor be replaced by Jean Negulesco, the director of *How to Marry a Millionaire*, whom I got along with well back then. With its new director, *Something's Got to Give* (I hope it isn't me) is scheduled to resume shooting in October.

Gratefully yours,
Marilyn

JULY 29, 1962

(With apologies to Christina Georgina Rossetti)

When I am dead, my Shrinker,
Sing no sad songs for me,
Write thou no tributes of my gifts,
Nor tell the world of me.
But be the Shrink for many
In perpetuity.
Think of me as when we met
But not with misery beset,
And if thou wilt, remember,
And if thou wilt, forget.

Dear Shrinker,

Not good! Not good!

Bobby told me, over and over, that he loves me and wants to marry me. Now he's trying to distance himself from me, and I don't understand why.

The special number he'd set up for me to reach him on at the Justice Department is now disconnected, and I've been frantically trying to reach him on the department's main Washington switchboard number, RE 7-8200. But he hasn't answered or returned any of my calls.

Then, in today's mail, I received a note from him, telling me never to call or try to contact either him or Jack again. He even intimated that I'd not been a serious contender for the affections of the President, but "just another of Jack's fucks." He didn't go into detail, but just wrote a cold hard statement that sounds more like Jack than Bobby.

I alternate between tears and rage. I called my friend Robert Slazer, and blurted out that though it was Jack Kennedy who had first cut me off cold, it was Bobby I couldn't get out of my mind.

Slazer only made me feel worse. He said, "Wake up, Marilyn! Where's your common sense? It's preposterous for you to think that the attorney general of the United States would destroy his career and endanger the presidency to marry you. He's a happily married man with eleven children. I can believe he had a fling with you—what hot-blooded man wouldn't want to bed Marilyn Monroe? But anything more is in your head. Be sensible for a change. Come down from the clouds and forget the whole thing."

I expected better from him. Anyway, I don't agree. Maybe some terrible error has been made, like the telephone company mistakenly turning off the wrong phone line. Or it's possible that the note Bobby sent me was meant for someone else, and he'll come crawling back to me on his hands and knees, just as Joe DiMaggio did when I told him I was filing for divorce.

I called my good friend Truman Capote and told him about the way the Kennedys were treating me. He tried to comfort me and said, "Don't cry over Jack Kennedy! He and Bobby together can't even raise a decent hard-on. If you brought all the Kennedy men together in one place, you couldn't conjure up a single good man. I know. I lived near them and saw them go for a nude swim many a time. They're like dogs. They can't go near a fire hydrant without pissing on it." He had a point there.

Late last night, I was so lonely that when a taxi driver drove me home, I invited him in. I wasn't sorry. His talents in bed far surpassed those of the President of the United States. It helped—for about five seconds.

Speaking of loneliness, I needed to hear the sound of a human voice so badly that I called radio station KRLA in Los Angeles on a call-in line. Tom Clay, a well-known disc jockey, asked for my name. I said, "Marilyn Monroe." He answered, "Yeah, and I'm Frank Sinatra," and hung up. I was really mad and called him back and told him off. Then I felt bad that I'd been so angry with his perfectly understandable reaction and invited him to come and have a cup of coffee with me.

He came and we talked mostly about his wife and children. I told him how lucky he was to have a family and how lonely I was. He said, in surprise, "How can you be lonely when there are so many people who love you?"

I said, "Have you ever been in a house with forty rooms, Tom? Well, magnify my loneliness by forty, and you'll understand just how lonely I am."

Love,
Marilyn

AUGUST 3, 1962

Frank Sinatra was my good friend
Up until the bitter end.
I'm crushed that he turned out to be
So poisonous a pill for me.

Dear Shrinker:

Whoever thought that Frank Sinatra would prove to be the straw that broke the camel's back? After all our years of close friendship, it's unfathomable that this should happen now in the time of my greatest need.

Whenever I'd needed him, he was always there for me, and I can't understand what's made him change. When I separated from Arthur, for instance, Frank was right there, as solicitous as any man could be.

Like the stinker he is, Arthur had taken my basset hound, Hugo, with him when he skipped out. I missed the dog more than Arthur. Do you know that Frank bought me a replacement for Hugo "so you won't be so lonely"? The dog became my new love, and I called him "Maf."

(Joke! Joke! I think that's hilarious, even if you don't. We know, Doc, that your sense of humor is not terribly well developed.) "Maf" is short for Mafia, and I don't have to tell even you about Sinatra's connection with the Mafia. Anyway, I love Maf dearly, and he goes everywhere with me.

From the first man in my life—my father—to the last, dear Frankie, men have always let me down. I can now accept the truth—that it's simply the way men are, and there'll never be a dependable one in my life. What good is it if all the men in the world love you from afar, but up close, you don't have a single one of your own? I have had it with men and with life!

Besides my emotional distress, my health is atrocious. Endometriosis keeps me in physical pain most of the time, and I'm told it'll continue to get worse as long as I live. It's resulted in the worst sorrow of my life—my inability to carry a baby to term.

In 1949, I contracted Ménière's disease, which, as you know, gives me dizzy spells, and left me with a partial loss of hearing in my right ear. (Not good for my business! I have to ask actors to repeat their lines over and over. They think I have a terrible memory, because nobody knows I really can't hear very well. Let them think what they want. I'm not going to enlighten them.)

While I was waiting for my divorce from Jim Dougherty, I got a bad case of trench mouth, with sore gums that trouble me to the present day.

I've also had raging attacks of the flu, bronchitis, bronchial pneumonia, laryngitis, and several severe viral infections, the last one just a few weeks ago.

I won't even mention the numerous colds and cases of severe exhaustion which have landed me in the hospital, and the diarrhea and constant constipation for which I have to take enemas.

As if these ailments aren't enough, I had to have my gall bladder removed last year, which left minor scars on my formerly perfect body.

I was often sick as a little girl, and developed a terrible case of whooping cough, and a chronic problem with rickets. I was not a well child, though that should come as no surprise. There was nobody to take care of me—nobody to even see that I was eating properly.

Things haven't changed all that much since then. These illnesses leave me very little quality time, which gives me nothing to live for. With such bad health and almost constant pain, can you blame me, with or without Jack or Bobby Kennedy, for wanting to kill myself? I'm flabbergasted I'm still alive.

I felt desperate enough to call Bobby at his home in Virginia to find out from him personally if there'd been some mistake. He was furious. "How dare you call me at home?" he hissed and hung up on me without another word. Then he went completely incommunicado. I won't stand for that. I will get my revenge! In the meantime, I have nowhere to turn but my pills.

To make matters worse, even creature comforts are hard to come by these days. Around midnight last night, I got hungry and went to make a steak. None were there. In fact, there was nothing at all to eat, so I went to bed hungry. I don't know why Greenson is so fond of my so-called housekeeper, Eunice Murray! I don't like her at all, and think he may have placed her here to spy on me. I think I'll fire her. I may just fire him, too.

You were right when you said my inner emptiness was keeping me from feeling pain. This is the worst agony I've ever known, except maybe when I was a little girl and hurt because I had no father. I've become a pain so big there's no Marilyn left. Emily Dickinson said it better than I can: "There is a pain—so utter—it swallows substance up."

Anyway, remember my poem, "Shrink Shrank Shrunk, I am not a drunk . . . Or am I?" Well, unfortunately, I can respond to that question now. The answer is yes.

Here's what happened with Frank: You know how heartbroken and distraught I've been about the rejection of the Kennedys. Also, even though my lawyers patched things up with Fox and are confident that *Something's Got to Give* will resume filming in October, with me reinstated at twice the salary, I'm still upset about being fired. I don't care about the move, but an orphan thrown out of so many foster homes doesn't so easily get over rejection. I feel fragile—the most fragile I've ever felt in a life not noted for its emotional strength.

To doctor myself, I've begun drinking even more than usual and binging on pills.

Over the phone, I'd complained to Frankie about how miserable I was and why. Frankie, kind friend that he still seemed to be, felt sorry for me and invited me for the weekend to his new Lake Tahoe hotel, the Cal Neva Lodge. He even sent his private plane to pick me up. He said, "Sometimes a person just needs to get away from it all." I was delighted at the invitation, and hoped that his company and the weekend rest at the lodge would make me feel better. Never have I been more wrong!

When I arrived, I thought I looked very chic. (You'll be happy to hear, dear shrinker, that I can still shine when I want to, without anyone knowing that my gloss is often just a thin veneer.) I was dressed all in green. Everything I was wearing matched—my green silk Pucci coat and blouse, green velvet slacks, green Hermés scarf, and jade earrings that Frank had given me. My red-rimmed eyes were hidden behind huge black sunglasses.

Frank, Peter Lawford, and a group of people lounging outside of Frank's bungalow applauded me as I got out of the limousine. So the visit got off to a good start. But unfortunately, that was the last good moment I was to experience, there or perhaps anywhere.

Frank soon left the scene. I'd expected him to take care of me, as was his custom, but forgot that he would need to prepare for his evening performances. Having been deprived of his company, I felt more miserable and lonely than at home, so I went to my bungalow and turned even more heavily than usual to liquor and pills. It would've been all right had I stayed in the room and slept it off, but of course, I didn't.

"I came here to see Frankie and his show, and that's what I'm going to do," I muttered aloud as I staggered out the bungalow door.

As I entered the showroom, Buddy Greco was just finishing his warm-up act. I paused, and must admit, stood there, swaying in the doorway. Suddenly, the room grew as silent as a churchyard, as if somebody had just turned off a blasting TV. There was a nightmarish quality about it, and my head swirled.

Frank was glaring at the doorway where I was standing so unsteadily. Given my history of chronic alcohol and drug abuse, which he was well aware of, his reaction was surprisingly sinister. When Frank had opened the refurbished Cal Neva a month ago, he and I got dead drunk, but then he got angry with me over my addictions and threatened to end our relationship if I didn't get over them. Of course, I didn't believe him. Why would he give up a relationship which included sex with the great Marilyn Monroe?

But this past weekend, recalling his lectures, I became drunk *and* defiant. Who the hell was Frank Sinatra to tell me what I could and could not drink and swallow? He was a nothing—just a little Italian boy from Hoboken—and no better than a little orphan girl. I was furious and said loud enough for the whole room to hear, "Who the fuck are you all staring at?"

Frank was more than a little irritated. He must've thought I was messing up his precious new nightclub. If I'd been in his shoes, I would've put my friend's interests before the club's. But he's not me, and he took action immediately.

He gestured to his bodyguard Coochie to get me out of there—fast! Coochie was a great big bodyguard. He picked me up, threw me over his shoulder, and carried me out kicking and screaming, "I'm not going anywhere!" I shouted. "Put me down! I came here to see Frankie's show!"

Coochie didn't. And I didn't. Even worse, my dress slipped up my legs, and you know I never wear underwear. I never was so humiliated in my life—the great movie star carried off the night club floor, kicking and screaming, her naked ass up in the air!

Well, come to think of it, I had been equally humiliated once before, when, as a child, I was beaten on my bare buttocks by Wayne Bolender.

Coochie carted me to my room, dumped me on the bed, packed my suitcases, and drove me to Sinatra's plane, which immediately flew me home to Hollywood.

Like everyone else, my "close friend" Frank Sinatra has abandoned me to my fate. But I will have my revenge. If I know Frank Sinatra, he'll be very sorry in a few days. Maybe all his life. And so will Jack, Bobby, Arthur, Twentieth Century Fox officials, and all the stinkers in my life back to Wayne Bolender and my S.O.B. father.

I'm going to go to bed with a bottle of pills and some champagne. I hope the combination will knock me out. Maybe I'll be lucky and never wake up again.

Love,
Marilyn

AUGUST 6, 1962

<u>Analyst's Note:</u> I felt dizzy the moment I saw the large words boldly printed in black on the familiar cornflower-blue envelope, stamped "Special Delivery." I had to grab my desk to keep from fainting. I held the letter against my heart for a long time before I found the courage to open it.

TO BE MAILED IMMEDIATELY
UPON MY DEATH
Marilyn Monroe

Weep no more, my shrinker,
Oh, weep no more today.
Just sing one song
For Marilyn who has gone
To the place where she belongs
Where she will keep you with her every day.
You are my shrinker true,
My true shrinker still is you.
I cannot bid you adieu
Without saying I love you,
I love love love you, Darcey Dale

My dear shrinker:

I have a parting gift for you. It's in the form of my final dream. Someone once said that a dream is a gift from Freud. It would be more nearly correct to say that this dream is a gift *from* you.

You've always liked me to give names to my dreams. This one is called "The Empire State Building Dream." Do you remember the dream I once had of a glorious Persian rug of vibrant red, blue, and gold—the unsurpassable beauty created from millions of hand-sewn stitches covering the whole downstairs floor of the Museum of Modern Art? I called it "The Beautiful Persian Rug Dream."

You said that, in my unconscious, I knew I was a magnificent work of art that belonged in an art museum. I smiled and said, "Come off it, Doc!

You forget that, inside, I'm poor little Norma Jeane, who was brought up in an orphanage, where we were lucky if our floors were covered in linoleum!"

Well, my unconscious seems quite persistent, even if I'm not. "The Beautiful Persian Rug Dream now reminds me of "The Empire State Building Dream"—the last dream I'll ever have, unless one dreams in Heaven, which I don't suppose is necessary in the land of milk and honey, where all wishes are granted and all dreams come true. (I can only hope!)

Last night, I dreamt of the Empire State Building, the highest building in the world. You always say that everything in a dream represents the dreamer. If so, I'm the Empire State Building, and I tower over every other building in the world.

You believe the unconscious always tells the truth. If so—and I hope you're right—I'm leaving behind a heritage I can be proud of, and can depart knowing my years of misery have been lived with a purpose. I've always belonged to the world, as I never have to any human being. So it makes sense that I see myself as a giant of a building, belonging to the world.

You've been like a mother to me. I'm very grateful, and only wish you'd been my real mother. Then I never would've needed to write this letter.

Thank you, Darcey, for being there for me when I needed you, and for not interfering when I didn't. Thank you for the many beautiful hours we spent together, and even for some that weren't. Thank you for caring, for never disappointing me, and for understanding, as I know you will, why it's right for me to make my exit now.

At the end of his life, your boy, Sigmund Freud, said to his doctor, Max Schur, "My dear Schur, you certainly remember our first talk. You promised me then not to forsake me when my time comes. Now my life is nothing but torture and makes no sense anymore." Schur reassured his patient that he'd not forgotten, and promptly administered to Freud a fatal dose of morphine.

I think of you as my Doctor Schur, and believe you eventually would do for me what Schur did for Freud.

But above everything else, dear Darcey, I want to thank you for making it possible for me to understand this dream. I can go in peace now, feeling I've left a monumental heritage behind.

Goodbye and much love,

Marilyn (Norma Jeane) Monroe

BIBLIOGRAPHY

Anderson, Janice. *Marilyn Monroe*. New York: Crescent Books, 1995.

Arnold, Eve. *Marilyn Monroe*. New York: Harry N. Abrams, 2005.

Arnold, Eve. *Marilyn Monroe: An Appreciation*. New York: Knopf, 1987.

Badman, Keith. *Marilyn Monroe: The Final Years*. New York: Thomas Dunne, 2012.

Banner, Lois and Mark Anderson. *MM—Personal: from the Private Archive of Marilyn Monroe*. New York: Abrams, 2001.

Barris, George. . New York: Citadel Press, 1995.

Baty, S. Paige. *American Monroe: The Making of a Body Politic*. Berkeley, Los Angeles: University of California Press, 1995.

Bigsby, Christopher. *Arthur Miller*. London: Weidenfeld & Nicolson, 2009.

Braver, Adam. *Misfit*. Portland, OR, New York: Tin House, 2012.

Brown, Peter Harry and Patte B. Barham. *Marilyn: The Last Take*. New York: Dutton, 1992.

Casillo, Charles. *The Marilyn Diaries*. Los Angeles: Charles Casillo, 1999.

Churchwell, Sarah. *The Many Lives of Marilyn Monroe*. New York: Picador, 2004.

Clark, Colin. *The Prince, the Showgirl and Me: Six Months on the Set with Marilyn and Olivier*. New York: St. Martin's, 1996.

Clayton, Marie. *Marilyn Monroe: Unseen Archives*. Bath, UK: Parragon, 2005.

Cunningham, Ernest W. *The Ultimate Marilyn: All the Facts, Fantasies, and Scandals about the World's Best-Known Sex Symbol*. Los Angeles: Renaissance, 1998.

De La Hoz, Cindy. *Marilyn Monroe: Platinum Fox*. Philadelphia: Running Press, 2007.

Dougherty, Jim. *To Norma Jeane with Love, Jimmie*. As told to LC Van Savage. Chesterfield, Missouri: BeachHouse, 2001.

Druxman, Michael B. Marilyn Monroe. In *Once Upon a Time in Hollywood: From the Secret Files of Harry Pennypacker*. Tucson, Arizona: Wheatmark, 2008.

Evans, Mike. *Marilyn Handbook*. London: Spruce, 2004.

Freeman, Lucy. *Why Norma Jean Killed Marilyn Monroe*. Chicago: Global Rights, 1992.

Gilmore, John. *Inside Marilyn Monroe: A Memoir*. Los Angeles: Ferine Books, 2007.

Guiles, Fred Lawrence. *Legend: The Life and Death of Marilyn Monroe*. Chelsea, Michigan: Scarborough House, 1991.

Guiles, Fred Lawrence. *Norma Jean: The Life of Marilyn Monroe*. New York: Paragon House, 1993.

Hanks, Tara. *The Mmm Girl: Marilyn Monroe, By Herself . . . .* London: UKA, 2007.

Haspiel, James. *Marilyn: The Ultimate Look at the Legend*. London: Smith Gryphon, 1991.

Haspiel, James. *Young Marilyn: Becoming the Legend*. New York: Hyperion, 1994.

Jasgur, Joseph and Jeannie Sakol. *The Birth of Marilyn: The Lost Photographs of Norma Jean*. New York: St. Martin's, 1991.

Jordan, Ted. *Norma Jean: My Secret Life with Marilyn Monroe*. New York: Signet, 1991.

Kahn, Roger. *Joe and Marilyn: A Memory of Love*. New York: William Morrow, 1986.

Klein, Edward. *All Too Human: The Love Story of Jack and Jackie Kennedy*. New York: Pocket Books, 1996.

Lawrence, Lauren. *Private Dreams of Public People*. New York: Assouline, 2002.

Leaming, Barbara. *Marilyn Monroe*. London: Weidenfeld & Nicolson, 1998.

Lytess, Natasha. *My Years with Marilyn*. As told to Jane Wilkie. Harry Ransom Center, University of Texas, Austin.

McDonough, Yona Zeldis. *All the Available Light: A Marilyn Monroe Reader*. New York, London, Toronto, Sydney: Touchstone, 2002.

Mailer, Norman. *Marilyn*. New York: Galahad, 1994.

Mailer, Norman. *Of Women and Their Elegance*. New York: Tom Doherty, 1981.

Martin, Pete. *Will Acting Spoil Marilyn Monroe?*. Garden City, New York: Doubleday, 1956.

Mercurio, Jed. *American Adulterer*. New York: Simon & Schuster, 2009.

Miracle, Berniece Baker and Mona Rae Miracle. *My Sister Marilyn: A Memoir of Marilyn Monroe*. London: Weidenfeld and Nicolson, 1994.

Miller, Author. *After the Fall: A Play in Two Acts*. New York: Penguin, 1980.

Miller, Arthur. *The Misfits: An Original Screenplay*. New York: Irvington, 1989.

Miller, Arthur. *Timebends: A Life*. London: Minerva, 1990.

Monroe, Marilyn. *Fragments: Poems, Intimate Notes, Letters*. Edited by Stanley Buchthal and Bernard Comment. London: HarperCollins, 2010.

Monroe, Marilyn and Ben Hecht. *My Story*. Lanham, Maryland; New York; Boulder, Colorado; Toronto; Plymouth, UK: Taylor Trade, 2007.

Morgan, Michelle. *Marilyn Monroe: Private and Confidential*. New York: Skyhorse Publishing, 2012.

Oates, Joyce Carol. *Blonde*. New York: Ecco Press, 2001.

Pepitone, Lena and William Stadiem. *Marilyn Monroe Confidential: An Intimate Personal Account*. New York: Simon & Schuster, 1979.

Porter, Darwin. *Marilyn at Rainbow's End: Sex, Lies, Murder, and the Great Cover-Up*. New York: Blood Moon Productions, 2012.

Rattigan, Terence. *The Prince and the Showgirl: The Script for the Film*. New York: Signet, 1957.

Reeves, Thomas C. *A Question of Character: A Life of John F. Kennedy*. Roseville, California: Prima Publishing, 1997.

Riese, Randall and Neal Nitchens. *The Unabridged Marilyn: Her Life from A to Z*. New York: Congdon & Weed, 1987.

Schur, Max. *Freud: Living and Dying*. New York: International Universities Press, 1972.

Shaw, Sam and Norman Rosten. *Marilyn among Friends*. New York: Henry Holt, 1987.

Shevey, Sandra. *The Marilyn Scandal: Her True Life Revealed by Those Who Knew Her*. New York: William Morrow, 1987.

Spoto, Donald. *Marilyn Monroe: The Biography*. London: Chatto & Windus, 1993.

Steinem, Gloria and George Barris. *Marilyn: Norma Jeane*. New York: Henry Holt, 1986.

Strasberg, Susan. *Marilyn and Me: Sisters, Rivals, Friends*. New York: Doubleday, 1992.

Taraborrelli, J. Randy. *The Secret Life of Marilyn Monroe*. New York: Grand Central, 2009.

They Fired Marilyn: Her Dip Lives On. 1962. *Life*, 22 June.

Wolfe, Donald H. *The Assassination of Marilyn Monroe*. London: Little, Brown, 1999.

Zolotow, Maurice. *Marilyn Monroe*. New York: HarperCollins, 1990.

ACKNOWLEDGEMENTS

I would like to express my gratitude to the following people, without whose help I could not have written this book:

My brilliant son, Jonathan Halbert Bond, frequently called "the Guru of Advertising," for his longtime help in publicizing my books.

My son-in-law, Sam Brill, whose generous help with the business of living enables me to write books.

Danielle Gilardi, Director of Emerging Technology, BigFuel.com, for her assistance in promoting my books on Facebook.

Dr. Cassandra Langer, Dr. Jill Morris, Karen Lane, and Carol Calhoun, all members of my writing group, who have listened to many versions of my books over the years.

My cousin, Sylvia Williamson, for her first editing of this book.

My cousin, Beatrice Weis, for a lifetime of encouragement.

Bruce Bortz, my wonderful editor and publisher, whose idea it first was to write this book.

Harrison Demchick, the talented co-editor of this book.

Shani Sladowski, for bringing great value to the final edit.

Lydia Olszak, Ph.D., Reference Librarian, Bosler Memorial Library, for her valuable assistance in obtaining rare books for me on Marilyn Monroe.

Dr. Sam Hijazi, my excellent webmaster for many years.

Afton Monahan, whose work with me has enabled me to devote my time to writing this book.

Michael Monahan, librarian, who has been most helpful in locating articles on Marilyn Monroe and making them available to me.

Karolina Zdanowska, for her help with PowerPoint presentations for my books.

Professor Nancy C. Mellerski, for kindly allowing me to audit her film class at Dickinson College, and for agreeing to read an early draft of this book.

And to my good friend Dr. Kleona Corsini, for reading the manuscript at a formative stage.

ABOUT THE AUTHOR

 Dr. Alma H. Bond is the author or co-author of twenty-one published books, including this one. Among her others: *Jackie O: On the Couch; Lady Macbeth: On the Couch; Michelle Obama: A Biography; The Autobiography of Maria Callas: A Novel; Margaret Mahler: A Biography of the Psychoanalyst; Camille Claude: A Novel; America's First Woman Warrior: The Story of Deborah Sampson; and Who Killed Virginia Woolf? A Psychobiography.*

Dr. Bond received her Ph.D. in Developmental Psychology from Columbia University, graduated from the post-doctoral program in psychoanalysis at the Freudian Society, and was a psychoanalyst in private practice for 37 years in New York City. She "retired" to become a full-time writer.

Dr. Bond is a member of the American Society of Journalists and Authors, the Dramatists Guild, and the Authors Guild, as well as a fellow and faculty member of the Institute for Psychoanalytic Training and Research, the International Psychoanalytic Association, and the American Psychological Association. She was one of the first non-medical analysts to be elected to the International Psychoanalytic Association.

Dr. Bond grew up in Philadelphia, where she obtained her undergraduate degree in psychology from Temple University, and following voluntary military service, moved to New York, where she earned a graduate degree in psychology from Columbia University.

A longtime resident of New York City, she lived for nearly a dozen years in south Florida, and now resides in Carlisle, Pennsylvania.